ENEMIES OF THE EMPIRE

ROBB PRITCHARD

Foundation of the Dragon

Book III

To Jose Rui Santos

King of Kings

Força, mano

Enemies of the Empire: Foundation of the Dragon Book 3 by Robb Pritchard

Published by Robb Pritchard

www.robbpritchard.co.uk

Copyright © 2023 Robb Pritchard

All rights reserved. No portion of this book may be reproduced in any form without permission from the publisher, except as permitted by U.S. copyright law. For permissions contact: robb@robbpritchard.co.uk

ISBN:

Cover and maps by Sasa Juric (www.sassch.com)

Place Names

The Wall	Hadrian's Wall, England
Eboracum	York, England
Deva	Chester, England
Segontium	Caernarfon, Wales
Lutetia	Paris, France
Treverorum	Trier, Germany
Mediolanum	Milan, Italy
Massilia	Marseilles, France
Constantinople	Istanbul, Turkey
Traiana	Xanten, Germany
Lugdunun	Lyon, France
Aquileia	Aquileia, Italy
Emona	Ljubljana, Slovenia
Siscia	Sisak, Croatia
Poetovio	Ptuj, Slovenia

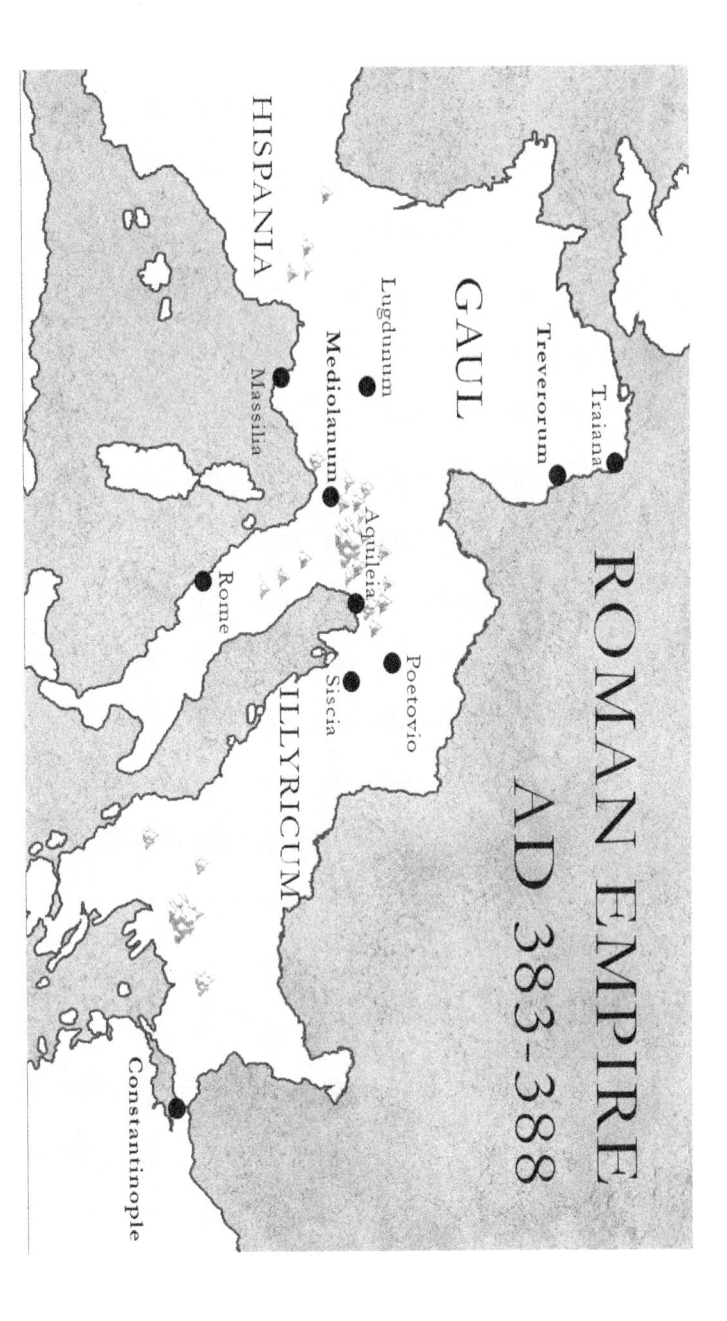

PROLOGUE

THE WALL. LATE WINTER 383

In the weak light around a wildly swaying lantern, streaks of snow whipped sideways through the crenellations on top of the Wall. As Magnus shuffled along through the drifts that were beginning to build up along the walkway, the biting cold seeming to be able to find every gap in his clothes, a spectral shape loomed before him and his breath caught in his throat. Some spirit the barbarians worshipped, come to seek his soul? He cursed himself for being so stupid and a few cautious steps closer, he saw that it was just the next guard.

"Salva," he shouted, but his words were taken by the storm wind long before they got anywhere near the soldier's ears. He had no choice but to walk closer. When he cleared his throat a few paces away, the boy snapped straight, either in fright, or just a more corporeal fear of having a superior's attention on him. To grab his spear he had to let go of his thick woollen cloak, and despite his best efforts to tug it back into place, it flailed around him.

"You're doing a good job," Magnus said, patting the guard's shoulder. The top of his cloak was covered in little clumps of ice. "Vital work." Even as he said it though, he knew how hollow his words sounded.

"Yes, sir!"

Head bowed, cloak tugged around him as tightly as he could pull it, Magnus trudged off towards the warm light flickering invitingly in the window of the tower. Every civilised man held a deep-rooted fear of what lay beyond the borders of the empire, but he couldn't help but think that the thousands of soldiers standing guard this night did so against something unnatural, that the blizzard blasting in from the untamed wilderness wasn't from the world of man.

At the thought of horrors from the north, he imagined Padarn somewhere out in that impenetrable darkness, over endless tracts of nothingness that would be bleached pure white–if the sun were ever to rise again. The leader of the Votadini tribe would be sitting at the head of a hearth fire, nothing stronger to protect him against the enraged elements than a hut made of mud and roofed with straw. Even the Wall, made of stone, eighty miles long, and the height of two men, felt vulnerable.

Since the day he'd set his red cloak over the Votadini's shoulders, a year and a half before, there hadn't been a single incursion, so the half-frozen guards stood in the darkness night after night, with both bodies and minds numbed, standing against nothing but bad memories. *Soon there would be a better purpose for them to serve*, he thought as he finally got to the relative shelter of the tower.

He tried the door, now desperate for the heat of the brazier inside. It was stuck fast and the thought of freezing to death caused such panic that when he set his shoulder to it, he pushed much harder than needed and fell into the room with a curse rather than a greeting.

A haze of charcoal smoke filled the small stone-walled room. Fraomar sat behind a small desk, brow creased in concentration as he carefully positioned a measuring weight along the arm of a small steelyard bar; a pile of variously sized silver ingots in the process of being counted.

Magnus wondered if any of the silver would make it into Padarn's scarred hands. The old man had kept his word so far, but Magnus had never forgotten how he'd made the blood oath to kill his own son. His palms and fingers had been cut deeply by the sword he'd grasped. A night like this, when the spirits seemed to rage, loudly enough to strike terror into the hearts of hardened soldiers, would be a good time to make plans for revenge.

The large fort on the other side of the deep ditch behind them stood at the junction of three roads, so much of the trade between Britannia and the tribes to the north came through here. Fraomar would take a cut out of every transaction for taxation, and like almost every official who had ever lived, would surely take a cut for himself. Magnus hoped that what he was about to offer the old Goth would be worth a lot more than some syphoned off slithers of silver.

He looked at the other man in the room, who was hunkered over the small brazier, palms offered to it as though it was an altar and he was begging God for some favour–for some sun and its attendant warmth, probably. Magnus assumed he was a trader, a Roman citizen who had for some reason chosen to earn his living by doing business with those who called the wilderness to the north their home.

Fraomar unhooked the leather bag from the scales, tossed it to the trader, and with a subtle nod of his head, indicated he should leave. Despite the storm, the man donned his thick cloak wordlessly and slipped back outside into the wind and snow. Whatever business couldn't wait until a better day, Magnus didn't want to know about it.

With relief, Magnus squatted down before the glowing coals and angled his aching knees as close as he could to the glowing charcoals.

"Dux Britanniarum," Fraomar said by way of greeting.

Ten years it had been since Magnus had watched the commander of the just defeated Lentienses tribe sign a treaty in front of Valentinian I. A scratch of some ink on a sheet of vellum and his men were to serve half their lives in the Roman army. Magnus couldn't have known they'd end up manning the Wall, a place so unforgiving that on nights like this, it wasn't a surprise to find a guard in the morning frozen stiff, still crouched up against whatever it was he'd tried to find shelter behind. They were still some years from being even halfway through their tenure. For that, Magnus couldn't help feeling a little sorry for them.

From the lines in his skin, the greying hairs at his temples, those years had been hard for the commander as well. The Wall, on any day, but especially in the grip of a bleak mid-winter, was no place for soft men.

"I think I know what brings you to the end of the world," Fraomar said. Even his voice sounded rougher than Magnus remembered, but breathing charcoal smoke in a small room six months of the year would do that.

"Do you?" Magnus replied uncertainly. For a summer and two winters he'd been collecting men to his army. It should have become easier, but the closer he got to openly declaring himself against the three emperors, the surer he was that someone had betrayed him and that the very next message from Eboracum would be a denouncement from Gratian.

"Tonight the wind screams, but sometimes it whispers," Fraomar said, "and what strange stories it tells me; ones of ambition, of power– and great risks. If I am right, it is a dangerous game you have come to ask me to play. Great risks, indeed."

"And great rewards," Magnus added.

"So it may be, so it may be." Fraomar hooked another bag of small ingots onto the scales and moved the dangling weight to balance it. With a grubby finger he slowly slid the weight back towards the middle of the mechanism so the silver sank down. "So?"

"Tell me what you want, and we can work back from there," Magnus said, trying his best not to admit anything explicitly.

"Well," Fraomar mused, "I think you have come to see me because you want me to take enough men from here back to the east of the Rhine, where we feign a military manoeuvre to draw Gratian's army away, therefore allowing you to land in Gaul unopposed."

Magnus could only nod. He could count the number of people who knew everything about his plans for the purple on the fingers of one hand, so it was deeply unnerving that Fraomar had managed to work out such an understanding from just the rumours that had come to him, and it begged the question, who else knew his plans so well?

Despite the bitter cold outside, it felt as though he was standing on ice that was becoming dangerously thin.

"Some of my men could die for that." In the silence, Magnus expected Fraomar to name his price, but he carried on tapping the balancing weight. Finally, he said, "I would suspect that if you were to remove the emperor from his position and take all that is his, you wouldn't be too keen on keeping his Alans as your personal guard."

"Of course not," Magnus agreed. "If any still live afterwards, I'll have them chased all the way back to the grasslands."

Fraomar was quiet again and Magnus wasn't sure if he should wait for him to suggest it, or if it would be better to make the offer himself.

Fraomar kept on gently tapping the weight.

Magnus gave in. "I would be happy to have you and the men you select to be my personal guards. I invite the rest to make up the imperial city guard at Treverorum."

At last, Fraomar slid the weight a little along the steelyard, but still not all the way to the notch where it would balance the bag of silver. "Double pay," he said, "and land for every man in the heart of Gaul; not up here in this forsaken place."

Magnus started to worry that he'd run out of things to offer anyone else he wanted to join his alliance. "If any man remains loyal to Gratian, his lands and titles shall be forfeit. Those, your men shall have."

Fraomar nodded. "The commanders of the order army down the Rhine are with you?"

It was as though the Goth had been in the room when Magnus had discussed his plans with Marcellinus and Andragathius. "Not yet, but I won't move until they are."

Fraomar finally knocked the weight into its notch. The bag of silver slowly rose and the scales were balanced. For the first time, Fraomar looked Magnus in the eye. "When do we leave?"

Magnus allowed himself a smile. "As soon as we can."

"Spring then." Fraomar nodded. "Seems we will have more to look forward to than just the coming of the sun."

He was now risking his life, just as much as Magnus was his. They would either die as traitors, heads on posts for the crows to peck at, or both of them would live the rest of their lives as they'd only ever dreamed of.

I

EBORACUM EARLY SUMMER 383

From atop one of the sturdy Constantine-era bastions in the city walls of Eboracum, Magnus looked down over the houses of the settlement that had grown on the other side of the river. Over the clusters of buildings, roof tiles still glistening wet after the last rain shower, a line of glimmering lights caught his eye. He knew it to be a long column of men, shields slung over their backs, trudging down the slope of a hill. Their long training march was almost done.

The summer was past its zenith, but the days in Eboracum were only just starting to get warm—not like how he loved it, though. He'd grown up in the fierce heat of Hispania when, at this time of year, the sun was well on its way to scorching anything in the landscape that had been green, to browns and yellows. Britannia's summers were the same muggy cloying heat of a bathhouse tepidarium and the humidity made it a living nightmare for the men to march their twelve miles in full kit. He did not envy them.

It was his third summer on the island, and he was very glad it would be his last; one way or another. It would be the same for a good number of the soldiers too. After the fifteen peaceful years since the Conspiracy, he was sure many would be glad of the war he was about to lead them into. Years of endless drilling and manning walls against nothing but the wind, was enough to drive bored men mad with the need for blood. Also the prospect of loot, rather than poor wages, would make men desperate to leave their tedious posts, but although Magnus would soon lead thousands to battle, he'd be giving them the strictest instructions not to fight; it was Gratian's surrender he needed, not his death, and a pitched battle between two armies was not something the empire could afford.

But he was getting a little ahead of himself though, as everything depended on the little piece of parchment the messenger had just left with him. It was from Andragathius; news about his efforts to get the commanders of the Rhine defences to declare for him. He had two confirmed already. This would be the third–and the last! He tapped it in his hand.

Gratian had recently moved his imperial court from Treverorum near the border, all the way south to Mediolanum. Putting weeks of delay between the frontier and command had dismayed every senior officer stationed along the river–so much so that two now supported Magnus. Between him and Treverorum there was only the commander of Bonnenusis. It was his answer that would be in the note.

It would be simple enough to unwind the binding and see what his future held, but there was something stopping him. This moment, just before the final decision had to be made, everything seemed so utterly calm, like the cool of a summer's dawn before the sun rose and began filling the day with its heat.

There was one thing he wanted to do before he found out about his future. He made his way down from the perimeter wall out of the sturdy gate and over the bridge into the town, and along the wall that blocked his large house from the street. Almost the size of a country villa, it wasn't quite a palace, as there were no really grand houses this far north, but it was well appointed, without being ostentatious, and that suited Elen perfectly. For Magnus' liking, it was too far from the fort, as he wanted Victor to grow up surrounded by the constant bustle and cooking smoke of the army.

The guards on the street opened the gate as he stepped into the verdant courtyard lined by the three colonnaded wings of the house. As usual, Elen was surrounded by her attendants, all hovering around her. Some, seeing Magnus, scurried off to make themselves busy, but

Eugenius stood to attention. Magnus wondered how many men in the empire were confronted with their wife's lover every day. Maybe they weren't together in the way of the flesh, as every spy he'd sent to watch them had confirmed, but her heart was Eugenius' as sure as a sword that rested in its scabbard.

His and Elen's marriage was convenient for them both, as it brought the two powers, native and Roman, together, and he was close to launching his bid for the purple–in the great part due to the local connections that she'd inherited from her infernal grandmother. But what he craved right now was a little genuine affection–little reassurance, a few words of support.

"What worries you?" she asked, as ever not missing a thing, but also as ever, he was sure her concern was more for herself, for her precious Britannia Secunda, than it was for him.

"Nothing but the weight of the empire," he said.

"As usual." She smiled politely.

Little Sevira, born a few months before, was wrapped up in swaddling at Elen's breast, but it was Victor who was special. With an excited lurch of his stomach, he saw his pride and joy, his progeny, who, if the dice rolled in the way he wanted them to, would grow up to one day rule the world. He was burrowing under some bushes in the little garden, probably finding unsavoury things to put in his mouth.

With a nod at the note in his hand, Elen asked, "Good news?"

He held it out to show her that he hadn't opened it yet.

"And if the last one declares for you?" she asked despondently, her true feelings about his plans were betrayed in how her face had turned ashen.

"Then we will be leaving soon."

At the wave of her delicate hand, the rest of her nurses and servants backed nervously away. All of them were freed women who'd chosen to stay and attend Elen. One came to take Sevira from her. When they were alone, her guards a few paces away, she stared up at him with a look of thunder. "Our agreement is that you take a *third* of the soldiers and a *fifth* of the garrison from the Wall; no more! A little quieter, she added, "A man more than that, and you will not reach Londinium."

For a moment, it seemed her words frightened him as much as they enraged him, and he shivered to hear the voice of her grandmother so clearly. The old woman was years dead, yet he still feared her. "One fifth of them. No more," he said. "It is enough. I will not undo the years worth of work it took to make Britannia secure." Besides, if he was to lose Britannia to the barbarians while fighting Gratian, no one would trust him to be emperor.

"And you return them as soon as your battle is won."

All he needed was a force so overwhelming that as soon as he arrayed it before Gratian, the boy would understand the full scale of his unpopularity and would surrender on the spot. If he didn't simply flee for his life, he would beg to sue for peace and terms. Despite Elen's ultimatum for leaving Britannia adequately defended, he was sure he'd still have an army big enough.

"It's not too late. You don't have to do this."

Magnus' heart sank. She still didn't support him. "My fate was sealed the day your men acclaimed me on our wedding day," he said. "From that moment, it had to come to this."

"But you risk *everything*!" she hissed. "Not just your own life and Victor's."

"The whole of the empire, I know." He looked her dead in the eye. "Even with every important man from here to Treverorum declared for me, you still don't think I can win? You think I could lose against the boy?"

"It is not *you* I doubt, dear husband. There is a lot more to successfully ruling an empire than military might. It matters not if every commander in the empire switches allegiance to you, if all the priests and powerful men stand in opposition. Those in Londinium, Treverorum, Rome and Constantinople, whose influence you will disrupt, will all become your bitterest enemies; and those you cannot fight with a sword."

"You still have no faith in me?"

Elen rolled her eyes. "Why do you still doubt me? In you, I have invested the future of my people, as well as that of the whole of Britannia. A betrayal of you would be the betrayal of everything I hold dear and am sworn to protect."

Magnus sighed. She wasn't wrong. The world of politics he had, by necessity to enmesh himself in, had turned out to be much more dangerous and dirty than that of a battlefield. There, sword in one hand, shield in the other, the best prepared side wins. In politics, he'd come to realise that the opposite was often true, that the victor was the worst.

"Britannia is only a distant province," she said. "The imperial court is where the *real* power of the empire lies. My worry is that after the military victory, which you will surely clinch, the world of politics might prove not to be your strength."

"Fortunately, I will have Elen of the Roads at my side to advise me through the traps and weeds."

"Any news from Marcellinus?" she asked.

The sudden change of topic wrong-footed him slightly, like a sparring opponent coming with a kick instead of a swing, and his concern quickly flipped to his brother. Marcellinus' task at the court of Valentinian in Mediolanum, trying to entice the powerful bishop to come over to his side, was one of great risk.

For his glory, he'd put everyone he loved in jeopardy.

"Papa, look," Victor chirped. He was pointing to something in the soggy grass of the well-tended little garden in the courtyard. Magnus supposed it was an insect, as the boy had developed some inordinate fascination for earwigs, woodlice and grasshoppers–normal for a two-year-old, apparently.

Magnus bent over, but couldn't see anything.

"Papa!"

"He wants to show you something," Elen said.

To humour his son, he crouched down, but at the end of Victor's pudgy finger was nothing but wet grass. He looked worriedly at his son as, mouth agape, he rocked his little head from side to side, fixated on something invisible. Magnus felt a tinge of panic that he'd fathered a simpleton.

"Ray-bow," Victor gargled.

Fearing the worst, he looked up at Elen.

"I believe that in a dew drop at the end of a blade of grass, he can see the colours of the rainbow."

Magnus squinted, bent even further forwards, and as he moved his head, he saw that on the edges of the blade of grass, tiny points of light changed from red, through yellow and blue, to the colour of the cloak he might soon be wrapping around his shoulders. It was not something he'd ever noticed before, not something he'd ever considered. Nor was it something he was too comfortable with his son being so enthralled with.

"As above, so below." Elen smiled..

Magnus turned his head so she wouldn't see him roll his eyes. *Trust her to see a deeper meaning in something he considered meaningless*, he thought. "Maybe you could line up his toy soldiers for him?" he suggested, "Or take him to see some real ones in the fort?" That wiped the smile off her face. Sevira started wailing, and the rainbow died.

He stood back up again.

He had an almost empire-wide network of spies and informants, more or less at his disposal, as long as Elen agreed with his intent, and they were proving absolutely invaluable to his ambitions, but the warmth and support he wanted from her now, before he opened the message, he couldn't have. All she had to offer him was stone cold duty–and that duty was to the people of Britannia Secunda before him; a people so stubborn, that even after three hundred years they still thought of themselves as Britons first, then Romans.

He remembered how he felt in those strange days when his wine had been tainted with her grandmother's dream powder. The all-powerful, all-consuming love he'd felt for her. It worried him more than he cared to admit that claiming the Western Empire often seemed of equal concern to winning the heart of a young girl.

"How is our Sevira today?" he asked.

"Strong." Elen smiled, but only with her mouth, not with her eyes. "She will be a very strong woman one day."

"I don't doubt that." Magnus sighed. Any girl with the old woman's blood in her would surely be a force to be reckoned with. Sevira was only a few months old, but already he didn't envy the man she'd marry one day. He'd have to be the strongest man in the land to cope with her..

It was Victor as emperor that interested him more than the destiny of his daughter, though. Every single time he looked at that pudgy face, he felt a sense of relief that the boy's features were almost his own. He had Elen's eyes though. If he had Magnus' mind and Elen's stubbornness and strength, one day he would make an emperor whose memory would rival Constantine's–maybe even Caesar's!

"Before I read this note," he said, "I have a question for you. Do you promise me on the lives of everyone you hold dear, that the man who ordered the murder of my uncle Theodosius, was Valens, and that the man on whose sword his blood was spilled, was Merobaudes?"

She knew exactly how to look at him, that look of saintly innocence in her eyes. "Why would I lie to you about such a thing?"

"Merobaudes is master of infantry of the Western Empire's army; one of the most powerful military men there is, and also the one I depend on now, above all else, for my ascension."

"I give you my word, the Good Lord as my witness, according to my trusted sources, that this is the truth."

"So, to get what I want, I must make a partnership with my greatest enemy; the man I have wished a painful death upon for years? It is no easy thing to do."

"The higher you rise, the harder things will become," Elen said with a nonchalance that he hoped one day to emulate.

He stooped down to kiss Victor and the nurse hurried over with Sevira so he could do the same to her. He thought better of doing the same with Elen, and headed out of the town back over the bridge to the fort.

In one way, it all seemed so inevitable. On the other hand, if the note was bad news, he would breathe a sigh of relief–although he knew that wouldn't last for long as Gratian would surely have heard the reports of his popularity and how much the soldiers loved him. An unpopular emperor would have to find a way to deal with that.

At the centre of the fort, he stood before the twice life-sized statue of Constantine that had been erected in pride of place before the doors of the principia. Looming over him, strong jawed and thick necked, the likeness stared impassively out over the spot where some eighty years before, the Sixth Legion had proclaimed him emperor: the very same place that Magnus now stood. From here, the great man had gone on to become the sole ruler of the entire empire, and the last to be bestowed with the epithet of Great. Even though it had happened back in the days of the current soldiers' great, great grandfathers, the whole of what was left of the Sixth still felt a deep pride that it had been their legion who'd set Constantine on his way.

To give as good an impression of history repeating itself as he could, Magnus would declare himself on the very same steps.

The binding of the note was hard to undo with shaking fingers. His stomach twisted, threatening to turn inside out, as it did every time he was deeply anxious. Doubling over to throw up at the feet of the statue would not be the best way to start his journey to Gaul.

For the two years since the subjugation of the Votadini, he'd twice walked the length of the Wall, taking a few weeks each time along it's awe-inspiring eighty miles to stop and talk and to play dice with almost every soldier, all the time breathing fire on the rumours of Gratian's intimate relationship with his Alan guards, regaling all who would listen to the story of the day he'd seen them in *trousers* in the palace of Mediolanum. He'd done the same at Deva, Segontium, to the forts of the Saxon Shore on the southeast coast. He couldn't have done any more, but whatever Andragathius had written, yes or no, he knew that if he was to make any mistake in the days to come, any slight miscalculation, not only could his own life be forfeit, and Victor's, but also the empire itself.

He had to have a clear route to Treverorum. Three commanders of the border armies that were stationed between the mouth of the Rhine and the former imperial capital. Andreagathius had got one to declare himself to Magnus, had found men to agree to kill the second at the sight of Magnus' ships coming up the river, and now there was just Frontonius in Bonnensia.

Under the sightless gaze of the statue, he finally found the nerve to unfold the parchment. III was the code for the third commander. It was followed by another I, which stood for 'yes'. The entire Rhine army north of Treverorum supported him.

He reread it another few times in case he'd missed something and had confused its meaning, but knew that, at last, it was time.

Coelius, the legate of the remnants of the legion that still called themselves the Sixth, came out of the principia, his bright red cloak flowing out behind him, as if with some divine timing. Quickly understanding what Magnus was doing at the statue, said, "If you've come to ask Constantine for an answer to a question, that message in your hand must have been an important one!"

Coelius had become a good friend over the year and a half that Magnus and Elen had lived at Eboracum and readily agreed that Magnus in the purple would be an improvement for the empire – although Magnus couldn't help worrying that that was because with him abroad, Coelius would, by default, be the most powerful man in Britannia.

"Well then, that seals it. The clouds have been gathering for some time. Now the storm is here," Coelius said in his characteristic way of painting pictures with words. "Once the men return from their march, I will call them to attention, and you will make history before them."

Magnus looked up at the statue. A strange feeling was running through his blood. From the day in Segontium when he'd first met Elen and had seen through her grandmother's ruse, he'd felt in control–until now! Decision made, he suddenly felt as though he was on a cart rolling downhill, gathering speed, and at the moment he wanted the brake lever in his hand for security, he realised there wasn't one.

II

Magnus listened to the excited buzz of hundreds of voices in the streets outside the principia. The tension had been growing for some time, and now it was now close to breaking point. If Magnus was to wait any longer, they would burst inside and drag him out themselves.

Coelius looked Magnus up and down critically, as though he was a new recruit at muster. He adjusted the bright red cloak on Magnus' shoulder as though he hadn't quite learned how to dress himself properly. He took a long deep breath then clasped Magnus' shoulders. "It's time." And then he added an appellation that Magnus wasn't expecting. "Augustus." It made his heart skip a beat.

Magnus felt Elen's hand in his, and for a moment, he was glad of the rare display of support, even if any true affection was too much to hope for. But her nails began to bite into his palm. She looked up at him. "Beloved husband, I urge you to be cautious. A wise man does not bet everything he holds dear on a single roll of the dice."

"Your wife speaks like a senior military commander," Coelius laughed in a way that was bordering on being a little too familiar.

"I speak only through the love of my husband," she replied, meekly. "And the desire that he lives a long and godly life to bring up our children."

"Soon, we will sit together in the bathhouse of Treverorum," Magnus said, trying to sound confident. "And you shall be called Empress."

"Just as long as I am not an empress of a wasteland," she said, with more than just a hint of her grandmother's steel.

Coelius held his hand out to the principia doors in an invitation for Magnus to step into his destiny, but as he began to walk, far from feeling like a new emperor, he wondered if the deserters he'd crucified after the Votadini raid had felt something similar as they were dragged to the crosses they were to die on.

Coelius pulled the doors open and the cheer of the soldiers washed over him like a wave in a storm.

All were in full armour, but clamoured about in an unruly throng. Not only were the crossroads of streets full of soldiers, some had even climbed onto the barrack roofs to get a better look. It was almost unbelievable what power a simple rumour could have. One that men wanted to believe, that was shared well, could change the world.

Elen stood on his left, playing her role as a diligent wife. She still held his hand, but dug her nails into his palm again. A cat giving a lazy little reminder to the mouse that it had no chance of escape.

"Attention!" Coelius shouted in a voice very used to being raised, and the excited murmuring in the streets instantly ceased. "Some eighty years ago, on the very spot you are standing on, your forbearers of the Sixth stood here just as you do now." He paused for effect. "And they proclaimed their own man emperor! His name was Constantine, and you all know he became the Great! A man whose name and legacy will live on through the ages, spoken in the same sentence as Caesar himself. That moment in history happened right here, right where we are standing!"

He pointed at the statue and Magnus wondered if one of equal size in his own likeness would one day find itself on the other side of the principia steps. A matching pair of Greats.

"And today it is time for you to play *your* part in the history of the empire."

Magnus was impressed. Even his heart stirred.

But then Coelius changed his tone. "For too long now the Western Empire has been under the nominal rule of *children*. In truth, as we all know, power has been wielded by those in the shadows - and always to the detriment of the entire Empire. What soldier can be happy with all the stories of his emperor surrounding himself with our enemies? *Alans*! Our brothers on the Rhine fight and *kill* Alans!. Gratian even *dresses* like them. I fear not to say that this disgusts me! I am a *true* soldier, in the red all of my life, and what I want more than anything is simply to serve under an emperor who brings *glory* to the empire. A man who makes me *proud* to serve."

Several hundred men collectively held their breath. Coelius let the pause grow, and it seemed that the silence drew power to itself. "I give you Magnus Maximus. Emperor of the West!"

The wave of sound of the men cheering reverberated through his chest.

He'd lain awake many nights knowing this day would come, but he hadn't imagined it would be quite so glorious. Looking through the faces, wide eyes staring out through gleaming helmets, they really wanted him to rise to the purple. They believed in him. They wanted him as emperor. And they would risk their futures, their lives, for it.

"Aug- ust- us! Aug- ust- us!" rang out so loudly he wondered if Gratian could hear it over in Gaul.

"And now to the cathedral?" Elen asked, an unmistakable hint of urgency in her voice. A baptised man was immediately forgiven of all sins, which, for a soldier with a history like Magnus' was surely the sweetest gift in all of the world, but the price for it was high, for he was then forever sworn to God and had to live a Christian life... on the threat of the eternal damnation of his soul. But for the murder of his uncle, he would kill Merobaudes. Probably in a way that would make the devil himself blanch–and so he had to delay the ritual.

A little nervously, he felt the heavy pouch of gold coins under his armour. Weighty gold for the weighty sin he was about to commit. Bribing a bishop probably wasn't the worst thing he'd ever done in his life. One more added to the account wouldn't make too much difference. Hopefully.

The excited soldiers parted to let him, Elen and Coelius through, but there were so many that from the principia to the southern gate they had to pass through in single file. The noise of them shouting their approval was absolutely deafening.

Out under the sturdy gate house, saluted by those up on the wall on duty, a long chain of soldiers followed them out, some trying to start up the chant of Au-gust-us. Coelius walked on Magnus' right, Elen on his left, her hand still in his, sweaty now, but not lessening the grip.

She wasn't walking with him; she was leading him.

As the mass of soldiers behind followed them onto the bridge the planks under his feet shook so much he was suddenly fearful that the structure would collapse, dashing him, and hundreds of soldiers, into the river below. It would be an act of God because He knew what blasphemy Magnus was intending to voice in the church.

The gates of the town were even more impressive than the ones of the fortress, thanks to the restorative works funded by Constantine. Nowhere was Magnus more comfortable than in a fort, shoulder to shoulder with soldiers, men he both understood and had command over. The town was run by different rules with administrators and justices–and most pressing of all, clergy. The bishop he was about to try and bribe held Magnus' future in his hands.

He felt the bulging coins at his hip again. The movement of his hand to the hilt of his sword would be enough to make a soldier or ordinary civilian fear for his life. That wouldn't work so well with men of God who were often more than happy to be made into martyrs. All he had to make sure that the rest of his life went the way he wanted it to go was gold. It was a method of persuasion he wasn't completely comfortable with. A sword at the throat meant exactly the same thing to every man, but offering a bribe was a much more subtle thing, and ran on some sort of scale dictated by the importance of the person against how much of a risk you wanted them to take.

Along the side of the forum, only a street away from his house, they turned the corner and stopped at the steps to the cathedral.

The idea that having his head anointed with water was all it would take to instantly be absolved of all of his sins seemed incredible. Almost too much to believe. All the men he'd hacked down with his own sword, all those he'd given the order to be put to death, all of the women and children of enemy tribes he'd let blood thirsty soldiers under his command take their frustrations out on–and probably plenty of other mortal sins he couldn't even recall. And if he was to die a moment after having his head anointed, he'd be welcomed straight through the gates of Heaven.

And one thing he understood about the church, as priests were fond of announcing it at every chance they got, is that there was no sin great enough that it couldn't be forgiven.

He was about to test that statement.

He felt the gold again, then made his way up the small steps.

For those coming from the north, the cathedral might be an impressive building, as after days travelling through the sparsely-inhabited, windswept hills from the Wall, stepping inside might have felt like the first taste of real civilisation. Coming from the south though, it would do nothing but remind you that you were in a rough hinterland in a city that knew it wasn't too far from the edge of the empire.

The doors were almost as sturdy as those of the city gates, which Magnus thought was a bit unusual for a place that was supposedly always open and welcoming.

As he walked slowly through the cool and curiously still air towards the bishop of Ebarocum, the noise of all those shuffling in behind him, hobnailed boots scratching on tiles echoing off the thick curving walls, sounded like a heavy waterfall.

"Welcome," the bishop said.

Even though it was a small provincial church, one of the furthest from the heart of the empire as it was possible to get, the bishop thought he was administering in the heart of Mediolanum. Magnus had often wondered at how the attire of those high up in the holy orders far outdid that of a mere emperor. The bishop was dressed in what looked like so many layers of cloth that he was standing stiffly– and he would have been pretty well protected in a sword fight. The crooked top of his staff was made of more gold than a real shepherd would make in a lifetime.

His stole was adorned with two large embroidered crosses and in a sickening hot flush, the memory of the deserters Magnus had crucified came back to him.

More excited soldiers pressed in behind and there was a bit of a commotion at the door as those lucky enough to get inside shouted at those still on the street that it was full. Someone even bumped into Magnus' back.

His voice raised over the noise, Magnus asked, "A baptism is between a man and God?"

The bishop nodded and his tall and oddly shaped hat accentuated the agreement.

"Perhaps we could arrange it so that it is a more *intimate* ceremony?"

The bishop understood, agreed, and with a couple of hand movements ordered his nervous acolytes to usher the soldiers back out.

Quite a few voiced their protest, but the young priests weren't going to raise their voices to an assembly of soldiers, and so, it was Coelius who bellowed the command that made his men turn around and hurry to get out. His voice sounded even more impressive inside the church than it had in the fort.

"Everyone," Magnus said and although he saw the disappointment on Coelius' face and the distrust on Elen's, they both left. It was the height of impropriety for a married woman to be out on the street among the soldiers, but having her in earshot of what he was about to say to the bishop would be much worse than her nagging him about accepted social conventions.

When the doors were closed, the sound of him being cut off from the outside world rang out through the hallowed building.

The thought of being able to leave a lifetime of sins behind and walking back into the light of day without them weighing on his soul was very tempting, but the problem with a baptism was that it could only be done once. One time in one lifetime was a strict prescript and he didn't think that there would be any exemptions made. Even for an emperor.

Once the acolytes had shuffled off into some side room and the bishop and Magnus were alone, he reached into his pouch and took a coin out. It was a gold solidus. The likeness of Constantine graced the front.

The bishop looked at it curiously. "Whatever you think you have come here to do," he said in what sounded like a growl, "I caution you that you stand in the house of God."

"I have a conflict in my heart," Magnus said. He was aware of how much he was shaking. It was probably the biggest gamble he'd taken on his journey so far.

"No doubt. Speak."

"I wish for baptism, I truly do. But I made a promise to God, a fervent one, that I would mete out justice to a man who committed a heinous crime. A murder."

"If it is as you say, why do you not have faith that this man will be subjected to *divine* judgement and punishment?"

"It is *my* judgement and punishment I wish to subject him to."

The bishop nodded with understanding, which was a good sign. "Which you would be damned eternally for if you were to do it after you are baptised."

"Exactly. As I said, I have a conflict."

"There is no conflict!" the bishop snapped, his booming voice echoing around them. "God will be the judge of this man," he said, a little impatiently, as though he was annoyed at having to explain something so obvious. "So speak and be judged."

"All I wish to do is *postpone* my baptism."

The bishop looked confused. "So come back when you believe yourself ready to receive God's grace. It is very simple."

Magnus sighed. "I would be happy to do that, of course. But the thing is, right now, I need everyone outside to believe that it happened."

"You wish to make a *bargain*? With *God*? With coin? You wish a *false* baptism because you harbour a plan of murder in your heart? You come to stand before me not just in sin, you have come to speak *sacrilege*!" the bishop's angry voice reverberated around them. "Put your coin back, turn around, and leave the sacred space before you cause yourself to be indelibly damned."

It was going badly, but he couldn't just walk out, shrug his shoulders and tell all the soldiers outside he'd been kicked out of the church and so he'd get baptised some other time. He looked again at what the bishop was wearing. Even for those who professed to not be interested in worldly trappings–the gold threaded clothes, jewel encrusted staff–not even a purple toga would look as rich.

Magnus knew that every man, no matter his standing or station, had a price, though. The only difference was that some men's price was higher than others.

Instead of leaving, Magnus took the pouch full of gold and set it down heavily on the rim of the large font, opening the drawstring so the bishop could see how full it was.

"There is absolutely nothing you can offer," he seethed, sounding offended. But his beady eyes lingered on the bag of gold with an expression that Magnus hoped was longing.

"I have just been proclaimed emperor."

"In front of men, not God."

Magnus reached out and touched the side of the font. Despite how well it had been crafted, he could still see some of the craftsmen's chisel marks down the side of it. "I do not presume to understand anything of God. But one thing I have noticed is that he does not build his own churches. No chorus of angels descend from heaven and by some miracle a new church is plucked out of the air overnight."

"The men who build them are guided by God's hand," the bishop said through gritted teeth.

Magnus pointed to the chisel marks on the font. "By men's hands with men's tools."

"Guided by God..."

"Land and materials are bought by men's coin. Their wages are paid by men's coin."

"Guided by God," he said again, slowly. "I warn you to caution with such words."

If Magnus had misjudged him and he was about to be tossed out onto the street, denied his baptism, his journey to the purple would be almost impossible. But it wasn't simply gold he'd come to offer.

"What is the most number of people you've baptised on a single day?" Magnus asked, attempting a different tack. "So many soldiers will want to come and be anointed after me, bringing their wives and children that this church won't be big enough for those who will want to come to your mass. Christianity will have a day of flourishing here the town has never seen before, under your hand. We'll need a bigger church–and *that* is what I offer. Not just a bag of gold. I have more bags like this, more than I can count. More than I know what to do with. Honest coin. The profit from my lands in the south. And so, why don't you and I honour God with it by building the largest church in Britannia, right in the heart of Londinium? Guided by God, of course. One dedicated to whoever *you* choose. And once it's built, it will need its own bishop. One that I, as emperor, can choose and appoint."

The bishop's face was turning red, as though he'd stopped breathing and was about to burst.

"Or maybe we can leave the appointment up to whomever God chooses?" Magnus suggested.

He watched the Bishop's eyes widen slightly. "As glorious as the Ambrosius' cathedral in Mediolanum?" he asked.

Just as a fisherman feels the pull of the caught fish on his rod, Magnus knew he had him. "Just as glorious." He smiled. "But even bigger."

The bishop's eyes widened a little more. "You risk a lot," he said as he dipped his hand into the holy water of the font.

"I risk it all." Magnus grinned.

The bishop nodded. Magnus wondered if maybe there would be trouble for his soul if something went wrong. As a bishop, he'd have more to answer for before God than Magnus would. "Take off your armour. You'll need to wear nothing but the white tunic."

"And my wife must know nothing of this."

"Of course. Only you, and I, and God will know."

III

Every joint in Andragathius' body creaked with the movement of the horse under him. He'd been in the saddle for days, and had ridden so hard he'd barely had time to eat or to rub salve on the sores on the insides of his legs while the next horse was prepared.

Close to the city of Treverorum now, he looked at some of the tombstones lining the side of the road. He was so exhausted, he felt close to joining them in their eternal slumber, and thoughts of lounging in the bathhouse appealed to him much more than the meeting he had come to have.

He wondered how imperial messengers spent their lives galloping the length and breadth of the empire, yet could somehow hand over their letters without crawling on the floor as though they'd been beaten half to death. He was glad it was only battles he had to kick his horse into a charge for.

As he approached the walls, he looked in awe at the imposing gate. Enough to protect an emperor. Its two towers in the northern wall rose up four stories high and he shook his head in disbelief that Magnus believed he could just walk straight through it and be welcomed inside. Either he was the most confident commander he'd ever met and would usher in a new age of peace and prosperity for the empire, or he was a fool who would get them all killed– and make the empire even weaker than it already was. But if there was any man in the empire who could pull off such a coup, it was Magnus.

Andragathius was glad that such weighty concerns were not on his shoulders... as they soon would be on the unsuspecting Ausonius.

The spent horse caught a hoof on a raised flagstone and the poor thing needed a few steps to right itself.

When he was close enough for the pair of guards to see the grime his face was covered with, he called out in a voice roughened by dust and a lack of water, "Message from Magnus Maximus, Dux Britanniarum, for Consul Ausonius. Urgent!"

"Hand it over. We'll get it passed on," one of the guards said, none too politely.

"Utmost urgency. Matter of empire. Spoken message only."

The soldier clearly took offence. "And your name?" he asked..

"Andragathius of the Batavi. Master of cavalry of Britannia."

The soldier might not have known the name, but from the humorous way in which his face contorted, Andragathius wondered if he was trying to work out how many ranks there were between them. "Right away!" he said, and added, "Sir!"

The gate house was one of the grandest buildings he'd ever seen. From the colossal stones at the base, it towered above him and it hurt his stiff neck to look up at it. It had stood for so many years that it was beginning to get stained from the smoke from the city.

A guard took an already saddled horse from the stable just inside the wall and tore off to inform the relevant people while another held on to Andragathius' reins in case he had any idea of charging off into the city by himself. While he waited, he thought again of the bathhouses Treverorum was famous for. A well-oiled young boy working the tension out of his back and applying balm to his chafed inner thighs was exactly what he wanted.

It didn't take too long for the rider to come back, pushing his horse to its fullest, sending the terrified people shopping at the stalls lining the street scattering. "At the basilica," he said to his superior a little breathlessly. "He'll see him immediately."

The other soldier handed Andragathius' reins back, and as he rode, he leaned forwards in the saddle, trying to take some pressure off the places that hurt the most. Something ran down the inside of his leg. Hopefully it was only sweat, not blood.

After so long travelling through nothing but rolling countryside, Treverorum, with its streets laid out in a neat plan lined with well looked after white-washed buildings, seemed a paradise, but the basilica was an altogether different level of grandeur. He wondered how the high wall could contain so many huge windows. With their domed tops, it looked more like a large bridge spanning a valley floor than a building in the middle of a city. It was an apt place to be for the man Magnus had chosen to decide the fate of the empire.

The elderly consul was waiting for him outside. The old man's toga was the whitest he'd ever seen. In the sun, it almost hurt his eyes to look at it. He looked like an angel the Christians liked to talk about.

It wasn't God's will on earth they had come to talk about though; it was Magnus'.

"Consul. Andragathius of the Batavi, master of cavalry," the soldier proclaimed in a loud voice. "With a message from Magnus Maximus, Dux Britanniarum."

"Andragathius," Ausonius said. "I know the name, and now I will have the pleasure of knowing the man. For the Dux Britanniarum to send his master of horse with a message, it must be important news."

"Yes, Consul." He'd soon find out just how important, but the street was not the place to tell him.

"Well..." the old man said, seemingly amused. "Would you like to give it from horseback, or perhaps we could go somewhere a little more comfortable?" With that he clicked his fingers, and without even blinking, the soldier slid out of his saddle and handed his horse over, took a knee and cupped his hands together for Ausonius to use as a step.

"Just a few more steps and your journey will be over. For today at least." Ausonius smiled.

Andragathius groaned at the thought of having to ride back north to Magnus without resting.

They could have walked, but after his journey, Andragathius would have limped all the way, and he was definitely not a man for the silks and perfumes of an emperor's litter. The fact that Ausonius seemed to be aware of that from the first glance made him a little nervous that he was out of his depth. Again, he worried that Magnus should have sent someone better versed in the arts of diplomacy for the delicate task at hand.

A toga wasn't easy to ride in, but with it bundled up over the saddle, Ausonius looked easy enough on horseback, although his pale-skinned, spindly legs gave an indication of how old he was. He led Andragathius along rows of large houses to a building almost as magnificent as the basilica.

"It's even more impressive on the inside," Ausonius quipped, and Andragathius realised that his mouth was hanging open. "After travelling so far, you'll feel like you've died and gone to heaven, I don't doubt."

For a man well known for craving power and influence, Andragathius wondered if his host would feel something similar once he'd heard the news.

He'd heard stories about the sizes of the palaces emperors lived in, but he could barely believe that the huge building Ausonius led him to was just a bathhouse.

"No frigidarium, I'm afraid," Ausonius said as an expressionless young slave unwound his toga. "Constantine left here and it was never finished. But the caldarium is the best in the empire, I promise you. Several emperors have told me so."

Andragathius wondered if another emperor would soon be enjoying it.

Even though it was empty, it was still ready for bathers as the humidity instantly made him too hot in his layers of armour. He was impatient with the pair of slaves fiddling with the straps of his lorica squamata and the clumsy way they tugged the heavy chain mail shirt over his head made him think that they didn't have too many heavily-armed soldiers to tend to.

He was almost embarrassed by the state of his tunic. Sweat-soaked and encrusted with patterns of dried sweat, the slaves had to practically peel it off him. He'd seen cleaner ones laying on battlefields, bits of their former owners splashed over them.

But standing naked before the old man, any shame in his condition was quickly dispelled by the state of Ausonius' age-ravaged body. Seeing the skin sagging off his bones, like the top of a milk pudding left too long, the consul's power seemed to wane in Andragathius' mind. And he noticed how wistfully Ausonius glanced at him. A few hard years past his prime he may have been, with grey hairs streaking his beard, but the food at Magnus' table was plentiful, and he'd filled out appreciatively over the last couple of years, like a bear before winter.

A man with Ausonius' wealth and power could have almost anything he wanted, but the vital strength of youth was something long denied him.

"Is your message so urgent that we should forgo the oiling and strigil and head straight to the bath?"

Andragathius wanted nothing more than to slip his aching muscles and sore skin into the hot water and soak the long days of hard travel away, so nodded his consent. A slave squatted down to slip a pair of thick soled sandals on his feet.

In any bathhouse Andragathius had ever set foot in, the pool had been murky from the dead skin and dirt scraped off the patrons, so his first impression of the imperial one was how spotlessly clean everything was. He could almost see the bottom of the hot pool.

He carefully made his way down the steps into the scalding water. It made the chafed skin on the inside of his legs sting, he supposed that the people who usually frequented the place didn't usually moan so loudly.

"You look like you have ridden all the way from Britannia," Ausonius chuckled as he gently lowered himself in.

Andragathius' stomach turned at the memory of the sea crossing. "I have."

There was a quick flash of distrust in his old eyes, but Ausonius asked pleasantly, "How fares that strange little island?"

Being so close to the most powerful people in court with all the intrigue, power plays, desires and treasons he must have seen over the long years, Andragathius was sure the old consul wouldn't be too surprised to learn of Magnus' plan. Many men had proclaimed themselves emperor over the years. "It is well. Magnus easily quelled the only uprising, and that took the fire out of the tribes at the borders. They have been settled since. He is very popular among the soldiers."

"So I have heard," Ausonius said, a bushy eyebrow raised. "But that is a very dangerous statement to make so close to the seat of imperial power." He slipped further down in the water so that it was up to his chin. Strands of his white hair floated on the gently steaming surface.

Andragathius was sure that Ausonius, a man famously adept at manoeuvring in the murky world of politics, must know he'd not come to divulge any normal message. He took a deep breath. "A storm is coming."

As Ausonius nodded, little ripples spread out across the surface of the pool. "It seems that, for all of my lifetime, the storms have never stopped. One disaster with so little time to recover from before the next one strikes. With things as they are these days, the empire takes not one man to rule, but *three*!"

And now the time had come to let Magnus' secret fully out into the world. Andragathius hoped that the way his heart was pounding wouldn't disturb the water to betray how nervous he was. "And now a fourth," he said and watched the change spread across Ausonius' face. The old man groaned and pushed himself up a couple of steps, perhaps suddenly feeling a bit too hot in the steaming water. "I knew this would happen," he growled. "Justina and Gratian were both worried about him brooding alone in Rome, watching the rest of us trying, and failing, to cover the cracks in the borders... stem the tide... mop up the shit Valens left us with. They thought that putting him on a soggy little island would give him everything he wanted and they could forget about him. I warned them to be wary of him! Maybe I wasn't insistent enough. Have I brought this calamity on us myself?"

He seemed to be speaking to the nicely decorated domed ceiling high above them rather than to Andragathius, so he let him continue.

"But no, no, this is a disaster that can be averted. Yes, I know what to do. I will promote him to Governor of Britannia. That should satisfy his lofty ambitions. And he can stay on his little island and leave us here in Gaul to worry about the Goths, Alemanni and Huns. I can write a prescript for him right now. Gratian will agree. That should be sufficient." He looked again at Andragathius, little ratty eyes burning with panic. "You shall leave tomorrow and take this promotion back to him."

Slowly, Andragathius said, "We're a little past that."

Ausonius looked at him with suspicion. Maybe even hatred. "How far past?" He pushed himself a little further out of the hot water. "Please don't tell me he's in Gaul already?"

Andragathius nodded. "He should be crossing as we speak."

"What? He's come in person to negotiate such a thing! Then the man is a damn fool."

"Negotiate is perhaps not exactly the word for his intentions," Andragathius sighed. "And the five thousand soldiers he has with him seem to share that sentiment."

It seemed that Ausonius was looking right through him, his eyes glassy. Then his expression changed to anger. "He will rip the empire apart. He will bring ruin upon us! Two armies clashing will be an absolute disaster. The empire already hangs by just a thread."

"Magnus doesn't want a battle."

"Good. So he proposes to simply walk into Gaul and have Gratian hand over power, does he?"

"To avert a pitched battle, which of course would be disastrous and must be avoided at all costs, he invites you to support him in his claim as Emperor of the West."

Ausonius' nervous laughter rang off the walls. "Does he now? Does he now?" He looked up at the ceiling, trying to calm himself. "Do you understand what it is that you ask of me? I was a tutor to Emperor Gratian when he was but a child. He is as much a son to me as my *own* son is. Anything, *every*thing I have been bestowed on me by the house of Valentinian. *That* is who you ask me to betray. Magnus asks me to serve the empire by *betraying* its emperor! Do you know what an impossible thing that is to ask?"

"Magnus does not want Gratian dead. He is adamant about this. He took baptism on the same day as his proclamation in Britannia, so he wishes no harm to a fellow Nicean Christian. On the pain of eternal damnation. The boy will be allowed to live in the luxury to which he is accustomed, maybe even to hold an important position in Magnus' administration. Or maybe he could go east to Theodosius in Constantinople, if he wishes. He will be afforded safe passage."

Ausonius scoffed. "Tell me, from the whole of the history of this empire of ours, from Romulus and Remus, through the Republic, to this modern day, the name of any deposed ruler, who lived more than a few days."

There might have been some, perhaps one or two, but Andragathius couldn't think of any names.

"Treason. He asks me to commit treason, which will not only result in my long, drawn-out execution, but that of many men I hold dear."

The long sigh Ausonius let out sounded like the death of hope.

"Out of interest, theoretically, just so I can get the measure of the man, what does the great Magnus think to offer me for such treason?"

"Apart from another consulship, a quiet retirement."

Ausonius chuckled. "Really? That's all. I am a little insulted. Besides, that is my plan under the *current* administration."

"Yes, but with Magnus here in Treverorum, your quiet, autumn days won't be interrupted by hordes of barbarians pouring across the borders." That made the old man think.

"You have to admit that Magnus will be a competent ruler," Andragathius said calmly. "He was not just taught by Theodosius the Elder, he was brought up by him and, as you must know, he has never lost a fight in his life. He calls himself the Great Greatest, which is an arrogant name for sure, but it is not one undeserved. His cousin is emperor in Constantinople and he is truly respected by his soldiers. He has to be better for the good of the empire than Gratian."

"It is the good of the empire he wishes me to consider, is it?"

Andragathius nodded.

"For the *good* of the empire?" he scoffed. "He is the *enemy* of the empire! How can you even be sitting here next to me saying such things! Do you come as some test of my loyalty to Gratian? Is that what this foolishness is? I should send for the guards and tell them to take your head!"

A threat from such a man was not to be taken lightly, and suddenly, it was Andragathius' turn to be too hot in the water. With a flush of sweat on his brow, he stood up, ready to suggest that they go to the cold room, but when Ausonius saw how broad his chest was and the heavy muscles that made men half his age jealous, he shied away.

"But anyway, this is all purely hypothetical," Ausonius whined. "What influence you think I hold here is, I fear, quite overstated. If you think I hold power over military matters, Magnus is very ill informed."

"All he wants from you is to persuade just one man to support him."

"Who?" he asked guardedly.

"Merobaudes."

"Gratian's master of infantry," he laughed, but his eyes remained rock hard. "The most senior military man in this part of the world. And what kind of influence do you think I have with a man like that?"

Andragathius shrugged. "Any intelligent man will listen to reason. And an irresistible offer."

"And what does Magnus think to offer Merobaudes for such a betrayal?"

"A second consulship."

That wiped the condensing smirk from the old man's face. He nodded slowly. "He does very well to offer Merobaudes something a man of his class could hardly even dream of. Perhaps Magnus knows well the hearts of men after all."

Andragathius didn't think it was the place to mention that it was Elen who had come up with the idea.

"Truely, you have given me much to contemplate," Ausonius said. "It will take some time to digest it all."

"I am afraid I can't offer you such a luxury," Andragathius said. "Time is what we don't have. He will be at the gates soon. I myself have just come from Bonnensia. the garrison there has declared for Magnus."

"That cannot be true," Ausonius gasped, his eyes narrowing as he suspected Andragathius of some easily disprovable deceit. "Frontonius is cousin to two emperors!"

"Indeed he is." Andragathius nodded. "Which is why as soon as Magnus' ships are sighted coming up the river, the broad-band tribunes, old soldiers who know all about the importance of military strength, will take it upon themselves to install a new legate. I believe they have already decided who that will be."

"They can't do that! Such treachery..."

"Will be rewarded by Magnus." Andragathius finished.

"No, no," the old man almost sobbed. "This cannot be happening." He leaned over, elbows on his knees, head in his hands. "You really wish for me to decide the fate of the empire tonight?"

"It is no small thing to think upon, I am sure. But I ride back tomorrow, so you can have until dawn. All he asks is that you put the good of the empire first."

Ausonius scoffed, squirming with the responsibility laid upon him.

"No small thing, indeed! You have just made me the most important man in the world!"

Andragathius almost felt sorry for the old man, but it was Elen he thought about. How a young girl could have known that he needed to sneak into the fort of Bonnensia and ask to meet a certain man in a certain place to discuss the murder of the legate was utterly beyond him. It was easier to believe that she wielded some kind of magics rather than that she'd simply inherited a network of contacts and informants from her family

Some time in the future, he could imagine needing the benefit of those contacts himself, so knew it would be wise to ingratiate himself into Elen's good graces. But what did he, an over-promoted Batavi horseman, have to offer a girl who was about to be Empress of the Western Empire?

IV

Kenon crouched down where he'd tucked himself away in the corner of the room, feeling the warmth radiating from the wall heated by the hypocaust at his back. It was midsummer, but he was almost cold enough to shiver. He was always cold these days. A constant chill in his bones he suspected came from spending too long in the wastelands north of the Wall as a captive of Padarn. It wasn't the cold that ailed him the most though; it was what was in his head. Today, the ringing in his ears was so loud it was a struggle not to weep. He scraped his knife on the floor to try and make some other noise to drown it out.

Doctors had told him the sounds were because he'd been hit in the head so hard by the Votadini that something in his ears had got damaged. Apparently, it happened a lot to soldiers who'd suffered a head blow. They'd said that it would get better with time. Except Kenon's had never ceased. Not for weeks, not for months. Now it had been two years. He knew it was no simple battle injury. He'd not mentioned it to anyone, but he was sure it was the screams of the girl he'd killed, and her mother, crying out to him from somewhere in the afterlife at the horror he'd caused; it was driving him right to the very edge of madness.

His hand clenched around the handle of his dagger. It was his grandfather's, the one that his father had taken off him before sending him off to the fort of Rutupiae. It felt good to have it back, but it hadn't been Octavius who'd returned it. The old bastard had died while still so disappointed with his son that he couldn't even speak to him. His last words would always remain, 'write to your mother'...

Words laden with the implication that his father did not want to hear from his son again.

Kenon was well aware that he owed absolutely everything he had to the popular Dux Britanniarum. He'd been spared crucifixion, and so he owed his life, but it went down to the water he drank on the farm he'd been sent to. And forgotten about.

The ringing was so intense it felt like a pressure—and there was only one way he knew of to quieten it. He inched his tunic up his leg and held the blade against the side of his thigh. The coldness of the steel against his skin was calming, but it was the agony of the cut he needed for a few moments of true silence. He felt the raised scar tissue of previous cuts for a smooth piece of skin. A tightening of the chest, a quick flood of nausea, and he pushed the blade into his flesh, then he breathed. The pain was like pulling a hood over his head to drown out all of the terrors of the outside world.

He sighed with relief as the screams quietened. His blood-letting brought a blessed reprieve from the torment, for a little while, at least, as he knew it fell well short of the absolution he craved, or the forgiveness he was so desperate for, but for now, his mind was stilled.

Magnus often talked about how much he valued the trust he could put in certain men in his circle. In the few times he'd seen Magnus since he'd defeated the Votadini, he'd told Kenon he found it in him. That was the day he'd handed his grandfather's dagger back. He'd meant it as a compliment, one he'd expected Kenon to value, but instead, it made Kenon uneasy, for how could a man on the cusp of such unimaginable power have such a deep misunderstanding of someone so close to him? A leader with such poor intuition, did not instil any confidence in him..

Often, when he tried to think about all that had happened north of the Wall, it was like a shield had lifted in his mind, as though his own brain formed a testudo to try and protect him from the horrors of the past. In moments of cold calm like this, his fingers sticky with his own blood, he could almost see the link between Magnus sending the Areani after him, so that the Votadini would be irresistibly enticed south... into the trap that Magnus had set. It was so very tempting to believe he was a victim of Magnus' convoluted plans, just as much as Padarn was, and that it wasn't simply because of his own stupidity that those things had happened to him. That he'd been betrayed by a master tactician, one of the most powerful men in Britannia.

The death of his father was also far too convenient, as well. It had come right at the exact moment that would benefit Magnus the most. Less than a week after he married Elen he became the owner of vast estates. It was nothing he could prove, so he'd never voiced it to anyone, but the grating feeling had never left him.

And if he'd have told anyone how much it burned in him that Magnus had taken away any possibility for his father to come to him and say, "Well done, son. I am proud of you", they would have called him mad.

So deep in his thoughts, he didn't notice his slave come in. Seeing the little pool of blood at his side, she almost tutted at him as though he was a disappointing child.

Another insult, they'd given him the ugliest, most dumpy slave in the whole province. The thought of seeing her naked disgusted him and he was sure he'd get more enjoyment from a conjugal visit to the farm.

She squatted down to hold a cloth against his bleeding leg, and pulled the knife out of his reach. At least she was so worthless that he didn't need to feel too ashamed in front of her, but then, having someone concerned about him, even if it was a slave no one else wanted, didn't feel so awful. With the weight lifted from his chest, he could breathe again, and think about how to find his place in the world, somewhere, far away from Magnus' imposing shadow.

Being in charge of the grain production in the Northwest province of Britannia Prima would have made many lesser men proud.

For Kenon, whose lands, if Magnus hadn't taken them for himself, should have been big enough that he'd need a week to ride through them. It was nothing but insulting. He knew it was just a way of keeping him quiet in a small farm, away from the fortress of Deva, and was probably something his sister had had to beg for.

The token wage was just about enough to spend in the brothels around Deva whenever he wanted–but although he'd been spared crucifixion, the soldiers of the Twentieth at Deva wouldn't treat a deserter too well if anyone recognised him, so, hadn't left the farm since he'd arrived. All he wanted now was to be able to afford a slave. One he could keep secret and in the darkness of the cellar under the farm and visit on to him all of the pain and humiliations he'd had to endure both above the Wall and below it. Do to him all the things Padarn had done. Maybe then he could find some comfort in knowing there was someone in the world suffering as much as he was. But to buy one, he'd need to go to Deva.

Suddenly, he heard voices–workers, calling out an alarm. With the terrifying fear that a horde of barbarians were coming up the path, fighting them was the last thing on his mind. All he could do was try and push himself harder against the wall.

"It's all right, Dominus," the fat slave said, trying to calm him, but her words only made him feel pathetic that a slave was braver than he was.

A worker was at the door, a look of concern on his weathered face. "Soldiers!" he gasped.

Kenon wanted to run, but didn't dare try to dash across the yard in full view of whoever was approaching–not that his legs would have let him anyway. He fumbled for his knife, determined that if they were intended to do what Padarn had done, they'd be doing it to his dead body. But then there was someone at the door. He couldn't look, couldn't move.

The intruder walked slowly, deliberately, and came to stand over him. He saw the knife. It wasn't too far away. If he made a lunge for it, managed to reach the handle with his fingertips, he could fight, but whoever it was kicked it away.

"What has happened to you?" asked a soft female voice.

Kenon forced himself to look up to see a girl standing over him with an easy authority. The light from the door behind cast what looked like a holy glow around her. "Elen?" he gasped. It was hard to speak as his throat was constricted with fear.

She, just as much as Magnus, was the architect of his downfall. Father had bequeathed all of his vast estates to her, and they'd therefore passed to Magnus when they'd married, and now she'd seen what he'd done to his leg. With the horrific shame mixed with all the injustices she'd heaped on him, he pushed himself up with the intention of snapping the bitch's neck. But from nowhere, a sword was pointing straight at his chest. He was too slow to react, as the tip pressed into his skin. He stepped back against the wall, but couldn't tell if the blood on his fingers was from what he'd done to his leg or from a new wound.

"Stay there," Elen's bastard guard growled.

Elen held an arm out to keep the soldier back, but even that was an insult. His little sister protecting him. "Aigla! Are you all right?"

She'd seen the blood and her first reaction had been to check on the slave!

"It's his," she said. "The same thing I told you about before, Domina. He's done it again."

Outraged at a slave freely divulging his deepest secret, Kenon spat, "You will die for that!" But with the sword still pointed at him, he didn't dare move to strike her.

"You will not touch her!" Elen snapped.

"She's my slave! I can do-"

"I am no slave!" the woman snapped, and it was as though she'd just slapped him in the face. Kenon was confused. For a slave to say that, she'd have her tongue ripped out. But Elen didn't look the slightest bit fazed. And then he realised. "She's not even a slave? You *pay* her to be here with me?!"

"You know I don't have slaves," she said. "I don't believe in subjugating fellow humans."

"Saint Elen," Kenon said with scorn. They couldn't even give him a slave. They'd sent a spy to him, instead, and the bitch had been telling Elen, and therefore probably Magnus, everything about him.

Another betrayal.

He should be used to them by now, yet it still made something in his chest burn.

Still reeling from being spoken to in such a way by his little sister, he was in no mood to offer her any pleasantries, so spat, "What do you want?"

"I have come with an offer. I'm sure that you want to leave this place, don't you?"

If he'd had anywhere else to go, he would have left long ago. He could think of no articulate answer to give her though, so just scoffed. "Where to?" he managed as the idea of going back to Deva or Segontium to have his nose rubbed in all that he'd lost everyday did not seem so appealing.

"Gaul."

"What? Why?"

"Magnus has been proclaimed emperor."

"Again?"

"Yes. But this time, he accepted, and he is going to face Gratian."

"And he wants *me* to go with him?"

"Of course. You are my brother. He has not forgotten what you did for him outside the walls of Rutupiae – your bravery."

Kenon's mind reeled. The man he'd just been dreaming about killing was now one of the most powerful men in the whole of the empire? He hated him with all of his heart, but at the same time he thought of all the powers an emperor could bestow on those he favoured, and in Gaul, no one would know him. Kenon's mouth watered at the prospect. Maybe something that would be enough to drown out the dead girl screaming inside his head. If he was honest, running out between two armies that day had more to do with stupidity than bravery, but it seemed Magnus couldn't tell the difference.

And Kenon wasn't honest.

V

They said that massive responsibilities sat on a man's shoulders like the globe did on Atlas', his back bent, knees buckling, as he struggled to bear its crushing weight. Many learned men held the words of the old Greeks in the highest esteem, but about that particular idea, Magnus wasn't so sure that he agreed. It wasn't a weight he felt, it was more as though the fist of the colossus that used to stand over the harbour of Rhodes had a tight grip on everything in his chest and guts. The crushing pressure was so great, he could feel it in his eyes, his heart felt laboured and each breath came only with effort, but even worse was how his stomach, already churned by how the boat lurched over the swells, was threatening to empty over the side of the ship. He couldn't be sick, not now. He could not afford even the slightest show of weakness. With the white cliffs of Britannia now far behind them, the fleet now out of sight of any land, for what was coming he needed nothing but good omens. His future depended on it.

The wind was gusting. It was square behind them, which was good, evidence, if the men needed it, that God was supportive of Magnus' cause and was helping it along. When it blew, he felt it as the breath of destiny itself urging him on towards glory, but when it calmed and the sails hung limply from the rigging, he couldn't help panicking that the lull was God literally and figuratively taking the wind out of his ambitions: A sure sign he should have stayed in Britannia, content with his posting.

He stood at the prow of the ship, ahead of the rest of the fleet spread out behind, looking at the white tops on some of the waves.

The hull connected with a large one and he got splashed with salt water. He didn't envy the soldier who'd have to rub and oil every piece of his armour clean once they'd made it to dry land. There must be ten thousand or more individual rings in his chainmail shirt.

If it was to get much rougher, some of the ships would be in trouble. The liburnas, the sleekest and fastest ships on the seas, were notorious for needing calm weather to travel.

Wobbling as she tried to balance herself with the movement of the ship, Elen came to stand at his side, looking almost as green as Andragathius had when he'd sailed the other way three years earlier. It was good to have her with him. Not because she gave him any genuine support or affection, but because it was good for the men to see them together. Taking his wife and his two children over with the soldiers made it seem a foregone conclusion that they'd be sitting in Treverorum's throne room in a few days.

So Elen had told him.

The real reason she was with him was because she had insisted on it, and when Elen insisted on something, she usually got it. What influence over the coming fight with Gratian she hoped to wield, he had no idea. Nor what ambitions of his she hoped to stifle.

"Is that it?" she asked as she pointed to the indistinct horizon.

Her eyes were better than his, but he assumed that she could see land. He thought she'd be a bit more excited about her first sight of Gaul than that, but he'd long since ceased being surprised about how she reacted to things. Admittedly, the low spit of land was only just visible between the sea and the sky didn't look that epic.

They hit another big wave. He reached out to support her, but she twisted away from his touch.

"You think of me as an enemy?" he asked.

"I think of you as someone whose ambition is aligned with my own," she said, which was not something a wife usually said to her husband. Then she added, "Presently," which was probably even less common.

"And what about when I am emperor?"

"The peace and prosperity of Britannia is my only concern," she said with a sweet smile that he'd long ago learned not to be disarmed by.

"We will live in the palace of Treverorum."

"We'll be back in Britannia soon enough," she replied, confidently. As an equal. "If your plan fails, we return. If you win and you stay to rule from Treverorum or Mediolanum, then I will come back to Britannia with the soldiers to make sure her borders are secure. It is what we agreed, and the agreement stands no matter which side of the sea we are on. Isn't that true?"

His way forward had been paved by the contacts Elen's grandmother had gifted to her. Men, either loyal, or paid well enough, had been spreading rumours against Gratian and his despised Alan guards, but had also told stories about a great general amassing support, who would come and put right all of the empire's ills. If she was to stop all of that, and start spreading unflattering rumours about Magnus instead, he could probably say goodbye to all of his dreams of the purple. All she asked was for Britannia to be well protected from sea raiders and those north of the Wall. For what he hoped to achieve in a few days, the price didn't seem too high. "Yes, dear," he sighed.

She'd given him a son and that was all he really needed from her. Once he was emperor, things would change. He was very confident about that.

What he was less confident about was Fraomar's mission. Half a month ago he'd sailed from the Wall fort of Arbeia with three hundred of his men. They would have docked somewhere on the far side of the Rhine and should by now be engaged with Gratian's troops, drawing his forces far enough away that Magnus would have the time he needed to stop at the three forts along the Rhine before the inevitable showdown, but–just as had been the case when Kenon had gone north of the Wall to bring a barbarian army south–all of

Magnus' hopes of success rested in someone else's hands. It was something he was sure he would never get used to, and one that he would do his best in the future not to repeat. There were a few more trials yet to come along the river before he got to Treverorum with the purple cloak on his shoulders.

The mouth of the Rhine was wide, its low banks lost in the tidal marshes and swamps, but with the sea behind them, they were in Gaul now. As an invasion force.

Just as his capable captain had planned it, they caught the incoming tide and, along with the stiff wind at their back, it felt like they were being drawn towards Gratian. But first, it was a man called Nannenius that Magnus had to meet. As he prepared himself for putting his fate in yet another man's hands, one he'd never met, it felt like he was playing a full-scale, life or death, game of ludus. And the board that the pieces were arranged on was the entire empire.

Rolled up and kept in a leather pouch around his neck, he had Andragathius' notes assuring him of the backing of the three commanders, but he still couldn't trust that it would be as easy as docking at the harbours and being acclaimed, as he'd been in Eboracum.

So much could still go wrong, and if it did, he'd long ago decided to throw himself on his sword if there was no hope. It wasn't worth any soldiers dying for nothing. Not when they were so desperately needed to shore up the frontiers, and nor would he be taken in chains to be humiliated by Gratian before being executed.

A snapping taut of the rigging and another gust of wind filled the sails. The ship lurched to the side and Magnus came even closer to heaving.

In single file, the ships sped down the middle of the wide river. People on the western bank stopped to stare. The soldiers manning the watch towers returned the salutes Magnus gave from his position up on the bridge, and by late afternoon the northernmost fort came slowly into view: Traiana. Dull walls, squat towers and partly obscured in a haze of smoke from cooking fires and industry, the town didn't look like too much. That wasn't such a surprise though. Positioned so close to the long border of the empire's mortal enemies, these days it was only the barbarians who'd been allowed to settle, who lived here.

The captain expertly guided Magnus' ship to nudge softly against the jetty, but the rest of the fleet stayed anchored in the wide river with sails trimmed, and if they had rowers, the lines of glistening oars were lifted out of the water. The captains had been instructed that if something should happen to Magnus they should turn around as quickly as they could and sail straight back to Britannia.

The crew of Magnus' ship tossed the mooring ropes over where they were caught by the dockers, so he knew that once again his fate was out of his hands.

Magnus walked along the sturdy wooden jetty and saw the man who must be Nannienus waiting for him in front of the gatehouse and was struck with a profound thought about how power shifts among men so fleetingly in times of turmoil, like a butterfly in a summer breeze, settling on the shoulder of one man here, another there. In one moment it would be Ausonius, an important advisor of Gratian's, then one of his generals would find himself the most important man in the world for a little while. Right now it was Nannienus.

Magnus wondered if it was a smile on the commander's face, or a scowl. If he had a sword in his hand, Magnus was sure he could beat almost any man in combat, but if the commander was set against him, and he was walking into a trap, then his fate was already sealed.

Arm out, palm facing the ground, then a fist pummelled against the chest, it was either a genuine greeting, or Nannienus' next gesture would be for the soldiers to cut Magnus down where he stood. He imagined he could hear a counter being slid across the ludus board, moved to a square that would either make the next move easier, or would end the game.

"Perhaps inside would be a better place to talk than on the street?" Nannienus said.

Magnus couldn't disagree. If Nannienus intended to chop his head off, it would be better for it to be done out of the sight of Magnus' men. If the roles were reversed, he would have done the same.

Through the sturdy gates, it was a town Magnus was led into, not a fort. A guard of sixteen soldiers walked with them, making sure the workers and onlookers pressed back out of their way. There were a few market stalls and some serving food from shop fronts, but it was obvious that most of the people had moved to safer places inland, away from the threat of the Alemanni and Goths. By the state of the dilapidated buildings, tiles missing from the roofs of most of them, they had left some years ago.

Magnus fell into step next to Nannienus, who, unnervingly, still gave absolutely no indication of whether he was about to hail Magnus or have him bound in chains.

They walked to the forum. The wide open space, lined by elegantly colonnaded corridors had been the focal point for the townspeople but now it had been taken over by the border army and a good thousand soldiers had been brought to muster. All were in armour, although in many different styles. As Magnus strode over the uneven flagstones to the centre, they began slamming their spear shafts on the ground. He hoped it was a show of respect.

"Magnus Maximus," Nannienus called out to the assembled soldiers. "Dux Britanniarum."

Being addressed by the rank Gratian had bestowed on him made his heart drop and he was sure it was all about to come to a messy end. The fingers of his right hand twitched towards the pommel of his sword and he wondered how many he could take down before they overwhelmed him. He hoped that Victor would get back to Britannia safely and that Elen and her special guard would find a way to protect him.

"But here at Traiana," Nannenius said, as he turned to Magnus, whose heart seemed to pause. "We call you Augustus!"

The soldiers cheered loudly enough to be heard down at the dock. Magnus hoped his men on the ships would take it as a good sign and not that his severed head was rolling down the street. But after the giddying flood of relief came a surge of anger. Nannienus could have told him that as soon as they'd met and saved him the worry of wondering if he was walking to his execution. He didn't know if it would be best to demand that Nannienus got to his knees to beg forgiveness, or to hug him. With his legs so weak, the greeting turned into an awkward embrace.

"Two centuries I can spare you," Nannienus smiled. "A hundred and sixty men. Any more and it will be an invitation for the bastards over the river to get some silly ideas into their heads." He took a step back and his expression became more severe. "But only on one condition."

Magnus groaned. He was well used to his wife attaching conditions to every concession so braced himself for whatever he was about to be asked to sacrifice.

"I want them all back. Every last one."

Magnus laughed. He decided that he liked Nannienus. A man who could joke with someone he'd just bet his life on becoming an emperor was one worth having around.

He'd understood it before, but had never experienced it in such a raw form, but knew now that power was not something a man could ever just take for himself. It was something that had to be bestowed on him by others.

"I have spent too many years in the army, it's time for an easier life," Nannienus said. "So, if you have no other man promised for the job, perhaps you will need a protector for your young son, once you have settled into Treverorum?"

Magnus wasn't quite ready to be handing out positions to his new imperial entourage, so nodded noncommittally.

"Will you stay the night?" Nannenius asked.

"I will, thank you," he replied, "and we'll leave at dawn tomorrow. Time is of the essence. I want to be in Treverorum before Gratian even knows what is happening."

"Both the river and the roads are blocked to the south, so no messages will be going south from here. You are safe."

Safe for how much longer, though? Magnus wondered and noted that despite Nannienus being for him, the iron grip around his chest had not lessened.

VI

Magnus was uneasy.

After leaving Nannenius in Traiana over a week ago, everything had gone smoothly. The next two forts had been ready for him, and with no enemy behind him, he'd led his army inland to meet Gratian, but now the momentum that had felt like riding the tide with the wind in the sails had stalled; turned stagnant.

He tried to ignore the taste of dust in his mouth but was worried that if got too far in the back of his throat, he'd be coughing more than talking. The flies were even worse though, and he spat in disgust when one landed on his lip.

It was the fifth day they'd been out on the plain near the city of Lutetia. Five days of heart-crushing nervousness, on edge with every beat of his heart that an attack was imminent, or that someone in his entourage was about to betray him. It was swelteringly hot. Men who hadn't taken their three layers of armour off for almost a week were stewing in their own juices now, probably starting to wonder if pledging their futures to a usurper had been a good idea.

It couldn't go on like this for much longer. No matter how strong his support was among the soldiers, each man had a breaking point where the concerns for his own life and future overrode that of his superior's ambitions. A grumble with a friend about the deteriorating conditions, or worrying about when the next supply wagon would roll in, would be all that was needed for it to snap. All they would have to do was to drop weapons and run a mile or so across the open ground to the opposing army where Gratian would be so grateful for their desertion that he'd gift them with gold.

The flies were beginning to get unbearable. The previous day's rain had turned the camp into such a morass that his horse kept slipping. Soon would come the first outbreak of flux, and when men started shitting themselves to death, all morale would be lost.

The men had been standing in the field, ready to fight, since sunrise, lined up waiting to react to Gratian's equally large force. After a long day of doing nothing but stand ready to fight to the death, as the sun set, sore legs, aching backs and empty stomachs, they'd trudge despondently back to camp to eat and sleep – to repeat it all again the next day.

The tension had grown to be like that of an overwound ballista and he could feel the fibres in the ropes beginning to give. In his bones, he felt that they were drawing close to the flash point. He wouldn't like to chance waiting through a sixth day.

He pulled his horse to a halt in front of the first row of men, all lined up in a neat rectangle. "We do *not* fight!" he shouted, aware of how strange the words were for a lifelong soldier standing on a battlefield to hear. "I must have Gratian's *surrender*, not his soldiers' blood," he bellowed so those at the back of the rectangle of men could hear.

Maybe some thought him mad, but to make his rule legitimate, the boy had to hand over his power, not to have it taken from over his corpse.

He couldn't afford to let too many soldiers die either. As soon as news of an evenly matched battle between thousands of Roman soldiers reached the Goths and Alemanni, they wouldn't even bother to put their campfires out before flooding over the river, and the Huns would follow. As much as he coveted the purple, Magnus could not let that happen.

"I want those men on the other side to be with me. With *us*! They are your brothers who will stand shoulder to shoulder with you to protect the empire when this is done. I will *not* have them lying lifeless on the field. Defend yourself, kill your assailant if you have to, but for the good of the empire, this fight must be a bloodless one!"

Instead of the usual roar for the coming of bloodlust, there was a curious quietness among the men. The centurion nodded his agreement. It was he who would maintain the discipline of the eighty soldiers under him, to hold them back if the tedium of waiting got too much and they took it upon themselves to charge at Gratian's line just to get the fight over with.

"Bloodless!" he shouted again.

He turned to look at the line of Gratian's soldiers and tents on the distant ridge, smoke from their fires a dark stain in the air above them. The scales of fate were finely balanced. It wouldn't take much for them to tip one way or another. All he needed was for a few men close to Gratian to come over to his side. And once they started, more would follow. Yet, for some reason, everyone had held fast for days.

The iron grip of fear was close to squeezing the life out of this heart, but as he walked back to his huge tent, he felt oddly calm. He was sure that for the past couple of years, he'd done everything as well as he could, had developed strong alliances, and promoted the right men to the right positions. Victory or defeat was in the hands of a higher authority now.

As his eyes adjusted to the dimness inside he thought again of Merobaudes. He'd been sure another consulship, something unprecedented in all of history for a man of his class, would have been enough to convince him to swap his allegiance. He'd been disappointed and had no idea what more he could offer. Perhaps it was as simple as Elen had suggested; that he enjoyed being in a position where he could influence the young Gratian–something that would be impossible with Magnus.

He unstrapped his helmet, set it on the table and accepted a glass of wine from the young soldier whom he'd chosen to serve him this day. The dark-skinned emissary got up from his cushions and raised his glass in salute.

Magnus felt the sword at his hip; a gift from Marcellinus for his wedding. It was a fine blade, one that would have cost years of wages for a normal soldier. Hanging in its scabbard, it felt oddly limp, like being flaccid while standing in front of the most stunning pleasure slave. He wanted to fight – but now was the time for words, not steel.

"Gildo, the Count of Africa, considers you more than a friend," the emissary said with a serious look. It was a compliment, but one Magnus had heard repeated many times over the last few days, and it hadn't got any less hollow.

Magnus was a soldier, and soldiers generally held that politics were for weak men whose only weapons were words, but for someone well versed in the fork-tongued magic, the right words at the right time could be more effective than the sharpest blade.

He thought of Marcellinus still stuck at Valentinian's court in Mediolanum and wished he was here to negotiate this delicate situation for him.

Like most men from Africa, his skin was the colour of fresh alluvial mud. Men made from clay, Magnus thought. Genesis. He wondered if the man had just the divine breath of life breathed into him, and the sheen on his skin wasn't just sweat, but glaze like a freshly fired pot. He wondered if such men were closer to God. He took a long swig of the wine. He hadn't slept for what seemed like weeks but he needed to be alert now.

"Gildo's beloved brother Sammac commands Gratian's guard and his concern is not only about the fight in these fields here, but about what must come after. If you kill Gratian, you must know that you will turn the other two emperors into your strongest enemies, and where will that leave us?"

"Those other emperors you speak of," Magnus sighed. "One is a boy so young his balls have not yet dropped, and the other is my cousin."

"Forgive me," the emissary said, his beaming smile full of perfect white teeth. "But Sammac, who speaks for his brother, believes that Theodosius is emperor before he is your family."

Magnus couldn't imagine his cousin standing against him. They'd grown up together, stood shoulder to shoulder in more battles and skirmishes than he could remember, and if Theo had learned anything in his five years as eastern emperor, he must surely understand the benefit of having a direct family in power with him. If they were in accordance, between them they could rule over a much strengthened empire.

"Valentinian is only a boy, this is true," the emissary continued, "but he has powerful people around him; intelligent men with lifetimes of experience. The Bishop of Mediolanum, for example, and what if your cousin was to stand in opposition to you?"

Magnus scoffed dismissively. He wouldn't admit it to anyone, but that thought had kept him awake for many nights. For what he was doing, he'd not dared to ask his cousin's opinion, never mind permission. If Theo was to take offence, not only would he not get the legitimacy he needed for his rule, but the full armies of the East and West would end up pitched against each other. He tried his best to ignore the trickle of terror that made its way down his spine into the muscles of his legs. "On one side of his domain, Theo is bogged down by a marauding army of Goths that he isn't capable of meeting face-to-face," he said, trying to sound confident. "On the other, he has the Sassanids to deal with. Even if he wished me dead, there is nothing he can do about it, because as soon as he moves his army west, he would lose Constantinople."

"That may well be," the emissary said, wringing his hands together under the voluminous sleeves of his robe, "for the foreseeable future."

The dance of words was beginning to wear thin now, not least because time was running out. "For a year and a half I fought in Africa against Gildo's brother," he said, heedful of the pitch of frustration in his voice, but unable to temper it. "I sweated and bled under the sun in those infernal sands. I fought in full armour in the middle of a desert summer. It was I who caught Firmas, and so it was I who raised Gildo to the position he now enjoys."

The emissary nodded in what looked like agreement, but said, "As did your cousin Theodosius, who, as I understand, was at your side as an equal for all of those eighteen months. Perhaps he should be afforded an equal degree of gratitude?"

Magnus sighed and wished again that his brother was with him to help. Marcellinus had the gift of the golden tongue whereas Magnus' level of diplomacy was soon going to be his balled fist. Trying not to speak with gritted teeth, he said, "Gildo's brother can choose between Africa being administered by a twelve-year-old, or the general who gave him his power." They were far from the haughty, dignified words Marcellinus would have used; they even sounded petulant.

The emissary stayed infuriatingly silent for a few moments before offering his answer, "Well..."

But sick of going around in circles, Magnus cut him off. "I already have Britannia. I will have Gaul, and will take Hispania without issue, of course, as they will gladly welcome an emperor of their own blood. I also fully intend to have Africa as well. So tell me, how secure do you think Gildo's position will be when I take control of his province and I remember that in the moment I needed him to come to my side, he opposed me instead?"

"Perhaps the glad news has reached you, that Gildo recently welcomed a strong and healthy son into the world?"

"And what...?" Magnus gasped as this did not seem the time to talk about family occasions.

"And you, as I understand, have just welcomed a sister for Victor," he said in a suggestive tone.

Elen, forgotten in the dark corner of the tent, chose this moment to clear her throat. Loudly. He was about to snap at her to stay silent, but then it made him realise that the emissary was suggesting the betrothal of his three-month daughter to another newborn in Africa.

Every father knew a daughter was precious. Girls born into important families could be the keystones in very important alliances, but whatever Sevira might be useful for at some point in the future, he needed Gildo's men here at his side right now. "It would be a good arrangement," he said. "Then Gildo's son would be part of the family of the Emperor of the West. Has Gildo been thinking about how such a thing sounds to him?"

Elen cleared her throat again. Magnus understood it as a warning, but hoped she could read the expression on his face as he intended it. 'Don't you dare open your mouth...'.

The emissary nodded thoughtfully. "At this point in the juncture, let's call this an initial proposition, rather than an official offer. I will return to Sammac's camp now and come back to you with his reply, as soon as I can." He stood, gave a slow bow to Magnus, then turned to the corner to give Elen an equal show of respect. Magnus couldn't tell if that was just genuine deference to his wife or a veiled insult towards him.

As the man left, Magnus was about to offer a curse to his back, but it was a battlefield he was about to cross. If he was caught coming from Magnus' army by any of Gratian's men, his last moments of life would not be enviable. A politician he may be, but he'd have to be as brave as any soldier to cross the ground between the armies. For some reason, that made him think about Kenon, and how the idiot had run out between the two armies when Magnus had landed in Britannia as Dux Britanniarum. Brave or mad, there was a thin line between them sometimes, and if those armies had clashed that day, he probably wouldn't be standing on the brink of greatness. How such monumental moments stood atop a foundation of such seemingly inconsequential actions, often made him stop and wonder at how delicate even the most powerful things are.

He was about to offer some conciliatory words to Elen, but a roar came from his soldiers.

Heart gripped somewhere in the middle of abject terror and heady euphoria, he grabbed his helmet and dashed outside, but before he'd strapped the chin plates together, Andragathius was before him, face flushed, "Fraomar arrives!" he said breathlessly.

Magnus' heart leapt. "How many?"

"All of them. About three hundred."

"Bring them in across the front of the camp," he said excitedly. "Get the men to cheer loudly as they come in." Something Magnus had learned about leadership was that at least half of it was just show. "Go and explain to him that I *cannot* have any fighting against Gratian's forces. He must control his men."

Back inside the sanctum of the tent, Magnus felt such relief he had to double over and support himself on the edge of the table. For the first time in his life, his armour felt too heavy. He chuckled at the thought that as emperor he wouldn't have to wear it anymore.

From behind him, in a barely contained rage, Elen spat, "Playing games of power as though your children are just counters on a ludus board before they even *know their own names*! And for nothing but a soldier's favour. Is that what you have stooped to?"

He was close to assuming the mantle of emperor, yet he had no idea how to argue with his wife.

As out of place as her opinion on anything was, she had a point though. If he'd waited just a few moments longer, perhaps Fraomar's arrival would have been enough to get Sammac to reconsider his position. And he'd still have a daughter to offer to someone else.

Then Fraomar was before him. Magnus held his hands out in greeting and called out jovially, "My friend. What took you so long?" but then he noticed the look of anger on the Goth's reddened face.

"I was burying my dead!" he spat and Magnus was glad that someone had taken his sword off him before allowing him in the tent.

"Fifty men you owe me!" he snarled, finger pointed accusingly at Magnus' chest. "You told me Gratian has no military mind! He managed to outflank us! I came close to losing all of my men!"

Magnus couldn't afford to lose Fraomar's support, so he was cautious to speak in a consolatory tone. "The rest will have easier lives from now on," he said, but wasn't surprised to see that such empty words didn't change Fraomar's demeanour.

"You want us to fight for you again?!" he asked. 'You think I can trust you now?"

For a moment, Magnus was terrified that Fraomar was about to march his men off to swell Gratian's ranks, but he wouldn't have come to Magnus to tell him that to his face. He remembered their last meeting in the tower on the Wall that stormy night and how Fraomar had openly toyed with the balancing weight on the scales. "What would you like from me?" Magnus asked in a tone quite reminiscent of the emissary.

"Where shall I start?" Fraomar growled, but was interrupted by loud shouts from the front line ranks. The low hiss of the armour of thousands of soldiers snapping into formation washed over him like a stiff breeze through the trees. Usually, the last sound before engagement was a sound Magnus loved, but not today. If it happened now it would be the end of the world, and he would be the cause of it. His stomach lurched and he struggled not to throw the wine back up.

Squinting as he strode out into the bright light, he heard them before he saw them. Cavalry. Hundreds of hooves of armoured horses thundering over the ground. "Do not engage!" he bellowed as loudly as he could and heard his orders repeated by the centurions. Over the gleaming helmets of his lined up men, he saw the plume of dust rise and the moment of truth was upon him.

"Will you order my men to the flank?" Fraomar asked, perhaps thinking about his own escape rather than standing to defend Magnus.

"No," he said and Fraomar looked on horrified as the line of horses advanced, but before they met Magnus' men, they wheeled to the side and rode across the front, then stopped.

The roar that surged through Magnus' soldiers as they understood that they were close to victory almost brought tears to Magnus' eyes. He ordered that Sammac be allowed to approach.

The emissary would still be out in the field somewhere, if he hadn't been trampled down by his own men, so when Sammac had seen Fraomar's detachment ride in, he had come on his own accord. If the emissary was dead, then there need be no mention of marrying Sevira to his son. As the African walked towards him, Magnus wondered at how unconcerned he'd become of the lives of lesser men.

Sammac unstrapped his helmet, a sign that he came in peace, and held his arm out for Magnus to grab. Gripping each other's wrists firmly, Magnus knew he was now only a step away from soundly beating Gratian, and to get to this position he hadn't lost the life of a single soldier. All it had cost was a daughter. Maybe. Magnus turned to face the crowd, then raised the African's arm into the air. The men shouted their joy loudly enough for Gratian to hear.

Back in the tent, Magnus snapped his fingers at a soldier who hurried to pour wine. "My old friend," Sammac said as he took the glass. "A long way we have both come since the blood-soaked lands and the battles we fought against my brother Firmas. It seems it was he who brought us together to where we stand today, but he is still not worth toasting."

Before they could put the wine to their lips another great roar tore through the soldiers.

Instantly alert, neither man wanted to waste even the moment to set the glasses on the table and simply dropped them as they darted for the door.

"What now?" Magnus shouted.

Beside him, Sammac cursed at the sight of the whole of Gratian's infantry approaching. The young fool had decided to attack after all, prepared to risk the security of the empire for one last half-chance to keep his throne, but before Magnus shouted any orders, he saw that the shields of the running soldiers were still on their backs and they were coming towards him in a mass of men far too disorganised for a proper attack. When they were close enough, no volley of spears was made ready to be thrown, and in the middle their commander rode with his arm raised for parley. When the soldiers slowed down a few hundred feet away, the rider slipped out of his saddle and walked towards them, and it looked curiously like he was cradling a baby. As he came closer, Magnus could see that he was holding a bundle of cloth. A purple one.

The men around him, still nervous as a situation like this was far from anything they'd ever trained for, were still poised to fight, swords drawn, shields ready to be locked into formation. "Weapons down!" Magnus shouted as Merobaudes approached. He watched as the man he hated most in the whole world, his uncle's murderer, came to kneel at his feet.

It was done.

That strange sense of power that had been flittering from one man to the next over the last few weeks, that had for the last few moments been on Merobaudes' shoulder, now finally settled on Magnus. And he wouldn't be letting it go.

Sammac, understanding the import of what was about to happen, sure that his rank wasn't anywhere near high enough for him to be standing so close to Magnus, he took a few steps away from the new emperor. As Merobaudes reverentially held the cloth up, Magnus saw in his eyes a curious mix of fear and distrust, a look of a man who knew he was in a truly helpless situation. He had been powerful enough to take power from one emperor and hand it to another, but now he was fully at Magnus' mercy.

Magnus realised that his hand was clasped around the pommel of his sword. He would have cried out in ecstasy to see Merobaudes' head on a post, but if he was to do that he'd instantly lose the hearts of all the thousands of soldiers Merobaudes had brought with him. To assume his place as emperor, he'd have to let his bitterest enemy live.

His first taste of imperial politics was disgusting.

Magnus took the cloak and with a flare to impress the onlookers, shook it out. He then wrapped it around his shoulders.

He didn't allow himself a moment to bask in the glory though. "Where is Gratian?" he asked the still kneeling Merobaudes.

"Fled."

"How many are still with him?"

"A few cavalry. Nothing else. His whole army is now yours. You are victorious."

It was hard to believe that in just a matter of moments, nearly a whole army had simply turned and walked away from an emperor. "You are about to be a very busy man," he said to Merobaudes, "but I promise you reward and relaxation soon."

"As you wish, Augustus," he said. The man who'd had power enough to raise an emperor by himself, now didn't dare to stand before Magnus without permission, and while he'd given Magnus all he'd ever dreamed of, all Magnus could think about was how soon he could kill him.

"Come," Magnus said, permitting him to stand with a waggle of a finger. "One battle ends, but another begins."

VII

Elen listened to the roars and the cheers. Although she couldn't set foot outside, as a woman on a battlefield would be deemed a herald of terrible fortune, she knew what was happening.

From her place on the cushions, she knew the world had just changed.

The afternoon light streaming in through the door dimmed as Magnus came back in. He'd left the tent a few moments before as a man with his destiny in the hands of others, as helpless to his fate as he'd just made poor Sevira to hers. He came back in again as emperor. A man with power on Earth second only to God.

Elen wasn't sure if her future had just become easier, or much harder, but seeing how the man who occupied the twin roles of both her partner and her enemy, spun around trying to look at himself with the cloak on, she was terrified. She'd never got used to being the wife of the Dux Britanniarum and now the hard-won balance between them had just been knocked far out of kilter, and she wasn't sure what she could do about it.

She didn't know if she had the strength to fight an emperor. All she wanted was to bring her children up in the safe land with the man she loved. She remembered the day she'd secretly married Eugenius in the Old Ways on the shores of the sacred isle of Mona. She wanted to remember the feeling of holding his hand and looking into his eyes as the ceremony was performed, imagining that the whole world was hers, but try as she might, she couldn't shake off the feeling of being on the journey to him there when she'd hidden from any of Father's soldiers in the box under the seat in the litter: strictly confined, trapped and unsure of what she'd see when she opened her eyes again. It was just how she felt with Magnus.

She wanted to crawl back into Grandmother's dark little house in the Segontium vicus and have the old woman speak words of wisdom. *You are no ordinary girl*, she said silently to herself, trying to find some strength in the last words her grandmother had ever spoken to her.

"Where did the coward Gratian flee to?" Magnus snapped at the strong-looking soldier who'd followed him in. They seemed so alike in build and demeanour she thought Merobaudes looked more like Magnus' brother than Marcellinus did.

"Rome, I would assume, your Excellency. There is no love lost between him and his half-brother Valentinian. Or perhaps I should say, his mother Justina. So he would feel vulnerable in Mediolanum."

"Raising Valentinian to Augustus without Gratian's consent would do that, I suppose," Magnus suggested.

Merobaudes shrugged. "I serve the empire."

She wondered if Gratian's former master of infantry was aware that instead of rewarding him for bringing Gratian's soldiers to him, Magnus had long planned to kill him.

"How can I get through his cavalry and his Alan guards to get him alive?" Magnus asked.

Merobaudes raised his hands in defeat. "His Alans know that if he dies, so do they, so they'll protect him with their lives. Or if they are cornered, maybe they will kill him themselves in the hope that such an act will get them granted some form of clemency."

"Andragathius!" Magnus called. The Batavi had been standing just outside the door, ready to be commanded. "Get as many cavalry as you can, I want you to chase Gratian. Ride him down. Capture him. But he cannot die!"

Elen was disappointed. As usual, her dearest husband shouted orders without thinking the problem through properly. Not letting Gratian get to the safety of Rome, where he could raise another army was easy to understand, but tearing after him, threatening those who knew their lives were forfeit should the old emperor fall, was not the way to get him alive. She knew that if she were to dismiss Magnus' plan in front of his newest general she'd be tempting an apoplectic rage. But she also knew how much his success, and therefore hers, depended on Gratian being alive. "He will be going to Lugdunum," she said.

Magnus, predictably instantly full of rage at being interrupted by her, a *woman*, turned to face her, but before he could put words to his anger, she added, "His new wife Laeta is there. They are very fond of each other apparently. It is genuine affection." In front of a man with as much importance as Merobaudes she couldn't mention that it was her spies who'd informed her, so added, "If the rumours can be believed."

Magnus looked at Merobaudes for confirmation. "This is true," he nodded.

If Merobaudes was surprised at hearing a woman's voice behind him speaking uninvited words of advice to Magnus, he hid his reaction well. She would have to watch this one. If he was to live long enough.

It was amusing to see the expression on her husband's face as he fought with himself to work his wife's information into a plan he could act on. He couldn't though. "I need him alive," was all he could say. "How can I get to him?" he asked Merobaudes again.

Confined, unsure of what the immediate future held, part of Elen was still trapped in the darkness of the seat box of the litter, but now, instead of allowing herself to fall into the blinding clutches of terror, she saw a way to get to Gratian through his soldiers. "Get to Lugdunum before him, get a litter and take it out of the city for him," she said.

Her husband rolled his eyes. "What are you blathering about, woman? We are talking of serious things..."

"Then you inform him that it is his beloved wife waiting for him inside," she said.

"And what will..." his face began to turn red, but Andragathius understood her and chuckled.

Magnus looked at him, mouth open in mid-tirade, wondering what he'd missed.

"Your Excellency," Merobaudes said deferentially. "He will want to go to her for comfort, or for the need of a man to protect the woman he loves."

Elen was impressed that he understood. If Magnus didn't kill him straight away, maybe he would be a good man to help guide the new Augustus through his difficult first weeks in Treverorum.

"Either is a sufficient reason," she agreed. "Inside, in the compartment under the seat, one of your men could wait until he's inside, then jump out and hold a knife to his throat. In that moment, I am sure that Gratian won't be in too much of a position to stop the litter being carried away with him inside it. You could be riding back north with him before any of those still loyal to him have any idea what had just happened."

Merobaudes nodded slowly at Elen with respect. "And more than likely, the Alans would know that without his patronage, they wouldn't last a day alive in any town in Gaul," he added. "They'd just scatter and try to get back east as fast as they could."

"If I may make another suggestion, your Excellency?" Elen asked, not without a hint of forced politeness.

Magnus flashed her an angry look as though he suspected that instead of paying him homage with the title, she was trying to mock him with it, but he nodded for her to continue.

"As fighting is not the intent in this situation, maybe you could send just a handful of riders, few enough that, unlike Gratian's band, they will have no trouble exchanging the horses for fresh ones at the stations. They could therefore get to Lugdunum much quicker than he could with his thirty horses. Therefore we'd have time to prepare the trap."

"Ingenious," Merobaudes said and Andragathius nodded, perhaps as impressed as they were shocked that a mere girl could suggest such a thing. But at the look Magnus gave them, the smiles were wiped off both their faces.

"One more thing," she added, and saw how Magnus' complexion was beginning to match the hue of his new cloak.

"Yes," he said, close to a growl.

"You would have to put all of your trust in a girl you paid to be an actress, a whore from Lugdunum, perhaps, who agrees to do something so dangerous as being in the litter pretending to be Laeta. Perhaps it would be better to have someone there you could trust?"

"And who would that be?"

"Me!"

Magnus burst into laughter, but when he'd caught his breath and saw that Elen was still looking levelly at him, the amused grin faded. "You? You will ride for days and will help capture the emperor. The *former* emperor?" he corrected himself. Perhaps he didn't quite believe his new position either.

He looked at her again with an expression that spoke of some conflated mix of deep respect and deep hatred, but then it seemed that he had an idea. She wondered if it was about how she'd given him Victor now, so if something was to happen to her that wasn't his fault, he'd be rid of her without risking the support of the men of Britannia.

"So be it," he said.

Elen had ridden through the mountains around Segontium many times before, and a few of those times had even dared to push her mount to a full charge – until Father had found out and with his whip, persuaded her not to do that again, but nothing could compare to riding at a full gallop with half a dozen cavalry soldiers in tow. It was pure exhilaration. She cast a glance at Eugenius, almost in disbelief that she was sharing such an experience with him, but it was Grandmother who came to her mind. If only she could see Elen now.

The timid little girl who'd been frightened of her own shadow was now racing across Gaul, hunting down an emperor. She was a mother of two, and had two husbands... One of whom had just... She almost lost her balance and fell out of the saddle as she realised that she was now empress. Everything Grandmother had said, had come to be.

She was glad that her horse knew to run next to the others, as with the sudden tears, not helped by the wind in her face, she was practically blind. She owed the old woman so much. She'd seen her rise from the daughter of the governor, a commodity Father had tried to sell off to increase his business holdings, to the wife of the Dux Britanniarum, to be one of the most powerful women in Britannia, and now Empress Elen.

She remembered the last day that she and Grandmother had had together on the tiny island in the straits. Elen hadn't believed it possible a person could shed so many tears without simply shrivelling up into a desiccated husk. Leaving Grandmother alone to take her last breaths while she got in the boat to cross back on the receding tide had been the hardest thing she'd ever had to do.

In the long winter nights with Sevira suckling at her breast, she'd imagined the generations-old honour of a mother passing on all she knew to her daughter once she was old enough, teaching her all the names of those who'd come before her, all the way back to Heulwen, hundreds of years in the past. More tears came, bitter ones this time, as she remembered how Magnus had simply traded that precious future away in a moment, for nothing more than a few swarthy-skinned horsemen–but the betrothal would last for a good many years. Sevira had to be seven years old before they could be formally engaged. A lot could change before then, and Elen was no timid little girl any more. She could stand up to Magnus, could get things arranged behind his back, and so Gildo could find another bride for his son. Sevira wouldn't be growing up in the sands of Africa. Not while Elen lived to prevent it. Her daughter's destiny was for Elen to decide.

They were on a different road south to Lugdunum than the one Gratian and his remaining cavalry had retreated on. It was much easier to exchange their six tired horses for fresh ones than the thirty or so that were with Gratian, so although their route was longer, they knew they were covering much more ground every day.

No one at the roadside inns, where the horses of the imperial messaging services were kept, knew anything of what had just happened on the plain outside of Lutetia. They still thought Gratian was the emperor, and had no idea that Magnus had just taken absolute control of all of Gaul. It would be days before the news filtered down to them, but still, neither Andragathius nor Eugenius wanted to stay in a room, a place in which they'd be trapped if anyone still loyal to Gratian were to find them, and so, once they'd swapped horses for the last time that evening, they turned off the metalled road and made camp in a damp woodland.

Before looking after their own comforts, some of the men constructed a lean-to shelter for her of branches with a bed of moss and leaves. With their cloaks laid on top of it, it was more comfortable than her bed chamber, especially as she didn't have to share it with Magnus.

Just as he'd done on their wedding day, Eugenius got a fire going, and as she watched him, breathlessly, all of the need and desire she'd suppressed for two years came back to flood her heart, hotter than the fire Eugenius was breathing life into.

Every single day in all that time they'd been physically close to each other, but not once in all that time had they been alone. Not even an out of place smile had they shared, lest Magnus' men interpreted it as evidence of impropriety. Knowing they were about to have their first proper few moments together for so achingly long, every muscle in her body began to tremble.

Maybe he'd built fire up too much, but she was beginning to feel hot and pulled a little at her tunic at her shoulder, the hem a little up her leg.

She thought she heard Eugenius growl.

Crashing through the undergrowth, Andragathius interrupted them. Wordlessly, he squatted down and cut the head and feet off a rabbit. She'd never had an animal skinned in front of her, and how the Batavi simply pulled the fur off was both stomach-turning and fascinating at the same moment.

"Would you like first or last watch?" Andragathius asked Eugenius.

"I will stand guard over her the whole night," he replied.

"Noble," Andragathius chuckled as he handed over the rabbit carcass for Eugenius to prepare, "but we have a ride of many days ahead of us. If we need to fight, I need you to be rested, alert."

Eugenius had no answer for that. "First," he said with a reluctant nod.

Elen would fall asleep with him watching over her–except knowing that, she didn't think she'd be able to.

"How do you fare?" he asked Elen.

"A little sore," she said, "but the excitement seemed to help with my endurance."

"Soldiers sometimes say the same thing," he said with a friendly smile. "We made good time, and at this rate we'll get to Lugdunum days before Gratian, so if you are tired from too long in the saddle, we can always stop to rest."

"The sooner we get to Lugdunum, the more time we will have to prepare," she replied.

"This is true," he nodded, "then we ride at daybreak." He began to stand up, but stopped. "You know…" he said, suddenly looking nervous. Something she'd never seen on his face before. He knelt back down again. "Magnus has had me, and several others, watch you over the past few years. Even some of your women servants."

Suddenly Elen was terrified. "This is known to me," she said in her best imitation of Grandmother's voice.

Almost unnoticed, Eugenius changed how he held his knife so that it wasn't the rabbit it was aimed at.

"I know that there is something very powerful between the two of you," he added, which did nothing to lessen her panic.

"I have never... *We* have never..." she started.

"I know, I know," he said, trying, but not succeeding, to calm her. "No one has ever seen a single hint of anything inappropriate in all of that time. Never anything more than a look. but the thing is..."

He adjusted a couple of sticks in the fire sending sparks into the air and Elen saw that he was just as nervous as she and Eugenius were. "You may say anything you wish to me," she said. "I will not judge you. I swear, with God as my witness, I will not go to Magnus with your words."

The Batavi nodded. "A few of us, who are close to Magnus, *subject* to him, understand that the true power behind his rise - is you. Also that, bar none, you are the best advisor he has. He's taken us into very dangerous times now, and his–ambition–unchecked, has the potential to–"

The master of horse was uncomfortable about speaking poorly of Magnus. Anyone would be, especially now he had the purple cloak over his shoulders. He took a deep breath. "Magnus is emperor now, but in my heart I know that *you* are the key to a successful future. You must be the counterweight to his lofty ambitions, the reasoning voice to his rash impulses, so I just want you to know, if you ever need anything from me, if there is ever anything I can do for you, it will be done. Consider me you man."

Elen had half been expecting him to say that Magnus had ordered him to kill her in a way that would look like an accident. His pledging himself to her came as a surprise; she had no idea how to respond.

"Is this some kind of trick? A test?" Eugenius asked, still gripping the knife tightly.

Andragathius looked genuinely concerned that he'd upset them. "No. She–tempers Magnus. And it seems to me that he owes more to her than she does to him. Whether he understands that or not."

"What about the other men?" Eugenius asked.

"They are *my* men. And so they are Elen's as well. Anyway," he said, slapping his broad thighs as he stood, "Magnus has absolutely everything he wants, but he will always love himself more than anything else. So in celebration of his great victory, maybe some of us can also take a little of what we want?"

As he took a step away, he said, "Our camp is far away. If you need anything, you will have to shout very loudly. Otherwise, we won't hear a thing."

As the hulking Batavi slipped away through the trees, Elen's heart pounded as though she'd been running as hard as the horses. It was all she could do not to just jump up and throw herself into Eugenius' arms.

"Can we trust him?" Eugenius whispered.

"If I was to tell Magnus what he just said, his life would be in danger. He has just put a lot of trust into me."

For the first time in longer than she could remember, she looked at Eugenius without restraint, with unbridled desire. She didn't even care that his hands were covered in rabbit blood.

VIII

Riding so far and fast was hard, but although at the end of some days she needed help getting out of the saddle, it was by far the best week of her life. After years of fighting every day to suppress all of her feelings, being able to look at Eugenius without the concern that someone could be watching them, knowing that as soon as they stopped riding she'd be in his arms, was the most wonderful feeling in the world.

Her only regret was that those nights passed far too quickly and they got to Lugdunum much sooner than she wanted. She could have chased Gratian around his former empire forever, as long as at the end of each day she could lie in Eugenius' arms next to a fire. She looked at the walls of the city high on the hill and thought they were symbolic of those she'd have to put around her heart again when she got back to Treverorum, to Magnus. To the emperor.

Over the bridge and up the steep slope, they entered the city with the guards paying them only the most cursory attention. Elen had grown up at the edge of the empire, always aware that a coastal raid could come any day, so in a city nestled so securely in the heartlands of the empire, it felt strange that the guards couldn't care less about the comings and goings of the populace. A girl riding in with a mounted guard hardly warranted a raised eyebrow. The affairs of the senatorial class were not even a consideration. She wondered if Britannia Secunda could ever enjoy such a state of security.

As she shopped for the silk scarf she'd need to be able to disguise herself as Laeta for a few moments, she felt oddly close to her grandmother. She was preparing to assume power over one of the most powerful men in the empire. Also, she was the only one in the whole city who knew that the whole Empire had changed forever, that a new emperor had taken power. Knowing something so fundamentally important and using it to her advantage, while those around remained in ignorance was how Grandmother had lived. The notes and messages keeping her informed of the goings-on of important people, the coins passed out to pay for a little influence here and there, had given her a power few could match. And Elen could almost feel it.

As she paid for her new clothes, her heart felt close to bursting at the thought that the shop owner had no idea that she was about to impersonate the empress in order to capture Gratian, the man whose likeness was on the coins she handed over. It wasn't until she was walking away that, with another shock, remembered *she* was an empress.

But as she made her way back to her room, Andragathius' men following her, she couldn't help feeling deeply sorry for Laeta. Married only just a few weeks ago, perhaps she loved Gratian as much as Elen did Eugenius and would spend time on the city wall looking to the north, wondering what the man she loved was doing, whether he was thinking of her at the same moment. Elen wondered how she would feel if Eugenuis was being pursued and hunted like game.

Andragathius had no problem procuring a litter and its attendant slaves fit for an empress. The first thing Elen did was snatch the whip from his hand. The second was to make him swear he'd get them sufficient food and water. Then they started work on modifying the seat so that a large Batavian horseman could get inside it.

They hadn't ridden quite as fast as they'd thought, as it was only the next day that the scout came charging back to warn them of Gratian's approach. Elen hadn't even managed to get the smell of smoke from the campfires out of her hair.

The slaves carried her hurriedly to the place that one of the Andragathius' men had deemed suitable for the ambush. Andragathius shouted threats at the poor men, but at least he couldn't lash them.

The main road ran along an open ridge and a track off it led through a field into a dense forest. Andragathius suggested they set the litter down just before the trees and once Gratian was in, they'd take it into the woods, out of sight of his contingent. For a few moments she didn't understand why he was asking her, not telling her, but remembering her position again, she agreed that it was a good plan. Gratian's soldiers would wait, thinking he was doing what a man did when he'd not seen his wife for some time–while they were speeding away back to Magnus with him.

One rider stood guard at the road while the others watched, trying their best not to laugh as Andragathius struggled to curl up in the small space under the seat. Her amusement quickly turned to concern as she realised she wasn't just going to have to lure the emperor into the litter, she was going to have to distract him somehow as well, and no matter what ended up happening, she'd find herself between him and Andragathius.

"Riders!" the guard at the road shouted and so it was too late to do anything else now.

Before he pulled the seat down on top of him, Andragathius threatened the slaves with unimaginable horrors should any of them so much as flinch. Then she watched through the delicate fabric curtains as Gratian's riders slowed down to talk to the man blocking the road. Thirty men on horses had been a frightening enough scene to imagine, but seeing them mill around nervously, all ready to fight, filled her with dread. If anything was to go wrong now, they were badly outnumbered - and if anything was to happen to Eugenius…

As she arranged the cushions and adjusted the silk scarf over her face to obscure her features, she realised how much her hands were shaking. To try and calm herself, she imagined Grandmother, and how she would chuckle nonchalantly at the threat of a few mounted soldiers and an emperor young enough to be her grandson. She took a long, slow breath. All she had to do was fool a frightened man for a few heartbeats. It couldn't be too hard.

She'd married an emperor, so tried to tell herself that fooling one for a moment couldn't be too hard, but as a single rider approached, all the composure she'd managed to muster flitted away and left her. Gratian had ruled the Western Empire for sixteen years, since his father had proclaimed him co-Augustus when he was eight years old. Magnus disparagingly called him a boy, but he was a good few years older than Elen was and it seemed impossible that he'd be fooled by such a simple ruse by a young girl. "I am no ordinary girl," she whispered to herself, yet the words sounded hollow.

"You are the Empress Elen!" a disembodied and slightly muffled voice came from under her bottom, and she couldn't help but laugh.

Outside, Gratian dismounted. He was much smaller than she'd imagined. Most soldiers, from a life of constant training with heavy weapons and drilling, were burly men who she thought could snap a tree in half with their bare hands. Gratian was slender, almost effeminate. He had the body of a boy who worked in a bathhouse rather than that of a fighter. It was no wonder it was so easy for soldiers to believe the rumours she'd helped spread. He ran towards the litter like a little boy with a bloody knee coming for his mother, full of relief that his precious wife was inside. Safety. Comfort.

She almost felt sorry for him and wondered how Laeta would feel when she heard the story of what was about to happen.

She opened the door, waved at him to hurry, and then he was in, his arms around her. She needed the door closed so his men couldn't see, but in his need to be close to her, Gratian pinned her down.

"Door!" she hissed trying to sound like a girl from a good family outraged at the impropriety of the guards being able to see the hands of a man on her. "*Door*!" she said again and this time he reached back to close it for her. But as it clicked closed, he finally realised something was wrong.

"Now!" she shouted, and with Gratian's eyes wide in shock, Andragathius pushed up from under the seat. He didn't just burst out like they'd planned though, with Gratian on the seat, it was too heavy. Elen tried to pull him off. "*Now*!" she cried again.

Gratian knew he was in a trap, knew he was fighting for his life, and in his panic assumed Elen was his assassin. "Who are you?" he gasped as he grabbed her throat. As feeble as he looked compared to a soldier, he was much stronger than her. He crushed her head against the side of the litter, grip tightening to choke the air out of her chest, but then Andragathius had managed to get out of his hiding place. The look of rage on Gratian's soft face changed from anger to terror, and as Andragathius shook him like a doll, his grip was finally released from her throat.

Close to her face, there was a flash of steel as a knife was drawn, but she couldn't see who held it. "Don't kill him!" she gasped, in case it was Andragathius. "We need him alive."

Her words had the effect of a spell on Gratian, and all the fight left him.

"It's over," Andragathius said. "You will come back with us to Treverorum."

"To be your puppet? Your slave?" Gratian spat.

"We can negotiate for your life," Elen said. "Just let the knife go."

"No defeated emperor can live," he said with a scowl and with a jerk of his hands got his knife away from Andragathius. The Batavi naturally assumed he was still fighting, so expected to defend himself against the blade being stabbed at him. Instead, Gratian buried the blade deep into his own throat.

"Futuo!" Andragathius gasped and Elen cried out as the hot blood splashed over her face. She pulled herself from under him, scrunched her scarf up and pressed it against the gaping wound to try and stem the flow of blood.

"Slaves! Up!" Andragathius bellowed. "Walk to the woods. Easy."

Gratian was drowning in his own blood, coughing it into her face as the litter lurched. No matter how much pressure she put on it, she knew it was hopeless.

"Who are you?" he croaked.

She looked down into his terrified eyes. "I am Empress Elen," she said and let go of the scarf.

"Laeta?" he whispered.

"She is safe," Elen said. "She will not be harmed."

As the litter made its way into the forest as though they were two young lovers going for a private few moments, she watched an emperor die at her feet.

When they were deep enough in the woods to not be seen from the road, Andragathius called out for the litter to be set down and his shocked men bundled Gratian's bloodied body over the back of a horse. His blood had gushed all over her and she must have looked a terrible sight to Eugenius. Panicked, he looked for the wound and she had to snap harshly at him that it wasn't hers.

He helped her up into her saddle and she was about to kick her horse into a run, but heard Andragathius shout, "Kill the slaves!"

"No!" she cried as his men drew their swords. "Let them be free!"

Andragathius looked at her confused. "They will know what happened and which way we rode," he said dismissively and indicated for his men to carry on.

"And Gratian's men won't be able to just simply follow our tracks?"

The Batavi shrugged but didn't rescind the order.

"Are you my man?" she snapped.

"I err. Yes, Domina!"

"Then I *command* you to let them live!"

Covered in blood, shouting orders at one of the highest ranked officers in the empire, it wasn't Grandmother she felt like. It was Boudica.

To the slaves, she called, "You are now free, by the order of Empress Elen. Get yourselves to Treverorum, to the court of the new emperor Magnus Maximus, where you will be received warmly." To the Batavi, she ordered, "Give them some coin so that they may buy themselves food and shelter."

Andragathius nodded reluctantly, but did as she'd commanded, and a scatter of coins fell to their feet like rain. None of them made any move to pick any up, though. Elen shuddered at the thought of how badly they must have been brutalised to remain so subservient.

They charged off along the muddy trail, but no matter how fast and far they ran, she couldn't get rid of the sensation of Gratian's hands around her throat.

No one followed, which was a great relief, but no one thought that taking Gratian's dead body back to Magnus could be considered a victory.

As she bathed in the freezing waters of a stream, washing the dried blood of an emperor off her, she wondered if Magnus would react more harshly if he thought it was her fault or that of his master of horse. He would be apoplectic, whosever fault he deemed it. Killing Gratian would mean that the other two emperors would consider him an enemy.

They'd wrapped the body in linen, and to try and stop whatever it was that was oozing out, a day later, they had added another layer. Whenever they stopped, the stomach-turning stench of rotting flesh wafted around them. It made her so queasy that the slightest whiff caused bile to surge to the back of her throat.

Andragathius still deemed it too dangerous for them to sleep in any inns, so they made camp in the woods again. It was an arrangement Elen was more than happy with. Even if it rained.

That meant she and Eugenius would snuggle even tighter together.

On the evening of the fourth day, they led the horses in single file along a path into the trees. One of Andragathius' men covered their tracks so no pursuers would see where they'd gone. Eugenius found a place away from Andragathius' men to leave Gratian's putrid corpse. Elen didn't envy the poor soldier who had to stand guard all night to keep it safe from the wolves and foxes attracted by the smell. If she had her way, they'd just dig a grave and bury him, but she understood that Magnus had to see the body for himself, otherwise he would forever be paranoid that somewhere a deposed emperor was roaming the land gathering together the remnants of his shattered army, to one day come and reclaim what was rightfully his.

As long as she wasn't downwind, sleeping under the stars was a joy. Somehow hunting for dinner, building a fire, and listening to the rain on the roof of leaves made her feel closer to her ancestors, ones she hoped were proud of what she was doing–and who she'd become. While she missed having Victor and Sevira with her as much as though she'd lost a leg, the days on the road she spent with Eugenius had a magical, dreamlike quality to them. Especially at night. Feeling the warmth of his body next to hers, listening to his soft snoring whenever she woke, was what she'd wished for years.

"We should be back with the army tomorrow," Andragathius said with an apologetic look, "or the day after, if Magnus hasn't moved too far east."

It could be their last night together.

Elen lay listening to the fire crackling. It had become one of her favourite sounds. That, and the dawn chorus every morning. By the time the men came back with the spoils of their hunt, the fire was hot enough to cook the meat. She didn't think that fresh roasted rabbit would be on the menu too often in the palace she'd soon be living in, and she knew how much she would miss it.

But there was something else she'd miss far more when she got back to being the emperor's wife. She watched how Eugenius turned the strips of meat, diligently making sure each was thoroughly cooked, yet not overdone. Making sure each one was perfect for her. The thought of a life that could be as simple as just showing each other how much they loved each other almost made her weep. She wanted nothing more than a small farm, a little patch for herbs, and a house big enough that it had some spare rooms where troubled people could be offered sanctuary. What was ahead of her in the palace at Treverorum, the luxuries, the servants, the respect of everyone in the empire, held absolutely no appeal.

After the day's ride, they were ravenously hungry and after smelling the meat while it cooked, when it was ready they both tore at it like animals. Eugenius, with a huge smile on his face as he ate, watched her. She had something else to tell him, though. Something that might banish his special smile. She waited until she was sure that none of Andragathius' men were close enough to hear.

If she'd wanted to over the past two years, she could have found a way to tell him, but had kept it a secret in order to spare him the pain of yearning for something else he could see in front of him every day, but could never have. She couldn't bear the thought of him suffering any more than he already had to, but after these days together now she wanted him to know the truth. So that it would be something else they shared. "There is something I must tell you."

"Yes, my love?"

This last week and a half had been the only time since she'd wed Magnus she'd heard him speak those precious words, and the tears almost burst out of her at the thought of how many months, *years*, might have to pass before she could hear them again. "That night in the barn..."

"Our last together," he smiled. "Are you going to ask me if I still remember it?" He dropped a couple more chunks of wood on the fire and crawled back to her.

Her arms went around him and she held him tight. "I think about it every day as well," she sighed.

"You don't have to say it."

"I was married to Magnus a few days later. But we didn't..." It was too hard to say that she'd lain with another man, even though that man was her husband: her *other* husband.

"I know!" he said a little more forcibly, with a knowing smile.

"Know what?"

He rolled his eyes up at how slow she was. "Victor is my son."

"How can you..?" she gasped.

"I'm sure any father can recognize his son," he smiled.

"How long have you known?" she gasped.

"I suspected when I saw the bump, but I knew the first moment I saw him."

"Yet you never said anything?"

"What would I have said? If Magnus was to find out he'd have my head - and maybe yours as well."

She held him even tighter, the only thought in her head was that she never wanted to let him go.

IX

The next morning, Andragathius' men killed a deer, and while Eugenius wrapped the cuts of fresh venison so they could roast it that night, they sewed Gratian's body into the skin. It looked like a hunted doe slung over the horse instead of a body, which was a definite improvement, but it also kept the smell from assailing her.

When they were at a gallop, all she could think about was the drunken thrill of being on the back of such an animal, but when they slowed to let the horses catch their breaths, her thoughts were consumed with the terrible realisation she could have already had her last night alone with Eugenius. A few days of living the life she'd always wanted were nowhere near enough. Imagining not being able to hear his soft words, to look into his deep brown eyes again, brought her to tears several times through the day. And when Magnus' riders came to meet them with fresh horses, her heart broke in two, as she wouldn't even get to say a proper goodbye to him.

In an equally sullen mood, her true husband wordlessly stepped back into his role as her personal guard, and as he'd been for so unbearably long, was distant and untouchable again. By the time they rode along the narrow track between the ditches and rows of sharpened stakes of Magnus' sprawling camp, she still hadn't managed to put her feelings for Eugenius back in check. Every time she told herself that she was with Magnus for the good of her people in Britannia Secunda, it was like she was tossing more kindling on the fire instead of water.

Magnus' large tent was pitched in the middle of the camp. With a sinking feeling, Elen knew he'd been waiting for them and had been expecting some kind of ceremony with Gratian submitting to him in front of an assembled crowd before the city. All she'd brought him was a rotting corpse. Her mind wasn't calm enough to work out if that was symbolic of their relationship together or not.

She was about to swing out of the saddle as she'd got used to over the last days, but instead of Eugenius being there to help her down in his big hands, a soldier knelt at the side of her horse on his hands and knees for her to use his back as a step. She'd managed to forget she was an empress again.

She hoped that when Magnus found out what had happened to Gratian, he wouldn't do anything to make Eugenius feel like he needed to defend her. That would not end well. With so many soldiers so near, she couldn't even whisper a warning.

Through rows of guards, she walked to the tent that had been set up for her. An empress couldn't just ride all day after camping in the woods and present herself to the emperor. At least, that's what she told Andragathius to tell Magnus. She didn't care less what she looked or smelled like, and after a few welcoming words and a hug from Aigla, she began hurriedly sifting through the messages Aigla had hidden inside a few of the cushions. As her servant watched the entrance, Elen quickly read ones from Constantinople and Valentinan's court. Nothing but gossip, apart from a possible meeting between Theodosius and Shapur of the Sassanids. That one, she'd look into later. It was the ones from her mother that were the important ones, and they were enough to twist her belly into a tight knot.

Installing Padarn north of the Wal had been the best thing Magnus had done for Britannia, but tribes were well-known for fighting over succession. Padarn had no strong bloodline to hand power to, just a son who was not much older than Victor. With Padarn in failing health, Mother was begging Elen to do something about it. She stuffed the letters back inside the cushion with no idea what she could do.

A clean tunic, a few dabs of perfume, hair wound into a simple bun, and she went over to Magnus' grand tent. It was a canvas palace in the middle of the camp, but was no place of luxury; it was about to be the scene of a battle.

"Do you have him?" he asked eagerly, looking behind the other riders. No greeting. No question about how hard her journey had been. But maybe she should be concerned for *him*. It had been just ten days since she'd last seen her second husband, but it looked like he'd aged by years.

"We do…" she started and he gasped in relief and cast his eyes up to the roof of the tent, perhaps to offer some silent word of thanks to the Lord above for providing what he'd wished for. "But not exactly how you wanted," she added cautiously.

"What do you mean? No, no!" he started as he realised what her apologetic look meant. Then he saw the deerskin draped over the back of the horse.

"There was nothing we could do. He killed himself."

"I will have heads for this!" Magnus cried loud enough for all of Andragathius' men to hear.

"I will take responsibility." Andragathius started, standing stiff.

"No! It was *me*!" Elen said.

Andragathius shook his head, trying to get her to be quiet.

"What was you, woman?"

"I was in the way. He struggled in the litter. Gratian got a knife and killed himself with it."

Magnus looked at her as though she was talking nonsense.

"Who is to blame?!" he yelled like the worst tyrant over her head at Andragathius.

"Husband, listen to me," she implored. "It was *my* fault, no one else's."

"Really? You expect me to believe *you* fought hand to hand with an emperor?"

"Yes," she said. "So tie me to a post and whip me if that will make you feel any better." She was confident that he knew her well enough to understand that instead of being an offer, it was a threat. He didn't take her up on it, and so she hoped the dynamic between them hadn't changed too much.

"Bring him in!" Magnus snapped and Andragathius' men, ashen-faced with fear of the new emperor's anger, carried the deerskin in and set it on the floor.

"You might want to do that outside," Elen suggested as she backed towards the door.

As usual, the word of his wife meant nothing to him, and like an eager child with a new gift, he took out his dagger and cut the seams. Elen stepped away into the fresh air. Her belly was turning at just the thought of the smell. From the cry of dismay and the sounds of Magnus violently throwing up, he now knew she was telling the truth.

He barged past her and doubled over again. After a few moments, he managed to yell, "He was just a boy, yet you couldn't simply capture him? My brother resides at the court of Valentinian!' At the mercy of Justina! Alone in a nest of vipers!"

He turned to Elen, his face reddening, spittle on his lip.

"Everyone will think I ordered his half-brother to be hunted down and killed like a dog! What do you think will happen to Marcellinus now? You have killed *both* of them, you stupid bitch!"

Half-mad Magnus might have been, but about Marcellinus, he was right, as with Gratian dead, the chances of his brother making it out of Valentinian's court were pretty slim. But instead of trying to calm him, Elen thought it best to just let him shout himself out, like Victor in a tantrum. Or maybe Andragathius could say something to calm him.

The slap came from out of nowhere. She had no chance to react, to flinch away to lessen the impact. It was so hard it almost knocked her out and she sprawled on the ground, as though she'd been thrown from a horse. Before she could call out to Eugenius not to do anything, his hand was already on the hilt of his sword. He'd come within a heartbeat of drawing his blade against the emperor.

"Something you wish to say to me?" Magnus asked him and the wrath of the emperor was aimed hawk-like on the only man who made her life seem bearable.

"No, Augustus," Eugenius said, backing down and taking a step away.

Elen tasted blood in her mouth, but didn't want to show Magnus how much he'd hurt her, so swallowed it. She was sure that Magnus was going to try and push Eugenius to take his rage out on him, but she caught Andragathius' eye and with the wink he gave her, remembered what he'd said to her at the fire on their first night chasing Gratian.

"Just like that!" the Batavi said, interrupting Magnus. He pointed at Elen with an arm in front of Eugenius' chest, deflecting Magnus' attention. "That's how Gratian died. On his knees."

"Is that right?" Magnus asked, unimpressed. "And that is something to celebrate, is it? This is the story that will spread across the empire? To my cousin? He was on his knees and I had him killed?" He looked down at Elen, a look of disgust on his face. "You always know everything that I should do, and how to do it. Tell me, how do I get recognition from my cousin now? Theo will make war with me for this. Have you got any great plan to save me from that?"

He was right about how outraged Theodosius would be at the killing of the legitimate Augustus. As well as arranging the succession of the Votadini, she'd have to work to prevent the two halves of the empire from clashing into each other.

She wasn't enjoying being an empress so far. But at least he'd forgotten about Eugenius. And she was at least glad that Magnus hadn't killed Merobaudes, yet. He offered her his arm to help her up to her feet. But Magnus' reaction to the kindness was a look of such hatred, such seething contempt, that it was like another slap to the face. Despite still reeling from what Magnus had just done to her, the side of her face smarting, she could see Magnus' intention to kill the man who'd murdered his uncle, written on his face as clearly as words on a scroll. She could understand a man's driving need to reap revenge he'd harboured for years, but the look was so shockingly out of place because it was one an absolved man would never cast towards another. She was so sure that he'd somehow managed to get himself out of being baptised at Eboracum that Merobaudes had to steady her.

While she'd been out on the church steps, waiting with the excited soldiers, Magnus had been denying God so he could kill. Conceiving a cold-blooded murder before being forgiven of all sins. Instead of receiving absolution, he'd been making some sordid deal with the bishop, appearing in front of his men as though he was now a full Christian so they'd believe his march towards the purple was guided by the grace of the Lord.

When he'd come out in his plain white tunic, holy water dripping from off his hair, to the adulation of the soldiers, it had been as an even worse sinner than when he'd entered the church.

It was so unbelievably audacious that she couldn't even begin to fathom how he'd managed it,

She'd known him for two years, thought she knew exactly how ruthless and calculating he was, but had never imagined he was capable of such depth of deceit.

Such corruption stank more than Gratian's corpse and before she thought about what she was doing, she spat a bloodied ball of spit at his feet. "Unbelievable!"

"What now, woman? Haven't you given me enough grief?"

"Just one question," she seethed and looked him straight in the eye. "Tell me, husband dearest, what would happen to your soul if you were to die today?"

If she'd needed proof, the way his mouth hung open like it had the first moment they'd met back in Segontium, then his reaction was it.

"Leave us," he snapped at Merobaudes.

Merobaudes was almost as big as Magnus and had almost as many years in the army, and until he'd switched sides, had outranked the new emperor, but understanding what Elen's question meant, his face had blanched. Elen wondered if perhaps he'd made his gamble of bringing Gratian's troops to Magnus on the same calculation that, as a Christian, Magnus had renounced all ill will against his fellow men. Now he knew that instead of a man with a heart as soft as a lamb's, it was a wolf he'd pledged himself to.

Magnus ushered her into the tent, with a big hand between her shoulders, handling her much more respectfully than he'd done a few moments before.

Inside, Gratian's reek still lingered, but this was no moment to appear weak.

"How could you know?" he gasped.

With the balance of power between them seemingly restored, she decided to push a little. "In one way I am quite impressed," she said. "Such a risk you took. And it almost worked. I hope what you offered the bishop was worth it because you've damned his soul as well as yours."

"How could you know?" he asked again.

"Perhaps because I am a true Christian, I can tell when someone's covenant with God is actually a lie."

She flinched in anticipation of another slap coming, but while his mouth twitched as though he was about to say something, all he said was, "Leave me." He added, "Empress," but said it with such scorn, he almost spat it on the rug.

Leaving him was exactly what she wanted. To leave him far behind, until he was only a bad memory.

"With me," she said to her guards. Eugenius and the other three came to stand around her and they walked back to her tent as though nothing had happened.

X

After the weeks of travel and living so long in the middle of so many soldiers, Magnus was well ready for the luxuries that awaited in Treverorum. His first stop would be the famous baths to scrape the week's worth of sweat and dirt out of his skin, followed by some time in a soft bed with clean sheets, with a pleasure slave fit for an emperor: maybe more than one.

There would be a lot of urgent work to be done before he could truly relax though. Elen had made getting the recognition he needed, as a ruler of equal standing to Theo almost impossible. He'd thought that defeating Gratian would be all he needed, but now, with him dead, that was going to be only the first of many battles. But he had more urgent tasks at hand now.

Andragathius had taken a sizable detachment to round up those who'd abandoned the city and headed south when they'd heard the news. Dealing with them would be a lot easier than the ones who'd stayed. Working out in whom he could afford to place a modicum of trust for positions in his new administration, was not a job he was looking forward to. It had taken years for him to achieve that in Britannia. In Treverorum, he'd have to start from scratch, and he certainly didn't have years.

The very first omen wasn't a good one, as the huge gatehouse with its twin four-storey towers had its big doors firmly closed against him, and the wall was manned by what looked like as much of the city guard that could be spared. Perhaps they'd been hoping it was Gratian who led the army back. Magnus had disappointed them.

He'd already sent back all the soldiers he'd taken from the Rhine so the long border would not be undermanned for any longer than it had to be. And he'd kept his promise to Nannienus, as not a single one had been lost. A few men, he'd sent back to Britannia, a token number to appease his infernal wife, and so at his back he had some three thousand soldiers. Enough to blockade the city. Building siege engines and starving the inhabitants out, or breaching the walls so he could walk in over their disease-ridden bodies, was not how he intended to get to the throne in the basilica.

But with Gratian dead, there was nothing the city could hold out for. Valentinian wasn't about to storm north and liberate them. Ausonius assured him that the nervous city patricians just wanted reassurance that Magnus' army would make camp outside the walls rather than inside. They were probably right to worry, as the city was full of the spoils and joys that victorious soldiers often enjoyed. They hadn't fought, but while they'd still won, what would in time become a famous battle, their bloodlust had not been satisfied, so it wasn't an army that opened the gates, just an old man. From the stiff way Ausonius walked, his days in camp obviously hadn't been too comfortable. He was doing well for someone pushing eighty years old though.

Once he was close enough to the impressive gate, seemingly so small against it, using a stick to help him stand upright, he called up Magnus' reassurances. And that was all it took for the heavy gates to creak open. Magnus watched in awe, once again marvelling at how power could work. A frail old man with hardly enough strength to stand on his own two legs had more power than a whole army.

Magnus waited for Elen's litter to pull up beside him so they could ride in looking like he was a diligent husband escorting his family. It was just for show. After what she'd done, he couldn't even bring himself to look at her. Not so much out of anger for what she'd done with Gratian, but from fear. Days later, he was still shaken to his core at how she'd known to ask him about his immortal soul. Could she really see into him so well? Were his deepest secrets an unwound scroll for her, for any Christian? Many times over the years they'd been married she'd assured him that she knew so much only from her informers, not magic, but now he wasn't so sure.

He nudged his horse forwards. Looking up, he saw how wearily the guards on the wall watched him. It wasn't just for show that he was wearing full armour. As he rode under the imposing gate, his horse's hooves echoing off the large stones, his skin crawled with the thought of a spear or arrow sailing through the air aimed at the back of the man who'd just killed the rightful emperor.

Even wearing Gratian's cloak, he still felt like an imposter.

A usurper.

Despite coveting the purple cloak for so long, the very first thing he wanted to do with it was to get off and burn it to cinders. It was Gratian's, not his. Even over the stench of the town on a warm August afternoon, he could still smell its former owner's perfumes on it. Mixed with the effluent at the side of the streets, it was making him quite queasy. Recalling how Gratian's rotting body smelled didn't help.

The streets were oddly quiet and the market stalls lining the road were almost empty. The few people who dared to be out watched him pass with stony expressions, as though they were Christian martyrs in the arena wondering what the lions were about to do. It wasn't every day a new emperor rode past them, and such a change might come hard.

He wondered how long it could be before he was safe enough that he could walk around without needing an armed guard, and how long before the people accepted him. Probably not before Theo did, he thought ruefully.

Whether they knew it or not, the normal townsfolk didn't have too much to worry about. It was the men with real wealth, who had a lot to lose, who should be more nervous.

Under his helmet, sweat ran down the back of his neck. He couldn't take it off yet, though. The first impression he needed to give those waiting for him was of a hardened battle commander riding in, an image as different to a young effeminate boy as it was possible to get. He'd had his shirt of armour scales polished to perfection, so that each one gleamed in the sunlight.

Milling about in the space around the entrance to the huge basilica was a good-sized crowd of apprehensive men whose support or opposition would determine what kind of a ruler he was going to be: his new allies and enemies. Finding out which was which, was going to be like playing ludus with a hundred men at once, and he knew that for such a subtle yet complex and vitally important undertaking, he was far from prepared.

He looked again at the faces of the men of status and standing in the crowd. Magnus knew that although they would give a good show of greeting and pledging their allegiance, most would be just weak, unprincipled men come to try to ingratiate and worm their way into his favour and his administration, hoping to raise their stations into those vacated by those who'd fled over the body of a dead emperor. His first reaction was to shower them with the scorn they deserved, but he knew it showed that they were ready to trust in him and that they believed he could do a worthy job. If Valentinian was somehow able to bring an army north big enough to flush Magnus out, theirs would not be an enviable future. Supporting a failed usurper was at minimum a confiscation of everything that man owned. At worst, it would be his head.

In the coming days, Ausonius was going to be the most valuable man in the Empire, especially when he had to decide what to do with those who'd been caught on the road trying to flee south.

As he approached, they parted to let him through, but he had no idea whether it would be best to look as many in the eye as a personal greeting as he could, or remain aloof, almost divine, and treat them with contempt. There was so much to learn.

A soldier knelt at the side of his horse, ready to have his back used as a footstool, but Magnus swung his leg over the other side of the saddle and slid gracefully to the ground. Gratian would have broken his legs trying to do that in full armour.

He made his way through the small building at the foot of the basilica. Unlike the city gates, the doors were wide open for him, and he entered as emperor.

Three years of work, a thousand nights of worry, a thousand days of laying the foundations for this moment. It was all his at last.

"If you would," Ausonius said, holding his hand out to indicate the large wooden chair at the far end, framed by the huge windows in the curving wall of the apse. It took what felt like a long time to walk to it, his legs seeming to get weaker with each step. The hobnails under his boots sounded too loudly on the tiles. He had to stop himself thinking that the sound was of him walking to his glory over his brother's bones.

* * *

Elen's heart was trying its best to hammer itself out of her chest.

As she stepped tentatively behind Magnus into the grand basilica, the immense space opening up before her, the air was suddenly much cooler and more sweet-scented. It was such a stark contrast to the streets outside, that it felt as though she was entering a different world. With the change of atmosphere, a feeling of awe and wonderment at her surroundings, she wondered if it was similar to what dying was like–if it would feel like this when she got to heaven.

Victor, perched on a hip, felt as heavy as a horse and was slowly slipping out of her grasp. While she struggled along, she was aware of all the eyes on her as men made initial judgements and assessments of her and Magnus. She needed to portray the perfect wife at her husband's side with his young son displayed for all to see. Like a soldier about to fight, she couldn't show people who may well turn out to be her enemies, any weakness. She gritted her teeth and hefted Victor a little higher up her hip.

The scratching sound of Magnus' hobnailed boots made a horrible sound on the tiles. The basilica was no place for military men.

Victor seemed to like the sound though, and gurgled his approval, then yelped when the echo came back to him. Then he screamed with joy.

A little ahead of her, it looked like Magnus had to bite his tongue not to do the same.

It was the biggest space she'd ever seen. As a girl, she'd been enthralled by traveller's tales of the pyramids of Egypt and the Hanging Gardens of Babylon, but she couldn't understand why she'd never heard about this place. It seemed so big to her that surely the pyramids could fit inside.

She looked up at the ceiling. The square pattern of substantial timbers was laid out like an upside down ludus board, so impossibly high above her that she couldn't imagine how men, no matter how sophisticated their systems of pulleys and levers, or how many slaves had laboured at it, that mere men could have built it: how the light spilled in through the huge, double rows of huge windows. She wanted time to just stare in awe at the sheer size and grandeur of the place, to run her fingers over all the marble that lined the walls, but knew that if anyone was to see her gawp with an open mouth, they'd think she was a simpleton from the countryside. Despite feeling like that was exactly what she was, she had to be an empress now. At least, that is how people had to see her.

Although she'd been married to Magnus for two years, she'd never truly got used to being the wife of the Dux Britanniarum. Hearing people tell her that she was the most powerful woman in Britannia had always seemed unnatural, no matter who it was that said it to her. As Magnus turned around to take his seat, the one he'd been dreaming of setting his backside on for so long, now she was married to an emperor, it seemed as unreal as the dream Magnus must have had when he'd drank her Grandmother's herbs, and had slaves whisper stories about beautiful maidens in far-away lands into his half-asleep head.

Victor had almost wriggled free. She couldn't see a nurse nearby, so instead of setting Victor on the floor, she offloaded him onto Magnus. He gave her a furious look and she thought he was about to curse her in front of everyone. On seeing his puzzled expression, she leaned close to his ear and, as the line of nervous-looking men filed in, she whispered, "Doting father."

He nodded his understanding and Elen was deeply relieved. He hated her for all he was worth, but at least she still seemed to have some measure of influence over him.

As the men of Treverorum approached and fanned uncertainly out into a rough semi-circle, unsure of Magnus' intent towards them, the atmosphere quickly became painfully tense and awkward. Above all else, old, wealthy men desired stability: reliable trade, regular incomes, and predictable profits. A successful usurper came in and smashed the mosaics from under their feet.

There were plenty of younger ones among them though, and she wondered how many among those who were coming to stand in front of Magnus saw his usurpation as a great opportunity to assume the statuses they hungered for, but for whatever reason, they couldn't achieve under Gratian. In their excited greed, she imagined that they'd come like buzzards to feast on the carcass of the former administration.

Regarding military concerns, Magnus was the unquestioned master. There was perhaps no man his equal in the whole empire, and he'd bested Gratian without raising a single sword, just through his sheer popularity with the soldiers. For the coming days of balancing martial skills with politics and religion, which were of equal importance in days as delicate as these, it needed someone born to the role. Magnus had got himself to the purple, but she was sure that keeping it was going to be just as much of a challenge.

Silently, she prayed that his first words would be inspiring ones. Ones that would settle, not inflame.

"First, I want the best house in the town prepared for my wife and children. I want everything, every sheet, every drapery, replaced by fresh linen," he said in a booming voice. "New ones. I want everything in the rooms to have never been touched by Gratian. The same for this chair. I want a priest to come and clean this throne properly. To *cleanse* it. Purify it. And I want those who make the imperial togas and cloaks to come to me. I want my own, not this..." He pulled at the fabric as though he was offended by it, "secondhand one."

Elen hoped no one could hear her groan. He was obviously assured of his authority, but to Elen's ears, he sounded petulant. More like Kenon in one of his bad moods than the brave new emperor with concerns for the well-being of the empire that the men needed to hear. As the demure little wife and mother, all she could do was stand mute at his side while he set about alienating everyone. If they had been soldiers before him, perhaps they would be cheering. Politicians were different though, and he was quickly losing them.

"We are weak and vulnerable, while we find our feet," he continued.

The way the basilica walls amplified his voice was incredible. She knew it was just a trick of acoustics, but it gave whatever he said the quality of divinity.

"We now have the bitterest enemies close to us in the south. I care not for the spineless boy Valentinian, but as some of you here must agree, Empress Justina is a cold and calculating bitch. I am more than sure as soon as news of our victory reaches her, she will begin plotting to oppose me. Women are like that when they are given too much power. I want an army ready to march south before the end of the month. We will need to get through the mountain passes before the first snows."

Elen was suddenly uneasy on her feet. Maybe Magnus had also seen their unenthusiastic response and had reacted with all he knew, which was a rousing speech for soldiers. These men had just had their existences uprooted with a change of emperor; the absolute last thing they wanted to hear was that there was going to be more fighting. That Magnus intended another emperor to fall.

Mediolanum was in the complete opposite direction to Britannia. If Magnus was to leave at this time of year, when the snows came, they could be trapped south of the mountains until the passes thawed in the spring, and even if he could beat Valentinian as easily as he'd done Gratian, he'd then want to carry on to Rome. And Britannia Secunda would be completely forgotten. She couldn't allow that. Her mind ran wild with panic and it seemed that the last two years had been a complete waste, years she could have had as a paradise on earth with Eugenius. Magnus had just won his greatest prize, but she'd just lost everything. She felt as though she was falling. She imagined the long line of women, stretching all the way back to when the people of Britannia Secunda still called themselves Ordovices–and it had all come to an end with her.

She'd never felt so helpless.

She wanted to slap the new emperor, to make him wake back up so he could remember all the things he'd promised, but in the full gaze of over a hundred men, she couldn't move, couldn't even whisper a warning.

But no. Grandmother had spent her life nurturing a network of spies and contacts, and now they were Elen's. She didn't have to fight, to argue with the new emperor, all she had to do was to *think*. She had to get a message to the right person in Valentinian's court so that he'd order the mountain passes blocked. He had Bauto serving him, a man with a military reputation to rival Magnus'. Just a message.

It was frustrating having to keep standing still, doing nothing, when she was desperate to write the note and get it sent. It felt as though there wasn't a moment to lose.

She wondered what the assembled men would think if they knew that his demure wife standing at his side with a slightly strained smile was thinking of betrayal and treason.

What she needed was to stop him speaking the nonsense that was giving such an awful first impression. For a woman in the imperial court, there wasn't all that much she could do apart from looking pretty and attentive. She was far from being just an ornament though, and when a nervous-looking servant with a platter held in front of him as though it was the most precious thing in the world, tip-toed forwards, she knew exactly what to do.

On the platter was an ostentatious golden goblet with a bottle of wine next to it. She waved the boy over, filled the goblet herself from the ornate jug, and then bent over until her face was in front of Magnus' enough that he had to look at her.

"Perhaps a glass of *wine*?" she asked as sweetly as she could, but with her eyes, she gave a look to remind him that all he had now was given to him because an old woman at the far shore of a distant land wanted him to wed her granddaughter. That if it wasn't for her, all he could look forward to was staring at the wastelands over the Wall for the rest of his days.

The effect on his expression was just as though she'd slapped him, and he visibly paled.

"Well," he said, managing to rally himself impressively well, "I will get the best advice from learned men and decide what is best to do."

She gave him a nice smile–but he would not be going south. Not until he'd finished fortifying Britannia's borders. Once that was done to her satisfaction, only then could he go off and do whatever he wanted.

The men at the front parted to allow someone through to the front, a man even older than Ausonius Her heart fluttered. Martin, Bishop of Turones, the closest man to a living saint there was in the whole empire. She looked at his age-wizened face, the look of sad compassion in his sky-blue eyes as he looked around to see which men of the city had chosen to stay to throw in their lot with the new emperor, and who was missing. A cold calculation. He stood with a calm authority, one that in the tumultuous moment of a new emperor installing himself in the seat of the one he'd just killed, seemed almost divine.

As she recalled some of the miracles he was renowned for, she felt her cheeks blush. Exorcising demons, curing the ill, including lepers, even once bringing a man back from the dead by laying his body on top of what everyone had thought was a corpse. Sadly, she thought that Gratian's week-old corrupted flesh was beyond even what the holiest of men was capable of restoring to life. She looked longingly at his cloak. She'd heard that scraps of it had healing properties.

Before everything slipped through Magnus' fingers, she knew that if Martin was to endorse Magnus, half the men in the basilica would do as well.

She took the goblet of wine out of Magnus' hand and sidled up to Martin with it. Her arms and legs were trembling so much that she had to concentrate on not spilling any of it as she offered it to him. The smile he gave her, along with the little nod of respect, made her melt almost as much as Eugenius did.

The whole place was eerily silent at the spectacle of the empress handing Martin the goblet from her own hand.

As she stepped back to her place next to Magnus, she hardly dared to breathe… especially as she was suddenly terrified that such a man could see straight into her soul and knew she had two husbands.

She watched as Martin slowly lifted the goblet to his lips, feeling as though the whole world had come to a standstill. All he had to do now was to hand the cup to Magnus, indicating his acceptance of the new emperor and the rest of the men would do the same. One little gesture which would have far-reaching consequences.

She felt proud of herself that she'd thought of such a thing.

Martin took a slow sip of the wine and held the goblet out towards Magnus, a hundred men watching with bated breath–but while looking directly at the new Augustus, he handed the wine to the priest at his side. There was a collective intake of breath which the acoustics of the building amplified. A nod to the priest and Martin convinced his colleague to drink. It was the most horrendous insult to Magnus, of course, and she knew she'd be dealing with his rage at her for so completely misjudging the situation, but at the same time, it was the bravest thing she had ever seen, and she couldn't help but watch in awe. Martin had just risked his life to demonstrate that Christianity had risen to such ascendancy that it was now equal, perhaps even superior to the state.

Magnus was no diplomat, and all he could do was stare at the bishop, a shocked smile on his face. "You judge me just another over-ambitious usurper?" he asked, initiating the challenge that as a man used to fighting, he couldn't let pass.

"I don't judge you at all," Martin said in a friendly tone, but then his countenance changed. "That will be for God to do, not me."

Somehow, Magnus mustered a smile that was actually a fair approximation of a genuine one. "Don't you know that I only accepted the position as the soldiers were guided by divine will when they chanted for me to be Augustus, just like they did with Constantine himself before me, and from the very same spot where the great man stood."

"Divine will," Martin said, with a reverential nod. "Don't you think it strange that for over-ambitious men, divine will often seems to align with their own will?"

Inwardly, Elen groaned. It was going badly. At least half the men in the basilica were against him, the bishop was against him, and as soon as they found out what had happened to Gratian, both the other emperors would be against him. And the biggest traitor would be his wife. It seemed Magnus had hardly any chance of survival, but, if he was to fall in Treverorum, Britannia would be much worse off. So the task in front of her for the foreseeable future, was to negotiate a delicate balance between reigning him in and not destroying him.

It was the last thing she wanted to do.

She looked for Eugenius in the crowd. One day all of this would be all over and she could live an easy life with the man she loved.

One day.

XI

AQUAILEIA. SUMMER 388

Elen scraped at the mortar around the stone in the wall behind a chest in her room. Her tool was the nicest spoon she'd ever seen. The delicate patterns all down the silver handle must have taken a skilled craftsman many days to make, which she supposed was fitting for any object intended to grace an emperor's table. It seemed a real shame that she was ruining it, but the stone would serve an important purpose, so she kept working away at it.

Aigla came in and frowned in confusion at the pile of crumbled mortar. "You won't escape that way!" she said and Elen smiled at her servant. Mother of Publicus, Victor's best friend and constant companion, she was the closest thing she had to a friend in Treverorum, in the world, in fact.

"Your husband requests your presence, Domina," Aigla said, almost apologetically, and the way she intoned the word 'husband' explained exactly how she felt about Magnus.

"I will be there soon," Elen said. "Tell him I am fixing my hair."

Aigla half turned to leave, but then stopped.

Elen had done a good enough job of disguising her tears from most of the courtesans, but not Aigla. Before Elen had freed her, she'd been a slave for many years and had a keen intuition for when someone she cared about was suffering. "He wishes you harm, Domina," she said quietly. "I swear it."

Aigla's words were comforting, but the tears hadn't come because of Magnus, but because of what she was going to have to do in Britannia.

"I was owned by many men. I know a cruel man when I see one. I owe my life to you, Domina," she said. "I would die to protect you."

Since giving him a son and heir, and now that he'd beaten Gratian, her value to Magnus had decreased quite significantly, but if Magnus had wanted to harm her, he'd had many opportunities to do it in a way that no one would have found suspicious. Her concern was more for what he could do to the empire than to her.

Elen stopped scraping and tried to stifle a laugh at the thought that Aigla feared she'd gone daft. All she needed was one stone, but it had to come from the palace. That was important. Aigla could think she was mad for making a hole in the wall, but Grandmother would understand. "You are a freed woman," Elen said. "Not my slave. You are my equal in many ways. It won't come to that."

"Remember my words, Domina," she said with a look of such determination Elen shuddered. She put the spoon down and went over to hug her friend. With how much she craved that it was Grandmother holding her, tears sprang again. Grandmother would be able to tell her what she should do and give her words of comfort, as well as ones of strength.

Elen shoved the wooden chest back against the wall to cover up the incriminating scene, but she wasn't ready to go to Magnus just yet. He was not an easy man to be around when she had any doubt about anything in her heart. She was sure it wouldn't do the emperor too much harm to be kept waiting for a few moments.

"I need a moment," she said.

Aigla nodded and took a few steps towards the door.

Elen looked at the two letters she'd written again, both ready to go back to her precious Britannia and on to north of the Wall. One instructed her man in the Votadini tribe to protect a young boy, the other was an instruction to kill him. Another flush of nausea washed through her. The day before she'd thought it a good idea to send both, but with different messengers, so God could decide which got to her agent first. Today she understood what a cowardly way of trying to absolve herself of the awful responsibility that was. What had to be done couldn't be left to chance. She couldn't allow ambitious men to fight among themselves for power and the ruin that could easily lead to. Especially as Magnus had left the Wall dangerously undermanned.

Padarn's son Edern was the only man of Votadini blood she could trust to lead them, but she cringed at the memory of the dark red blood on Padarn's hands when he'd grabbed a soldier's sword to draw the blood for his oath. How he swore in the most public way possible to kill his only other son on sight was not an easy thing to forget.

She had no idea what to do and in frustration, she swept them both to the floor.

"What troubles you so much, Domina?" Aigla asked.

Elen had thought she'd left, but as grateful for the concern and comfort as she was, there was nothing her servant could do.

"Where I come from, we say a trouble shared is a trouble halved," she pressed.

"You come from the same places as I do!"

"Exactly!"

"I need to decide whether to order the killing of a baby or not," Elen sighed, thinking such harsh words might shock Aigla into not asking anything else.

She expected perhaps an offer of some kindness, or maybe another hug, which Aigla was just as fond of giving, as Elen was of receiving. Instead, she said, "Didn't Plato say that the measure of a man is what he does with power? As long as you are using your power for the benefit of the whole of Britannia, then what must be done, must be done."

It was something so similar to what Grandmother would have said, that Elen replied with what she was really feeling. "How sickeningly corrupt is the whole empire when instead of protecting and nurturing its young, its most innocent have to *die* for it?"

"One life for how many?" Aigla asked. When Elen didn't answer, she continued, "One child. If the Votadini weaken themselves enough to allow the Picts to come south, it could be another Conspiracy."

Elen nodded. It was what both her mother and grandmother had dedicated their lives to prevent happening again.

But if she ordered a child to be killed, she'd be no better than Kenon. The little girl he'd killed would probably haunt him until the day he died, and the thought of having to live with such guilt was enough to fill her with dread. It was an even deeper fear that she voiced to Aigla though. "And what about my soul? It will be forever damned."

She was expecting some soft words, but as stoney as her Grandmother, as Aigla bent down to pick the letters up, she said, "One soul for how many?"

So that is what it would take to keep her province safe.

"What must be done, must be done," Aigla said again.

Elen took the parchment with the instruction to spare the child and scrunched it up so tight her knuckles blanched white.

If her soul was what it would take to protect Britannia, then so be it. She wondered if in hell, Magnus would still be emperor.

Sevira was sound asleep in her cot, adrift in the deep, carefree slumber that only children and blind drunk men could know. Elen was a little jealous. Between a four-month-old baby, a toddler who was desperate for the amount of attention he was used to before his sister was born, and an emperor in a constant foul mood, she hadn't managed a good night's sleep for longer than she cared to remember. Not since the woods somewhere in the middle of Gaul.

As carefully as she could, she picked her treasured daughter up and held her over her heart.

She wondered if, years ago, her mother had looked down at Elen's innocent little face with such an aching worry for the future. She'd kept her grandmother a secret until the last possible moment, trying to protect her from a generations-old responsibility, so the answer was probably yes. She thought again about how she should go about preparing Sevira for what she'd have to face in the years to come. How to deal with the powerful man she would one day marry, which while Elen still had breath in her body to stop it, would not be Gildo's son in the deserts of Africa.

It didn't matter if Magnus was her father, Sevira was Elen's daughter and she would one day grow up to be as strong as Grandmother.

She called an attendant who came over to fuss over her hair, making her look presentable as quickly as possible, and then she walked through the marble-lined corridors of the palace to attend to her husband.

In the huge atrium, Victor lay on his belly, his cheeky and infectious laugh echoing off the gold-streaked marble floor and walls. He'd been set in front of a ludus board, but Magnus' attempt at educating a toddler about the similarities of a game of counters and the running of the court had descended into a wrestling match between him and Publicus as they tried to get counters out of each other's hands. Each other's tactics also included a liberal amount of tickling. She waited for Magnus to snap at a pair of two-year-olds to be sensible, but his attention was on something evidently more important.

He shouted a curse at the man who was fighting a losing battle to not simply curl up in a corner to try and protect himself from the emperor's onslaught, especially when Magnus tossed a handful of parchments into the air. The poor man watched them flitter to the floor with eyes as terrified as a condemned man at his executioner's sword. Magnus not being in a good mood wasn't unusual, but while Elen couldn't imagine with what weight the rigours of his new role and its responsibilities pressed on him, no matter their toll, it was what he'd wished for, and so it was all his to deal with, no one else's. His face was so drawn, the rings under his eyes so dark and pronounced, she was beginning to wonder where his breaking point was, and what would happen when he couldn't control the maddening rage he was only barely holding onto?

The repercussions of his anger went a lot further than him just making her life miserable, though. Now they could be felt across the whole empire.

One of the parchments landed at her feet. It was a drawing for the design of the first coins to be minted in Magnus' likeness. The reverse had him sitting on an impressive throne, but she wondered who the figure kneeling at his side was supposed to represent.

Magnus turned from the artist to look at her. With his tired eyes devoid of all compassion, he asked her, "Is there any explanation as to why a group of bedraggled slaves are huddled on the steps of the basilica wanting an audience with me?"

Elen shrugged. Many men from all over Gaul, and from even further, had come to petition the new emperor for strange requests. It was to be expected in times of such change.

"They say that you freed them," he added.

Elen remembered the litter bearers she'd freed after she'd killed Gratian. She nodded. "I did."

"For any particular reason?"

"Andragathius wanted them dead."

"So why did you think to stop him?"

"Because I thought sparing them was the Christian thing to do," she said forcibly, staring him in the eye.

With the guilt he had in his heart from lying about his baptism, he couldn't hold her look. "And what will you do with them?" he asked, his tone a little softer, but no less strained.

"Nothing," she shrugged.

He rolled his eyes in exasperation. "Why not?"

"Because they are not slaves. It seems to me that if I freed them, then they are the masters of their own destinies. Just as we are of ours."

"You can't just keep freeing slaves," he said in frustration. He sighed, trying to think of a reply suitable for an emperor. "You'll begin to unravel the structure of society."

She couldn't help scoffing and had to bite her lip to stop herself from laughing openly in his face.

"What?!" he demanded.

"Unravelling the structure?" she said in a whisper so the coin designer couldn't hear. "So says the man who has usurped the emperor, to the girl in whose arms he died."

His eyes seemed to bulge in a way that might have been familiar to the residents of Pompeii who knew something terrible was about to erupt from Vesuvius. She thought about cautioning him that nothing good had ever come from a fit of anger, with Valentinian the First being a good example, but kept her tongue still as she knew such words would only make him worse.

Worried, perhaps, that the designer was listening to his wife speaking to him in such a way, Magnus picked up the parchment that had landed at her feet and flapped it around. "This one. The one where the emperor's wife is kneeling next to him in supplication, and he holds the world of worry and responsibility in his left hand. This is the one I want. Bring me the first coin struck so that I might judge it."

Elen shrugged again. If it was meant as an insult, it was one that affected her as much as water running off the back of a duck. He might have just about got himself an empire to rule over, but the only way he would have his wife kneel before him in supplication was on a drawing.

"Augustus?" a servant at the doorway said nervously.

All Magnus' servants were nervous. Elen thought Magnus liked them that way. "What now?" he bellowed.

"A visitor."

"Another?! Tell him to go and amuse himself in a brothel and leave me alone!"

The servant nodded his head, but before he turned to leave, Elen called out, "Who is it?"

The servant swallowed nervously. "Ambrosius, the Bishop of Mediolanum."

"What?" Magnus cried. "You idiot! Why didn't you tell me? I will have you whipped! Scourged!"

"Which brothel would you suggest for him?" Elen asked.

"Take him to the basilica!" Magnus shouted in a high-pitched voice. "I will come as soon as I can! No wait! Take him to the cathedral. I will receive him there!"

Elen only just managed to stifle her laughter, but it was no laughing matter. Apart from the three men in the empire who wore purple togas, the bishop was the most important man in the empire. Perhaps even more so than Emperor Valentinian, and so in the next few moments, the shape of Magnus' reign was to be determined. And by denying the bishop an audience in the grand basilica, he seemed determined to make an enemy out of him.

* * *

Magnus stretched out his shoulders and pumped his chest, just as he did before any fight.

Since he'd taken Gratian's purple cloak, he'd known this moment would come. He hadn't expected that the bishop could have made the trip from the court of Valentinian over the mountains from Mediolanum quite so quickly, though. The haste was an indication of the importance of the situation.

As much as he didn't want to keep the bishop waiting, a sign a man of his status and standing could take as an insult, maybe even contempt, he wanted a moment alone with Victor before facing him. At first, his son protested at being pulled away from his best friend, but he always liked being held by his father, and for Magnus, feeling the warmth radiating from his little body was some kind of balm on his heart. Telling himself that all he did was for his son, helped alleviate some of the awful weight of responsibility, that the wave of trauma he'd unleashed over an already weak empire was all so that Victor would one day come to power and enjoy a reign as golden as Constantine's.

Magnus the Conqueror. Victor the Restorer.

He didn't truly believe it though, and he held no real hope that the bishop would either. Magnus knew he was no one special, no one god-ordained to the role he now found himself in. He was no more than an ambitious man gifted with the means to achieve a position almost every man born into the senatorial class would try to attain if they could. All thoughts of grandeur aside, all he'd done was rile up an army big enough that he'd managed to overthrow the former emperor. A popularity contest with a prize worth risking everything for.

The bishop seeing that in him wasn't a worry. What caused the stabbing terror in his heart was that as a revered man of God, he'd be able to see into a man's soul and know if he was baptised or not. If Ambrosius was to know of Magnus' deceit, that he'd lied about something so profound, so sacred, and announced it to the world, he was about to be in real trouble. If his soldiers were to argue about the right and wrong of it, some taking his side, others not wanting to risk their necks following a man whom God could smite in disgust at any moment, his advance south would be halted before it had even begun.

His place in Treverorum would even be under threat.

In his worrying little way, Victor bobbed his head from side to side, his eyes noticeably unfocused. "Want that," he said and with a chubby finger pointed at Magnus' head.

He took the golden diadem off. Victor grabbed it greedily and turned it around in the light in front of him, enthralled. Magnus supposed he could see his precious little rainbows in the way the sun caught the golden leaves. One day he'd enjoy the look of a sharp blade with an opponent's blood on it. Magnus was sure that it was of equal beauty.

He passed the future emperor to his wife and waved Ausonius and his personal guard to him, then walked down the corridor. He liked how his purple toga felt with its heavy folds wrapped around him, one part held over his left arm. He knew how important it was to present himself as the loving head of a family rather than a conquering soldier, a statesman rather than a military one, but heading out to a confrontation with someone while not wearing his armour felt very uncomfortable. The chain mail with its thousands of close-linked rings, the padded shirt and the outer shirt of hundreds of overlapping metal scales and his shield weighed about a third of his body weight, but he'd grown up in it, had worn it almost every day of his life, so despite its weight on his shoulders, it felt as familiar as a second skin. Dressed only in the toga and a pair of light sandals, he felt almost naked, as though he was in a bathhouse rather than hurrying along the palace corridors to meet one of the most powerful men in the empire.

He waved for Elen to hurry up. Victor was only two, but Elen was so slight she struggled to carry him. Not for the first time he wondered how it could be that someone so small and physically weak could wield such power.

"Erm…" Ausonius whined, also struggling to keep up. "Are you sure that you wouldn't rather receive him in the basilica? Surely a more fitting place for a man of his status."

"To be hosted in the consistory of the cathedral will surely be taken as a great offence," Magnus said. "But Valentinian must understand that I consider him an inferior. Not an equal."

As they made their way along the street, the guards fanning out to protect him from the townspeople, he noted the look of scorn on Elen's face for wanting to treat such a revered man in such a way but was glad that she kept her misgivings to herself. He hoped she wouldn't dare to do anything like she'd done with Martin.

Merobaudes, Ausonius and Nannienus wouldn't be offering too much to the conversation, but all of them were former men of Gratian, and now all stood loyal at Magnus' side in a show of power and confidence. Elen took her place on his left, with her odd brother. Magnus' reaction at seeing him was as though something was stuck to the bottom of his shoe. As soon as he could find a reason to send him away from Treverorum, far away, he would jump at it.

Despite his display being arranged perfectly, as he waved for the doors to be opened, his heart strained and his stomach churned.

Magnus watched as the bishop strode purposely towards him at the head of his entourage, feet kicking out his voluminous gown in front with each step. As he walked through the pools of light cast by the rows of windows, the gold sewn into his outfit flashed and the tall mitre on his head made him seem oddly oversized. Soldiers of Varro's legions might have felt the same terror as they watched Hannibal's armoured elephants charge towards them. Against an army, Magnus knew plenty of techniques and manoeuvres to protect his position or to launch a comprehensive attack, and he'd never once been defeated, but in the game of politics, he knew himself to be not much more than a novice. Against Ambrosius, the famously fire-tongued Bishop of Mediolanum, a man who was either about to be his closest partner or his absolute nemesis, a battle in which words would be weapons, he feared he was about to be horribly outmatched.

In front of a man of such standing, there should probably have been some decorum, some stoic, formal greeting, perhaps the exchanging of valuable gifts, but as soon as Magnus saw his brother, he sprang up with open arms and ignoring Ambrosius, bound over to him. Marcellinus pushed his way through the Bishop's entourage and did the same. They slammed into a hug so hard that the breath was forced from Magnus' chest. "You are safe!' he beamed. "Did they treat you well?"

"They did, brother, fear not." Marcellinus beamed. "And look at you now! How far you have risen!" He tugged at the purple toga, testing it between his fingers, and toyed with the diadem on Magnus' head, not unlike Victor had done. It was a totally disrespectful way to treat an Augustus, especially in front of such a prestigious audience, but Magnus would not have had it any other way.

"My brother!" Marcellinus beamed again and pressed in for another hug, but as he patted Magnus' shoulder, he whispered urgently, "They are in disarray. Strike now!"

But Magnus didn't have a single moment to consider those words as Marcellinus turned around to introduce the bishop. "My brother, who after so many nights of me regaling you with tales about him, as you can now see for yourself, I spoke not one word of exaggeration."

"Talking of *brothers* is the first thing on the agenda," the bishop said, giving a slow but shallow bow. Magnus hastened back to his seat, where he hoped he might cut a more imposing figure. He swirled the free end of his toga around, but before the bishop in the splendour of his gold-encrusted finery, he felt like a chicken before a peacock. Talking of Gratian's rotting corpse was not how he wanted to begin the conversation.

"Imperator Caesar Dominus Magnus Maximus Pius Felix Augustus!" the bishop said in the peculiar drone priests liked to speak in. It gave him a chill to hear his full title spoken by a man with such power. "Let us get the—unsavoury tasks out of the way first."

Magnus nodded his consent.

"Look to the man who stands at your right hand," Ambrosius said, holding his hand out towards Marcellinus. "Augustus Valentinian, when he had the opportunity of avenging his grief, instead, he sent your brother back to you loaded with honours. He had him in his own territory, and yet restrained his hand. Even when he received the tidings of his brother's death, he restrained his natural feelings, abstained from retaliation, and sent back your brother alive."

"He did," Magnus said, "and I am very grateful to him for it."

"Perhaps that gratitude could be reciprocated in kind? Do you restore Gratian to his brother at least now that he is dead?"

With his first words, the bishop had caught Magnus in a bind.

In the delicate few weeks after the shock of Gratian's killing had spread through the empire, there was no way Magnus could allow a state funeral for the emperor he was responsible for killing. Such a ceremony would legitimise Gratian's rule, therefore making it clear that Magnus was a usurper. And if the grief of the populace was to turn to anger. Quelling uprisings was not how he intended to spend his first months in Treverorum.

He could think of no quick yet erudite answer though, so deemed it best to simply dismiss it. "It is a matter I have yet to decide upon," he shrugged. "Perhaps we can dispense with the flowery formalities. I come to the throne not as an orator, no student of rhetoric, only as a soldier, as Constantine did. Swords and soldiers are my strength, not words."

"Indeed, indeed," the bishop said with a slow dip of his head, but one that was not low enough to worry the balance of his tall mitre. "The offer I come authorised to give from the esteemed Emperor Valentinian the Second is that if you were to accept Treverorum as your imperial capital, from where you will focus all of your efforts on the protection of the borders against the very real threat of the Goths, he will concede to you Britannia, as well as Hispania, a province that should be delighted that one of its humble sons has risen so far. He trusts that if you don't have any ambitions further than replacing his brother, you would be more than satisfied with this."

"Satisfied?" Magnus asked. He felt his face flush. He'd been prepared for a challenging discussion but hadn't been ready to be so insulted. He wondered how much of his disappointment it would be politically expedient to show. "How can I be satisfied?" he asked softly. "Rather, I am confused. It seems that it is no offer you bring me. Britannia is already mine by proclamation of its armies. By the will of God, of course."

"It is duly noted," the bishop nodded again.

"Furthermore, Gaul and Hispania were Gratian's, and now they are mine, so how can he think to grant me what I *already* have?"

"Absolutely, Augustus," the bishop said, clasping his hands together in front of him under his voluminous sleeves. "A mere formality, that is all."

Magnus sighed. If the bishop thought it acceptable to make outrageous offers, Magnus might as well do the same. "And Africa," he added.

"Well... That might be..."

"I fought there, spilled the blood of my soldiers and buried friends. When I stood against Gratian at Lutetia, Gildo's cavalry were the first to come to me from Gratian's side, and so I claim Africa as mine."

"It can be discussed, of course. But it is of course far, *far* beyond both my remit and power to agree to such a thing. I stand before you only as a humble emissary."

Magnus didn't think that there was anything at all humble about Ambrosius.

"I would also imagine Augustus Theodosius will have something to say in the matter, and should therefore be consulted."

"Indeed. And he will be, of course."

The bishop took such a deep breath that Magnus found himself preparing for an onslaught of superfluous verbiage. "While I am in the admittedly rather awkward situation of having to serve an emperor and his mother who are both sadly lost to the heresies of Arianism, I do, of course, understand the merits and the benefits of you and your esteemed cousin ruling the East and West in tandem. Two strong military men whose victorious exploits from all over the empire would take so much time to extol, but at the current moment, I would plead with you, as one man of God to another..." he droned on in his jarring monotone, obviously enjoying the sound of his own voice. Magnus was glad he hadn't received him in the basilica. The acoustics inside the grand building were extraordinary, so if Ambrosius was to hear himself there, he'd never stop talking.

As the soporific drone continued, Magnus' thoughts wandered off until he was looking at Marcellinus. If his brother's quickly whispered words were true, he could lead a lightning strike on an unprepared enemy before Valentinian could block the mountain passes. He could take Mediolanum as convincingly as he had Treverorum, and then he'd have the whole of Italy. His half of the empire. On the other hand though, if he was to leave with as many men as he could muster while things in Gaul were still in turmoil, the tribes crowding the eastern borders wouldn't hesitate to swim across the Rhine and swarm over the land like a plague.

The bishop cleared his throat and snapped Magnus back to the matter at hand.

"...as two Nicean Christians, esteemed proponents of the One True Faith surrounded on every border by ravenous barbarians, all eager to despoil the burgeoning light of Christ with their base, unenlightened pagan ways, I beg you, on behalf of every citizen and slave of the empire, at the beginning of your surely to be exalted reign, to see to the foundations of your administration, make them strong and sound enough to build the cathedral of your reign on, before you take even one single soldier away from the border."

On the face of it, making the borders more secure was sound military strategy, but for Magnus, how the bishop could say so many words in a single breath was both impressive and a little worrying. Although he had spoken just what Magnus was thinking, he couldn't help wondering if Ambrosius was uttering some kind of incantation to lull him into a supine state where he could wheedle anything he wanted out of him, and as untested as he was in matters of diplomacy, he was sure that while the bishop was speaking about the well-being of the empire, it was more for Valentinian's benefit that he was talking. They were desperate for him to stay put in Treverorum.

"I act for God, I will swear to that," Magnus said, guessing that such words were what the bishop wanted to hear. "My new administration is in the process of working out the details."

"Indeed, indeed," Ambrosius said, trying to assume a humble pose and failing. But then he raised his head, and looking Magnus in the eye, asked, "What do you want?"

The directness, stripped of all pretence, came as such a shock that it felt to Magnus as though he'd just had to deflect an unexpected sword stroke. It really was like sparring with a formidable opponent, only with words, not swords. Each sentence spoken was a probing for the other's weaknesses, and in this fight, Magnus was sure that the bishop had his measure.

It took him a moment to compose himself, but decided to give an equally forceful reply. "What I want is for Valentinian to come to me here in Treverorum, as a son comes to a father."

The bishop nodded thoughtfully. "An altogether reasonable request, indeed. Truly, I see a great benefit in having the youngster, a boy plenty young enough to be your son, an elder brother to Victor perhaps, to be here under your protection, and even more valuably, your tutelage. I regret though, that whatever position you believe I stand in, I do not have the authority to agree to such a thing. Be assured though, that upon my return to Mediolanum, I will be vociferously advocating for your idea, but alas, it does have a flaw; unfortunately, a fatal one."

"And what is that?" Magnus sighed.

"The days draw close to September. For me to return to Mediolanum will take, say, two weeks, perhaps a little more, perhaps the same again to make all the necessary arrangements for the journey back here, and by then we will be well into autumn. I cannot, in good conscience, suggest that with the severe weather, which could well be expected in the mountains this time of year, a boy with his widowed mother should travel. I will, however, give you my word that I will do all I can to make this happen for the spring of next year. I do not feel that it is beyond my powers of persuasion. I would definitely expect to see him here with you in Treverorum in just a few short months."

On the face of it, the bishop's words sounded easy to agree with, but Magnus' instinct told him that the bishop was just stalling. He recalled Marcellinus' words again.

"There is something you need to be aware of in such a situation though," Ambrosius said solemnly.

"What is that?" Magnus asked, cautiously.

"He will come with his *mother*!"

A few men in the assembly laughed at Empress Justina's expense, probably those who had had the misfortune of meeting her, but they did nothing to alleviate the tension in the consistory.

"And further to your words," the bishop continued. "I would suggest that official recognition from Theodosius would be a consideration worthy of your immediate concern. News of your elevation should have reached him by now. Perhaps the best way of getting your foundations secured would be to receive official recognition from Constantinople."

"Recognition is merely a question of time," Magnus said. "He is, after all, my cousin, as well as a fellow Nicean."

"Perhaps, perhaps," the bishop said in his annoying way of speaking veiled insults with polite words. "However, to get the pressing situation clarified, I would suggest that it is already past time to send an envoy out to the east. The sooner he returns with a proclamation that recognizes you as Emperor of the West, Gratian's successor, the sooner solid foundations can be laid for your good and godly rule."

It was the first thing the bishop had said that made real sense.

"The envoy should be someone close to you. By blood would be best, a brother, but I imagine Marcellinus would like some time to re-familiarize himself with his family and friends after his time in Mediolanum. My suggestion, therefore, is your wife's brother."

From saying something that finally made sense, he went straight back to speaking nonsense. Magnus couldn't trust his wife's idiot brother with anything that required even a hint of responsibility.

"It will be a long and fraught journey from here to Constantinople in these tumultuous times."

But then again, Kenon was certainly expendable and would be a worthless hostage if something was to go wrong. All he had to do was carry a message across the empire and bring another back. Surely not even Kenon could mess that up. "Done, then," he said, not even bothering to look at Kenon's reaction. "He can leave tomorrow."

The bishop smiled. "I shall write a letter to your esteemed cousin, for Kenon to take to him. I'll send it for your approval before the ink has even dried."

After a normal fight with a man, it was usually simple to know who the winner was, as the one dead or pleading for mercy was the loser. With the bishop, and the conflict of words, Magnus was not sure who the victor had been, But if the bishop wanted to spend time with Kenon, then Magnus had definitely come off best.

And as far as he could tell, Ambrosius hadn't seen the sin in his soul.

Perhaps Elen was a better judge of character than the bishop was.

XII

Kenon had been in Treverorum for a couple of weeks, but even though no one knew him, he hadn't found the courage to go out exploring. Even though he was further away from Padarn than he'd ever been, the thought of strangers on the streets staring at him, *through* him, still filled him with a crippling fear.

He didn't feel any safer with a pair of the bishop's guards flanking him.

The reason why the Bishop of Mediolanum had summoned him and whisked him out of the palace so secretly swirled around in his head as much as his guts were in his belly. From not having the courage to leave his farm for years, he was about to be sent to the far side of the empire. Memories of the crucified deserters, him kneeling before them, thinking he was next, came flooding back.

The inside of the house the bishop was staying in looked even more spectacular than Magnus' palace. The exquisitely crafted furniture, the piles of fruit stacked high on all of the bowls, the mosaics on the floor, the frescoes painted on the walls, everything was so sumptuous. Magnus was a military man down to every last bone in his body and after stripping out Gratian's gaudy trappings, but he hadn't replaced them with equally decadent things, so much of the palace had the austerity of the barracks, but for a reason he didn't understand, how the bishop, a man of God, was obviously so well acquainted with worldly luxuries, made him very nervous.

As he made his way into the open atrium a movement caught his eye at the base of the fountain. The large pool even had fish in it!

When Kenon had watched the bishop walk into the church to meet Magnus, he'd thought he was the most outrageously dressed man he'd ever seen. His attire was so ostentatious that the emperor, in his purple toga and simple diadem, had looked positively plain in comparison. Even reclining on the couch in the dining room, popping grapes into his mouth, in just a toga and embroidered tunic, he looked richer than any man Kenon had ever seen.

Ever since he'd been dragged out of the river, the day Magnus had captured the raiding Votadini, he'd been mortally terrified of powerful men and had done his utmost to keep out of their way, but now he was before a man whose power rivalled almost that of Magnus; perhaps even surpassed it. He felt like a dog tied to a post, utterly unable to take a step away.

With a wave of the wrist, lazy fingers dangling, as though he didn't feel Kenon was even worth the bother of extending a finger to point with, the bishop offered Kenon the couch opposite to recline on.

As he settled himself down it felt like he was getting ready for Padarn and his men. He tried to tell himself that he was being stupid, but as the bishop popped a couple of grapes into his mouth, he looked at Kenon, and his gaze lingered. It was the same glint of disgusting hunger that had been in Padarn's, and it was as though he'd been struck with the butt of a spear in the stomach. Bile rose to the back of his throat and he was instantly bathed in a sheen of sweat. He was glad he was lying down. If he'd been standing, his legs would have given way.

"You don't know who you are, do you?" the bishop said with a saccharine smile. "You believe yourself to be the vilest sinner, but in fact, you are as innocent as a babe."

That was not at all what he was expecting to hear, and in response, his tongue decided to freeze itself stiff.

"Don't worry," the bishop said in a smile that seemed far from friendly. "*I* know who you are. I know everything about you."

The thought that such a godly man knew Kenon's sordid secrets made it feel like a hundred filthy rats were crawling over his body.

"Everything. You see, I have my little ears and eyes at Magnus' court, of course – and in your sister's circle. A singularly incredible girl, that one, isn't she? I don't doubt that she'll be made a saint one day, but spies telling me all the rumours, as delicious as some of them are, are not what I mean. You see, ever since I took on this role, I have always felt an affinity with the afflicted and the tested. Do you know what I mean by that?"

Kenon didn't want to know, and shook his head.

The sound of the water trickling over the fountain was making him desperate to pee.

"The tested, those sweet souls who, by no fault of their own, are tossed into such awful circumstances, caused to suffer such privations and tribulations, that it can only be by God's hand the circumstances manifest. You still don't follow?"

Kenon shook his head again. The shame of what Padarn and his men had done to him was mixed with the confusion of not knowing what a man like the bishop could possibly want with him.

"Think of the finest sword, one that makes a man gasp at the beauty and perfection of it. Think of what it took for it to get to that God-like state of perfection, all of the infernal fires of the smith's forge, the hammering over the anvil it had to endure. And how terribly it must have suffered to become the blade it is now. Are you following me?"

All Kenon could think of was running away, all the way back to his farm in Britannia, and with weak legs he pushed himself up and looked around for the quickest way to escape. But the bishop's voice, laden with such authority, held him in place, as though he was a fish on a hook.

"For the greater good, the worst things could be done," he said. "Remember that, my boy. You are one of the lucky ones, my dear Kenon. You have been tested by God. The ordeals you endured, you were not cast into them by man's hand. No, God himself led you into them, and you *survived*. Therefore you are close to being perfect."

No one had ever said such words to him, but instead of it being a compliment, they filled him with more terror than any of Padarn's men ever had.

"Didn't you feel the touch of God when you were tested, north of the Wall."

It certainly hadn't been God touching him!

"I brought you here because I have something you want. Something you *crave*."

It was happening again. The worst moments of Kenon's life were about to be forced upon him again. The bishop was just as bad as Padarn. "And what is that?" he managed to croak.

"You know exactly what that is," the bishop scoffed and Kenon recoiled. "The thing you wish for more than anything. All you have to do is ask for it, and I will give it to you. You can ask me for it, can't you?"

"I don't know." It seemed so terribly wrong that the bishop would term something so disgusting as that as the touch of God.

"We will do it together, just you and I. Or, if you want, you may have some witnesses, I will lay my hands on you."

"Witnesses?" Kenon gasped.

"Of course. Sometimes men want their friends and family to watch. Often quite a crowd. Although some like privacy, as they prefer the *intimacy* of it. All you have to do, just so I know that you are ready, is to ask."

Kenon was so confused he wanted to scream. Sweat beaded on his forehead and it was getting harder and harder to breathe. He looked around for something sharp he could stab the bastard with, or something heavy to cave his skull in.

"Just say the word. Just ask for it. And afterwards, the whole world will be yours. As well as the afterlife."

"I don't understand!" Kenon whimpered.

The bishop sighed in a way that Kenon worried was impatience. He angled his open palms towards heaven. "Absolution."

Kenon scoffed at what he thought was a cruel joke, but, at the relief of finally understanding how utterly, sinfully, wrong he'd misunderstood everything, he burst into tears.

"Good boy, good boy," the bishop said, less in a mocking tone, more in a consolatory one.

Kenon didn't agree, though, and he was utterly disgusted at himself for thinking that a *bishop*, a man closer to the Lord than almost any other in the empire, could be as bad as Padarn. "The cleansing of the immortal soul through the blessing of baptism," the bishop added, "the wiping clean of every sin, every stain. This is what I wish to offer you."

"But..." Kenon said before stopping himself. All the things he'd done, the blood of the little girl he still saw on his hands. For all the suffering he wished on others. He was sure the bishop, no matter what dregs of society he tended to in his role, had never come across someone as wretched as Kenon.

"Anyone can be absolved," he said as though Kenon had been speaking his thoughts out loud. "No sin is so severe that to the truly repentant it cannot be forgiven. Even a tyrant can be forgiven. Even a *usurper*. What do you think about that?"

"Erm.." Kenon said, at a complete loss of how to reply.

"Would you like to be baptised. To be reborn into the Light of Christ?"

"I err. Yes!" he blurted out in case the offer would be taken away and he'd miss his chance.

"Very good. Very good. We'll do it very soon. But firstly, you must do something for me; a simple exchange. Something a little dangerous should anyone find out, admittedly, but then I will do for you the single most wonderful thing you have ever experienced in your life. Or ever will again."

Suddenly the sweetness turned sour.

Of course there would be a price.

"You see, Magnus is a powerful man, and no man could possibly get to the position he finds himself in without the divine grace of the Lord guiding the way, but I fear a man so wrapped up in his own ambition can somehow misinterpret the guidance of God, mistake divine direction for the voice in his head that presses him for more worldly power, more worldly glory. My duty, here on Earth, is to guide men towards the grace of God, and for that I need a man I can trust in the usurper's circle, someone close to him to be my ears, to report to me his plans, who he has meetings with. That sort of thing."

Kenon didn't know what to say.

"And one day, to betray him. Don't you agree, my dear Kenon, that the best man to do that would be someone who has been tragically betrayed by him? I don't *just* offer absolution," he added with a horrible smile. "I offer revenge, as well. But there is even more! I have something to enrich your life *after* your baptism. Those who do the Lord's work are rewarded in heaven–often on Earth as well. We all enjoy our earthly pleasures, don't we? Land, I can give you. It must eat at your heart terribly what Magnus did to you, stealing your inheritance like that. Such an injustice. But I can rectify that somewhat. And when I say land, I don't just mean a villa on an estate. I mean a *province*. In Gaul. For you to govern. I know, that sounds incredible, doesn't it? Almost too much to believe. Almost as though you are in a dream; but there is *even* more. I, of course, am in the confidence of many wealthy men, many of whom have daughters in need of the hand of a good man. I believe that I have found someone perfect for you. Ursula is her name. Daughter of Dionotus. A wonderfully godly girl. She has just begun an undertaking which she hopes will be a years-long pilgrimage around the holy sites of the empire. Once she has returned, she will want an equally godly man as a husband. One who has the power at the position to allow her to establish Christian centres for those in need. You will be happy to be that man, won't you?"

"I..."

"Just say you agree, and it is *all* yours."

"Yes!" he gasped.

"Good, good."

The bishop clicked his fingers and a moment later a man stepped into the atrium, but it was the timid young girl on his arm who Kenon stared at. She was the most gorgeous creature he'd ever laid eyes on. If she'd been offered in a brothel, he'd have thrown his full purse at the owner for a few moments with her; dark and sultry–but then he snapped himself out of such thoughts. Desires like that had no place in front of the bishop, and he made sure that his toga was bunched up over where such thoughts would be betrayed.

"Only an evening to get to know each other, I'm afraid," the bishop smirked. "Tomorrow she will be ripped out of your hands, as at dawn you will begin your journey to Constantinople. I will send you to Emperor Theodosius as my agent, but it will be him who gives you your mission."

XIII

Magnus scrunched up the parchment in his fist. Every note Andragathius had ever written to him before had contained good news. But not this time. All passes across the mountains were blocked, and the man in charge was Bauto, a general whose reputation had reached Magnus even in the north of Britannia.

He balled the note in his fist. It had been done too quickly The warning must have left Treverorum soon after he'd defeated Gratian. Which meant he'd been betrayed.

All hope of taking his brother's advice and storming Mediolanum while Valentinian was unprepared was gone. For the foreseeable future, the next few years at least, he'd be stuck in a defensive position, in charge of only half the Western Empire's army, not all of it.

At least he would have ample time in which to find out who the traitor was.

Another thing that had left a sour taste was not knowing why the bishop chose to serve an Arian teenager and his mother, whom he openly admitted to disliking.

He wondered if while Ambrosius had been speaking pleasantries to his face, he knew that Valentinian's best general was building barricades.

But there was another issue Magnus needed to address before he concentrated on anything else. With no military action imminent, there was a former master of infantry who had just found himself surplus to requirements.

He had waited years to repay Merobaudes for the death of Theodosius the Elder and he was quite disappointed when it had come to it, that he felt so reluctant. It would be a cold-blooded execution, but a whole cathedral was being built in Londinium to pay for the sin. Such a grand edifice to the glory of God would surely be payment enough for the life of one murderer, and once Merobaudes lay dead before him, he would submit himself to the holy waters and get cleansed of all sin.

He was sitting in the sun in the huge atrium in the palace that was now his, in the city that was now his, in Gaul, which was now his.

He turned his sword over in his lap.

He'd had many blades over the years. Spathas he'd fought with in Africa, and many of the shorter gladius', which were easier to ride with. Some he'd had to change as they were too old, others had been broken, but none had ever been as special as the one Marcellinus had gifted him for his wedding. The swordsmith in Deva had created a blade like no other. They'd had him grip a lump of damp clay, and from that they'd made the most perfectly fitting handle crafted exactly to the shape of his fingers, and his alone. The metal was the finest tempered steel and when he held it to the light he could see little rivulets of darker metal flowing through it, like currents in a stream. TO HIM UNCONQUERED was engraved on one edge.

In the three years he'd owned it, he'd not used it in anger, hadn't baptised it in the blood of an enemy. Until today. The revenge he'd waited so long to exact, on the man he hated more than any other in the world, was finally about to come to pass. He thought again of Theodosius the Elder. His loss was still a hole impossible to fill, even though he'd been gone for nearly ten years.

A tear splashed on the blade and he laughed at how Theodosius would have clipped him on the ear for getting salt water on it. As he wiped it off with the end of his toga he wondered if Merobaudes would appreciate its craftsmanship, as it sank into his chest.

Despite dreaming for years of blood and swords, he'd come to the decision that killing Merobaudes cleanly would be less of a sin than pulling him apart piece by piece, slowly, over several days. He would even allow him his own sword to make his execution a little fairer–at least to give the appearance of fairness. As emperor he could control rumours now, If he needed to, he could spread the story that Merobaudes had attacked him and he was simply defending himself.

He looked around the small courtyard, the graceful columns lining the open corridors that surrounded the open space. It was far too nice of a place for Merobaudes to die, but it was convenient as it couldn't be overlooked, the blood would be easy to clean off the flagstones, and his body could be disposed of without anyone seeing. But that still wouldn't be dead enough for Merobaudes. Magnus would do to his memory the same as he'd do to his body and would issue a damnatio memoriae. For a man twice awarded consulship, it would be a much worse fate than death. Killing the body was easy as everyone died, but killing the memory of a man, making it as though he had never even existed, not allowing a word to ever be spoken about him, was something dreadful. Magnus would tell Merobaudes of his intention a few delicious moments before he sank the blade into him so the bastard would know he was about to die in more ways than one.

He heard the loud confident footsteps of his enemy coming down the corridor. And then he was in the courtyard, and they were alone; no witnesses apart from God himself. "I made you this promise," Magnus whispered as though in prayer. "Now I will keep it."

At Magnus' drawn sword, Merobaudes knew that something was wrong. The guards slammed the door closed and at the sound Merobaudes knew that he wouldn't be leaving alive.

"Was it similar to this?" Magnus asked.

"Was what, Augustus?"

"The setting for my uncle's murder."

Magnus was quite impressed at how well Merobaudes managed to hold himself. There was no panic, no pleading. He looked around thoughtfully. "There are similarities," he said, "but that day, it was raining."

"Was there a rainbow?"

"I'm sorry, Augustus?"

"Never mind. Just tell me how it felt to kill him."

Merobaudes sighed. "It was a duty, nothing more."

"Just obeying a command?"

He nodded. "I was."

"From Valens?"

"Yes."

"And you didn't question it? Knowing that your actions would leave dead one of the greatest military minds the empire has ever known?"

He shook his head. "I serve the empire. It is not for men like me to question a command of an emperor; only to obey."

"Did you think about why he ordered it?"

"Because he feared for the lives of his nephews. He wanted to protect Gratian and Valentinian, the children of his brother. Theodosius the Elder would have made a much better ruler than both of them put together."

If Magnus could assemble an army to take Gaul, his uncle would have had no trouble at all in taking the whole empire for himself, if he'd had the inclination. And the empire would probably be in a much better state, as the idiot Valens would not have been in charge at Adrianople.

He put his fingers into the grooves in the grip of the sword and felt the perfect balance. "Just obeying a command?"

"I serve the empire," Merobaudes said again with a degree of pride Magnus wasn't expecting.

"And if I, your emperor now, ordered you to throw yourself on your sword here at my feet, would you do it?"

"I might have a few questions before I did. I might beg for my life. Might argue that bringing you Gratian's cloak and almost his whole army might have made things equal. But, yes."

"Because you serve the empire."

Merobaudes nodded, starting to get worried now. "I do."

Watching Merobaudes kill himself in front of him might be a lesser burden for Magnus' soul, but it wouldn't give him the satisfaction he needed.

"How did my uncle react?"

"He was brave, calm and…"

"Resigned?" Magnus offered.

"Yes. I think he understood why it had to happen."

"And will you?"

He shrugged and with a sigh said, "Yes, Augustus."

"Draw your sword," Magnus said as he stood up.

That seemed to confuse Merobaudes.

"Draw your sword!" Magnus snapped angrily. "I command it!"

Slowly, uncomfortable with the action, Merobaudes slid his blade from the scabbard at his hip. The blade flashed as it caught the light. Magnus knew he was in no danger, but facing a man with bare steel in his hand still had the effect of quickening his blood, shortening his breath, and bringing into perfect focus only that which was right in front of him.

"You think you could beat me?" he asked, amused at the thought.

"Even if by some miracle I could, I wouldn't."

Miracle… Suddenly Magnus had an awful thought that struck him like a thunderclap. And then, like something out of a bad dream, Merobaudes raised his sword upright so the hilt was in front of his forehead. As he lowered it to over his heart, Magnus groaned. "Are you baptised?"

"I am," he smiled as he moved his hand across the front of his chest, completing the cross.

"When?" Magnus gasped.

"A couple of years ago."

"After you killed Theodosius?"

"Yes."

"So you are forgiven? Absolved?" he asked, fighting the feeling that something terribly important was being wrested from his grip.

Merobaudes nodded solemnly.

It had been many years since he'd done anything but spar with a partner, but even with just the chain mail shirt on under the purple toga, swinging his sword still felt perfectly natural. He felt the easy weight of it, as perfectly balanced as Fraomar's scales. "Come," he said.

Looking like a raw recruit about to get his first disciplining from his centurion, Merobaudes reluctantly lifted his sword and moved his feet into a defensive position. Magnus went at him in a barely controlled rage and it was only with an instinct to save his life that Merobaudes fought back.

The flash and clash of steel was like some kind of elixir to Magnus, and he suddenly felt twenty-five years younger. But something he had not considered until now was how stupid it was to try and fight in a toga. The heavy folds of cloth slipped down around his arms and if Merobaudes had really been fighting, Magnus would be dead. His opponent waited while he unwound it and tossed it to the floor. One of the most precious objects in the empire, something half the men alive aspired to, discarded as though it was a dirty rag.

They clashed again. The shock of each steel on steel connection shooting up his arm was a thrill. But Merobaudes was only defending, he wouldn't give a single attacking thrust, and that made Magnus angry. With a couple of hard strokes, he managed to catch a glancing blow at the side of Merobaudes' head, just above his eyebrow. Blood ran through his sweat and quickly streaked the whole side of his face.

"You served Gratian," Magnus said, pausing for a moment,

"I did."

"And yet you betrayed him."

"Only at the very last moment, when I realised I would better serve the empire by pledging my men to you."

"And do you regret that now?"

"I serve the empire," he said through gritted teeth and angled his sword ready to put it back into its scabbard. "Killing you is not serving it."

There was a banging behind them, then a woman's shrill voice. It could only be Elen, but he'd posted guards at the door, so she would not be coming in.

"Magnus!' she screamed like a harpy and at the grin from Merobaudes that was almost mocking, he struck at him again with all the strength he had. Merobaudes only just managed to flinch backwards and save himself. The next time he ducked under Magnus' swing and Magnus almost lost his balance, and before he could get his feet under him for another strike there was a flurry of colour in front of him, a shriek like a bird of prey, and his eyes refocused to see Merobaudes pulling a girl behind him, protecting her, hand on his pommel, ready to draw. When Magnus realised it was Elen, the shock was as though Merobaudes had stabbed him in the chest and he almost dropped his sword.

"Stop it! Stop it!" she cried, from under the protection of Merobaudes' arm. "Put your swords down! Both of you! I command it!"

As Merobaudes' sword clattered noisily to the ground, Magnus wondered if he could take both of their heads off and relieve himself of two problems at once.

"Do you want to rule like Constantine?" she wailed. "Or like Nero? You have that choice. Merobaudes has been baptised. His sins have been forgiven. What do you think Constantine would do now? What do you think any good Christian would do?"

Magnus was gripping his sword so tightly that his hand was beginning to ache.

"The Lord has seen fit to forgive Merobaudes of his sins," she continued. "If you don't, doesn't that mean that you stand opposed to God?" As she often did, she had words to best him better than any swordsman could.

His sword was too nice to let simply fall to the floor though and so he stabbed it down between the joints of a couple of flagstones and left it gently swaying before him.

She was admonishing him as though he was a recalcitrant little boy. And he thought about killing Merobaudes just so he wouldn't have to endure the shame of being spoken to by his wife in such a way.

Elen bent down to pick Merobaudes' sword up and tried to pull Magnus' out from between the tiles. He hadn't wedged it in too hard, but it still took her a few tries to get it free. She wasn't too small to carry them properly, but she dragged them behind her and the metallic scraping noise seemed to fill his head.

Once she judged that they were far enough out of reach, she put them down and came back to Magnus. "What good is an empire run from hatred and founded on the need for revenge?" she asked. "Isn't the role of a good Christian emperor to make sure that God's will is carried out on earth as it is in heaven? We serve the empire," she said forcibly. "And we serve God. What you are doing here serves neither! Speak words of peace together!" she said.

Merobaudes picked up the discarded toga, shook it out and dusted it off. There was no point putting it on, as neither of them could wrap, fold and bunch it as well as the palace servants.

Magnus watched Elen go, too dumbfounded to do anything but stare as she left. He supposed the expression on his face was just as shocked as the guards she strode past.

"I serve the empire, I serve God, and as long as you serve both, I serve you," Merobaudes said, which was a very bold statement for a man who had just come so close to death.

"And if I don't?" Magnus asked guardedly.

"I serve the empire. And I think now, I also serve your wife," he added,

"We both do," Magnus growled.

XIV

Kenon's journey was a lot more forced than it could have been, and for that, the only man he blamed was Magnus. If it wasn't such an urgent task for him to get to Theodosius in Constantinople, he could have spent his days reclining on cushions in a carriage rattling sedentarily through the countryside, rather than having to ride a horse over sixty miles a day.

Mostly though, he thought about the girl who'd been promised as his wife. Half a night of talking, of hearing her sweet voice, of speaking with a girl who wasn't disgusted with him, or was taking plenty of coin for the privilege had felt like a glimpse of heaven. The touch of her fingers on his had felt to him like a full baptism, and had instantly made him a better person. And the only price to have all that the bishop offered was to betray Magnus.

It was no price at all.

When he wasn't thinking about Ursula's green eyes, how the moisture on her lips had caught the candlelight, he looked at the view from the back of his horse, he found himself constantly excited at the new sights that arrayed themselves over the crest of every rise. Like most educated men, he'd often wondered what other parts of the empire looked like, and stories from travellers had never been quite enough to satisfy his curiosity.

What he enjoyed most though, was how the other road users, forced off to the sides as his entourage rode past, looked up at him. Awe, deference, fear! It had been so long since anyone had treated him as a superior he'd almost forgotten what it was like. Up to a few weeks ago he'd thought he'd never manage to summon the courage to leave the safety of the farm he'd been left on, but fortune could change quickly. Although at least several times a day it struck him as unbelievable, he really was a dignitary on official business between emperors. It was a role he'd never even dreamed of, plus what the bishop had promised him afterwards. And then he was thinking of Ursula again.

Every muscle sore from such a long ride, they trotted into Massalia, the horizon full of the glistening sea. Massaged in the bathhouse, a night in the plushest room of a nice inn, and at dawn the next day, with guards flanking him, he walked to the docks. Waiting for him at the busy harbour was the finest ship he'd ever seen. They weren't just getting a berth on a dirty room of a cargo ship; it was a liburna. Twenty-five oars to a side, the fastest ship in the Imperial Fleet. It was just for him.

His place was on a large chair just ahead of the tiller with a cover over it to protect him from the harsh southern sun. He watched breathlessly as in unison the rowers lowered the oars and with a similarly amazingly coordinated movement, slowly manoeuvred the ship out into open water. He was almost delirious with the soaring sense of self-importance as the prow turned to head in the direction of Constantinople, but it lasted all of the few moments it took to get to the open sea behind the harbour wall. Suddenly, the lurching of the ship brought back all the memories of being Padarn's captive and the terrible sea crossing in the barbarian's flimsy boats.

Panic gripped him and he couldn't breathe it felt as though he was flailing about underwater.

With tears springing to his eyes and bile rising in his throat, he slowly drew out his dagger from under his clothes and tried to get it angled towards the skin on the outside of his leg without anyone noticing. The overwhelming sensation though was the need to bring his breakfast back up. He didn't want to sully such a beautiful ship, so staggered to the stern rail–but dropped his precious dagger. It hit the surface with a pathetic splosh. He saw it under the clear water for a moment and thought it was floating, so, although he couldn't swim, was terrified of deep water, he almost jumped over after it. A big hand grabbing his tunic hauled him back onto the deck. He flinched away from the backhanded slap he was sure he was coming, but although the man was huge, the skin of his face weathered by years of salt spray like an old tree, he helped Kenon back to his seat and handed him a canteen of water. "You'll get used to it in a day or so," he said unexpectedly kindly. "A trick is to keep your eye on the land and try to breathe in and out with the movement of the boat."

"Thank you," Kenon said, but the loss of his dagger, the one that had been at the hip of his grandfather, hurt him deeply. It was the only possession he'd had left that connected him to his family. With it resting on the seabed, he had absolutely nothing to tie him to his past. He felt as adrift in the world as the ship was on the sea.

But he was going to Constantinople, an emperor's emissary, and with all the bishop's promises still all bouncing around in his head, he was sure that he didn't want to mess up such an opportunity.

With the two sails unfurled, one large one on the midship mast and a smaller one over the prow to catch the slight morning breeze, they cut through the water so quickly that he was sure they'd get to Theodosius in just a day or two.

Some hundred miles they did on that first day, according to the captain. Kenon had no idea how to judge a nautical mile but although it seemed unbelievable, he had no reason to disbelieve him. Setting foot on solid ground again was a relief–until it seemed as though it was still moving and he dry heaved. Unconcerned with the mocking laughter of the dock workers who'd seen him, he followed his little entourage to an inn, wrapping his sense of self-importance around him like a cloak.

The next day was much better. Once his stomach had settled, as the men rowed, the gentle rhythmic thrust of each stroke sent a thrill through him. It would have been an incredible enough feeling if the fifty men all working at their hardest at the heavy oars, sweating, straining, just for him had been slaves, but they were all being paid to row him from one end of the empire to the other. That was an exhilarating thought, even if every stroke took him further from Ursula.

But while he enjoyed his new exalted position, his was just one little ship, one almost anonymous in the crowded harbour they'd just left. From his throne in the basilica of Treverorum, Magnus had the same control over half of the empire as Kenon did his little ship. He tried his best to imagine it, but soon came to the conclusion that it was an inconceivable amount of power which, after betraying him so deeply, he did not deserve it.

The sails were full all day so the oars were raised like an upended insect. The sensation of speeding over the water only by the power of the wind was so profound that he wondered if the bishop felt something similar when he was doing God's work. He even began to feel better about losing his knife. Its loss was perhaps symbolic of the need to let go of the past. Maybe he could get himself a new one in Constantinople, one that would be symbolic of the future of his new connection to Emperor Theodosius.

As Kenon's station was so far above the rowers', they stayed at their benches below deck until after he'd disembarked. They were the oxen and he was the precious goods in the cart. He supposed they'd spend their evenings in a bathhouse, having their tired muscles massaged, and probably many would still have the energy to visit a brothel, but he was betrothed. Paying a girl for pleasure would be an insult to Ursula. The thought of her being disappointed, or even disgusted with him, was enough to keep him in bed alone.

On the third day the rough, but respectful, captain informed him that they were now off the coast of Italy, and looking at the changing land to their east, thinking about all the battles, intrigues and tragedies that must have taken place there, was another constant thrill. And one, as an imperial emissary, that he was now a part of.

The closer they got to Rome, the busier the waters became, and when they got to Ostia, Kenon looked out from his cushioned chair with awe. The port of Rome was heaving with ships of a dizzying array of shapes and sizes, many at anchor waiting for a wharf to become free, others weaving their way through them. Kenon was sure that some must have come from as far away as Egypt, full of grain. As soon as he set foot on land, he felt a thrill almost as though he was about to faint. Knowing he was so close to the Senate, the Palatine Hill, the Colosseum, the Pantheon, he felt a burning need to go and see them, to touch them, to make sure they were real and that he wasn't just dreaming everything about his journey, but with time being of the essence, there was no time for seeing the sights, and so he stayed in an inn just a few stinking streets back from the warehouses. It wasn't too awful. From the window, he looked out at the strange-looking trees in the grounds. With darker leaves, they were taller and thinner than anything he'd seen before; the sun too. It somehow felt different on his face than in Britannia.

He wondered if Ursula was thinking of him as much as he was of her.

The captain obviously knew the route well. Kenon supposed there would be a constant flow of messengers and emissaries travelling between the imperial courts from one side of the empire to the other.

Some days, when the wind was with them, they docked in the late afternoon, a hundred miles done. Others, when the going was a little harder, and the men had to row him all day, it wasn't until almost dusk that they pulled into the harbour of another port.

They sailed the straits between Italy and Sicilia, Kenon not knowing which side to look, and waited a few days somewhere in the south of Greece for a storm to pass. A liburna sped through calm waters like nothing else on the sea, but couldn't take choppy waters. Kenon walked around without an escort, feeling the age of the houses of the town, imagining that ancient philosophers and mathematicians had trod the same streets, and the sense of wonder never left him, especially as no one knew him. He could pretend to be anyone he wanted.

The days wore on into weeks and it seemed that he awoke more into his new life, his new position in the world. Every morning he was one day further from the haunting horrors of his past and one day closer to Ursula, through the many islands, up a narrow, but very busy, channel and a day later, the imperial city of Constantinople was finally before them, its grand buildings clustered on the hill like a city more out of a dream than one of stone and mortar.

The baths were the grandest he'd ever seen. No one here knew anything about his past, and so he could just about endure the touch of the slave oiling him and scraping the strigil over his skin. It was almost pleasant. No one dared remark about the scars on the side of his legs.

Adorned with the finest toga he'd ever worn, the strands of the most delicate sandals wound around his ankles, the imperial guard led him through the airy corridors of the grand palace where Theodosius was waiting for him.

Built by the most skilled architects in the empire and evidently without any restraint on cost, it really was like walking in a dream.

And then he was before the emperor. Magnus was undeniably a powerful man, more powerful than anyone else in the whole empire, bar one; but he was just an old soldier who'd exchanged his armour for a purple toga, with countless dirty deals made with different men to get him to where he was. Theodosius was truly majestic. A true emperor. The power seemed to radiate from him like the heat of flames from a fire.

"Kenon, my dear relative," he said and it was a thrill to hear his name on the tongue of such a man. "You are my cousin's wife's brother. Tell me, what does that make us?"

Kenon had no idea, but that the first thing the emperor had said was about their familial connection, his tongue tied itself into a knot. His warm words were another thing that set the cousins apart. Magnus snapped orders to his inferiors, but Theodosius was actually talking to him.

"Erm, related, absolutely, your Excellency," an old man said from the side.

Kenon hoped that his advisor usually had some more useful advice to give.

"Well, family, nonetheless," Theodosius smiled and reached out to lay a hand on Kenon's shoulder. It was a nervous, uncomfortable gesture, and Kenon was shocked that he saw in the emperor the same reticence for human contact that he had.

As he invited Kenon to the couches, he noticed how lightly Theodosius walked on the balls of his feet, more like a dancer than a soldier–or an assassin moving silently towards his victim. He reclined on a couch. It was the softest he'd ever felt, and was covered in the smoothest silk he'd ever touched.

"I know much about you, probably much more than you would be comfortable with me knowing," Theodosius said.

That was far from what Kenon wanted to hear, and that a man so exalted as Theodosius knew what Padarn had done to him, that he'd killed the little girl. It made his skin crawl with shame. He recalled how completely wrong he'd been about the bishop in Treverorum, so forced himself to at least appear relaxed.

"How can I know?" he smiled. "For men like me, spies are a form of currency, one often more valuable than gold. It is vital for us to know the movements and motivations of our rivals. And just as importantly, our partners. But don't worry. I don't judge. In fact, you have my admiration for managing to overcome such an experience. Not many Romans survive capture by barbarians. Only the strongest, bravest and cleverest, I would assume."

Kenon's head seemed to swirl with confusion. No one had ever called him brave or clever before. Not even those he'd paid to be nice to him.

"But not only survive. Look at you now," the emperor continued, "an imperial emissary. Although, now that you have arrived, I must tell you that an emissary, you are not!"

"I'm not?" Kenon asked, his mouth gone dry. All the dreams he'd had over the last few weeks suddenly started to drain away. "What do you mean?"

"He may be my cousin, but Magnus is no emperor. I consider him, as you have every right to as well, my enemy. An enemy of the empire! I brought you all the way across our sea because I want you to be my agent."

The horrible feeling of being used as nothing more than a counter on a ludus board was too strong to ignore. Just as Magnus had done with him, as the bishop evidently had, Theodosius was doing the same.

"Don't worry, the offer Ambrosius made still stands. All of it. Ursula and absolution. When the time comes, and the opportunity presents itself, which I fervently believe it will, all I wish for is that you deliver him to me."

Kenon swallowed. "How can I do that?"

"I think Magnus underestimates you; in several ways. All you need to do is to keep his trust and at the right time and place, feed him some false information."

In front of someone was such power, the answer was of course, 'Yes, Augustus!', but

"I tell you this, at some risk to myself, because it is important for you to trust me," Theodosius continued. "The empire is fractured. It lies cut into three separate pieces, ruled by men whose aims and ambitions are fatally misaligned. I have come to believe, that for it to survive into a future that can be anything more than just a shadow of its golden past, it must be reunited. So, to preserve the divine light of Christ in the world, it has fallen to me to heal it again: to make it whole. Strength, you see, is found in unity, not division, and I want you, Kenon, to be a part of this. A very important part."

There was no possible way to say no, but his reluctance to answer was because he feared the emperor had terribly overestimated him. Didn't know how weak, how broken, he really was. "How?" he asked. It came out as a rasping whisper.

There was a flash of disdain on Theodosius' face, but whereas Magnus or Padarn would have raged at what they would have misunderstood as an insult, Theodosius just smiled and nodded. "With the Sassanids to my east and the infernal Goths crawling all over the empire like fleas on a dog, my resources are stretched. But I believe both of these issues will be resolved to my benefit soon; a year, two at most. Then, I need Magnus to attack Italy."

It seemed that every time Theodosius opened his mouth he said something that made Kenon's panic grow to a new height. A year or two? He wanted everything the bishop had offered as soon as he got back to Gaul–but they wanted him to wait years!

"Upon your return to Magnus, you will tell him that your journey has inspired you to want to become a scout. This way, with the freedom to range far and wide, you will be safe to communicate with my men, free from any suspicion. You will be my treasured agent. One of many, of course, but the one Magnus would least suspect. You will help direct Magnus to his ruin. I need him to flush Valentinian and his mother out of Italy, into my protection. That will take care of one issue. Then he must move to confront me. At this time, with you free to move between his army and mine, you will find the perfect opportunity to betray him. Your revenge will also be for the glory of the empire. Before me, every man of the empire, and before God, you will be a hero, and you will be richly rewarded."

All Kenon could think of was that when they'd pulled out of the harbour of Massilia, he'd fallen into the sea after his dagger and everything else had been a very pleasant, but very unrealistic, dream.

PART II

XV

BRITANNIA SECUNDA SUMMER 384

Among the sprigs of heather, and other hardy little flowers he had no names for, Magnus sat with his back to the rocks of the cliff, trying his best to keep out of the incessant wind.

His cloak was of the purest and deepest purple, a colour that signified that its wearer was near divine, yet all he wanted from it was that it kept him warm. He pulled it tighter around him and clamped his legs together in a vain attempt to stop Britannia's bitter wind tormenting his nether regions with its frigid breath.

A man could have almost all of the power in the world, but a few greedy barbarians challenging their leader in a tribe that inhabited some waste in the unconquered lands, and it could all fall away. If the emperor couldn't keep the province that had proclaimed him safe, then what would he care about the rest of the empire? He had installed Padarn and his Votadini as a foederati tribe, but now with him worryingly ill, he needed to sort out his successor.

He'd let Elen think that she'd talked him into coming back, but he knew he needed to be here himself. Marcellinus was capable of looking after things in Treverorum, especially as he could end up being emperor himself one day. It would be good practice for him to run an empire for a while. The only thing was that he had no idea what to do about Padarn.

The only sounds that disturbed him were of the men building the watchtower on the top of the rocky hill behind him and the cries of the gulls. And the peculiar local birds that flapped ungainly and splashed into the sea like falling stones. His wife's land was a strange place.

He looked down at the waters around the headland of Mona shimmering in the light of the late afternoon sun. Where the sea was blanched silver by the low sun, he could make out the swirling currents, and the white crests of little waves where they met. When opposing forces came together there was always turbulence. It was some fundamental law of the world. And one day soon, once he could get his army over the high mountains that protected Italy and there would be a lot more turbulence. He would make big waves across the empire.

But when they settled, then he would set about restoring its glory.

A few black specks were dotted near the horizon. A flotilla of little hide-covered boats sailing down from north of the Wall. The sight of them caused his heart to flutter. A few years ago they'd carried vicious raiders, savage barbarians who'd plundered the lands around the fortress of Deva. They returned now, but for a different reason.

A slight nod and Andragathius let Edern, the man who used to call himself the Areani, approach. He stood up to warmly greet the man, who, perhaps more than any other, had helped him to the exalted position he now occupied. "Your father approaches these lands once again," Magnus smiled. "Should I be afraid?"

"Padarn was the fiercest man I have ever known, but you tamed that beast. I am sure that he returns today as a valued ally. He has protected against those from the north for years now. The only problem is that he makes the men on the Wall grow bored standing guard against nothing but the wind and sheep."

"He has done well," Magnus said. "But if the news was to be believed, that might not be true for too much longer. "How does he fare?"

"With your old cloak around his shoulders, it is said that he thrived," Edern smiled. "They even call him Padarn Beisrudd, which in the imperial tongue means Padarn of the Scarlet Cloak."

Not for the first time, Magnus thought it remarkable what the gift of life, gold and the inclusion into the empire could do to a man. "And yet you speak of the past?"

The smile left Edern's face.

"If the reports are to be believed, it seems that the years have caught up with him and that, of late, he fares none too well."

"I have heard this. I also heard troubling news of his other son."

"A very unfortunate thing," Edern shrugged. "Newborns and harsh winters north of the Wall are often a tragic combination."

"Do you know the truth of what happened?"

"I don't. Only rumours. Some are as wild as you would expect."

"Such as?"

"That it was your wife who ordered it."

Magnus scoffed, but saw that Edern wasn't joking. She certainly had the means to do it, but the motivation? He couldn't believe she'd risk the integrity of the Wall just to get Magnus to go back to Britannia. "It means that you should be heir of the Votadini tribe now."

"A very fortunate thing," Edern nodded.

Magnus didn't want to know if the Areani had had a hand in the death of an infant. Such a thing wasn't unheard of in the heart of the Empire though, never mind in the half-wild tribe of its foederati beyond the borders. "Apart from the fact that he made a blood oath in front of a whole legion to kill me. That might preclude me from taking over from him."

Suspicion of foul play had also fallen on a couple of Padarn's nephews, who were now fighting among themselves. The bickering of barbarians could easily end up with a significant number of powerful men dead. If that was to happen to the Votadini, Magnus might as well order the gates of the Wall open and let the other tribes flood south. He'd taken too many men to Gaul to be able to defend against a full invasion of Picts.

"And you want me to somehow arrange it so that Padarn rescinds his blood oath and claims you as his successor?" Magnus asked.

"The clean handover of power is beneficial to every party," Edern shrugged.

"Padarn doesn't strike me as a man to easily change his mind, especially about a blood-oath."

Edern shrugged. "Do you have any idea how to persuade him?"

"I don't."

Having Edern in place after a clean exchange of power was the only option that would work. If he was to push it though, he was sure that at the very least Padarn would take offence. He'd been brooding about it for months, but had come up with nothing. And the council was set to meet the following evening.

"I hear that your son is doing well, though. Remind me, what did you call him?"

"Cunedda," Edern said with a proud smile.

For some reason, a chill ran down Magnus' spine, a coldness that had nothing to do with the wind. Victor, Sevira and now Cunedda. All just children, babies. But one day it would be their names that would be spoken across the empire with reverence.

"Conceived on the night you reunited me with my wife. He turned three not so long ago. And he is strong."

"The same as Victor."

"My greatest hope is that one day my son will serve your son well," Edern smiled.

"Cunedda will be a great man," Magnus said. "His name will be remembered for many long years." It was a simple platitude, one spoken to many new fathers, but he didn't doubt that it was a truth he spoke.

"You feel it as well?" Edern asked. "That destiny flows through you and me?"

"You sound like my wife," Magnus sighed, feeling the need to pull his cloak even tighter.

"Elen is held in great esteem in these lands," Edern said with a serious look. "Some in Britannia would even look to her over the emperor himself."

"Is that right?" Magnus thought of Elen's grandmother and had to suppress the involuntary shudder at the power the old woman had wielded.

"Augustus," Edern said, suddenly more formal. "It pains me to ask, but I have a request to ask of you."

Magnus sighed. "Most of the men in the empire have the very same wish. Sometimes it seems as though my existence is to be asked, entreated and petitioned. What is it?"

"Would you grant me permission to join the council?"

"Why do I have the feeling that my wife suggested that you ask me that?"

Edern had a disarming smile. "In truth, she did. But I have no idea why. You might also be interested to know that she also asked me to bring my boy."

"Your boy? Your child? To a meeting of the council? Now I know my wife asked you. No sane man would come to ask me a thing like that."

"And one more thing," Edern said, looking at the impatient bishop next to Andragathius. "If I may speak freely?"

Magnus nodded, albeit with a little reluctance. He'd been emperor long enough to know that when someone asked for such permission, he was about to hear words he rather wouldn't.

"You would do well to have Elen featured prominently in the discussions. Her honour and importance is the honour and importance of Britannia. My father would understand that."

"My wife to host the meeting between the most important men of the land?"

"Elen of the Hosts?" Edern mused. "It has a nice ring to it. Do you feel the chill again? She did not ask me to put this to you, but perhaps she would have a better chance of changing my father's mind than either you or I."

Magnus was sure it wasn't the flow of destiny he felt, just the usual sense of discomfort whenever he was reminded that Elen was a lot more powerful than he liked to believe. But Padarn was a barbarian who'd dared to sail right in front of the fortress of Deva and had raided Magnus' lands. The thought that Elen could deal with a man like that was laughable.

The wind carried the bishop's unamused cough to them. Knowing his time was up, Edern hit his chest with his clenched fist then held his arm out, palm facing the floor.

"I will consider it," Magnus said, non-committally.

As Edern left, the bishop of Eboracum approached, treading uneasily on the narrow, rocky path. He was probably used to walking on well-polished flagstones where no loose stones threatened to twist an ankle.

Magnus stood up again. No affectionate greeting this time though, but the bishop held a secret that he could not afford to have spoken aloud, lest everything he had was to crumble around him like the walls of Jericho. 'I have come here through Londinium," he said with a strained smile. "The cathedral is coming on well. It will be a grand edifice, and will stand for hundreds of years as a glory to us both." In truth, he had been very disappointed at the slow progress of the construction and was sure that a lot of the gold he'd given for it had found its way to other places other than material and labour. This wasn't the place to make accusations of misappropriations, though.

"Which bishop had the privilege of anointing you with the sacred waters and absolving you?" he asked in a friendly tone, but Magnus understood that it was a searching question. "Britto, I would presume. Although I have heard no news of this."

"The privilege is still to be yours," Magnus said but watched the bishop's countenance quickly turn into a look of thunder. "Then the cathedral, and your rule, are built on blasphemy!" he hissed. He spoke quietly, as though he was afraid that the wind had ears. "Its foundations are built on falsehoods, its mortar binds the stones with deceit, its windows open to expose the lies. It is funded by a man who remains unbaptised. It will be consecrated with sacrilege!"

Magnus had worn the purple for almost a year and in that time he'd become well accustomed to being spoken to in a certain way, and to have powerful men literally prostrate themselves as his feet. He was in no mood to revert back to the times he had superiors to appease. He wrapped the cloak around him, perhaps just to keep the wind off him, perhaps just to display the colour to a man who might need to be reminded of Magnus' station. The bishop might be an intermediary between God and men, but he'd never before stood before an emperor.

"Your diocese is far from the imperial capital," Magnus said, staying calm, but making sure his displeasure was conveyed in his tone. "It was not in your lifetime that an emperor last set foot in Britannia. Perhaps you are unaware of the decorum expected. So I caution you that an unbaptised emperor is not a disrespected emperor."

"But..." the bishop said through gritted teeth. "You lied!"

"Did I not explain that I only wanted my baptism postponed?"

"I..." the bishop stammered, perhaps a little flummoxed at how unconcerned Magnus was.

"Is our church in Londinium going to be bigger than anything Ambrosius has built in Mediolanum?" he asked in a much lighter tone. "Do your peers in the clergy do you honour that you are the one overseeing its construction? That the gold for it flows through your hands."

The bishop didn't answer.

"Perhaps you could help me to simplify your sentiment?" Magnus said. "Are you trying to tell me that you no longer wish to be the next bishop of Londinium?"

He had to stifle a laugh at how the bishop struggled to find his next words.

"I didn't kill the man I postponed my baptism for," Magnus offered. "In fact, he enjoys a high standing in my administration. Does that afford me any clemency?"

The bishop's mouth flapped like a fish out of water, but he uttered nothing coherent.

"When we last spoke together, back in Eboracum, I was just Dux Britanniarum, but I am no ordinary soldier with a high rank now. I have returned to Britannia as emperor! And what bishop do you know of, have ever heard of, who has baptised an emperor?"

The bishop's eyes widened a little and his mouth flapped a little faster.

"Would you appreciate such an honour? Of course, if you think that I am too much of a sinner, a man beyond any hope of redemption, I can ask another."

"Well- no- I mean..."

"Could you recommend someone for me? Or shall I make inquiries myself?"

"A man cannot be baptised twice. One soul, one absolution."

"Of course," Magnus said with what was a real attempt at an innocent smile. "What we will do, we will call a symbolic ritual. Only you and I will know that it is in fact real."

"And God," he added solemnly.

"Of course."

"You've thought of everything, haven't you?" the bishop said with a hint of disgust.

Magnus smiled again, less innocently this time. "Which is what I must do, as emperor. And it will be two emperors you will get to baptise. I intend to announce Victor as co-Augustus, so you'll take us both to the river. And unlike last time we met, this time everyone needs to see."

Magnus stood up, and brushing the dust off his cloak, made sure to wave it around in the bishop's face so he could see the purple. "In Segontium, once all the deals are made. I will have the rest of the gold for the construction of our cathedral, and I will leave Britannia in peace, and will be able to sleep soundly. And God will be pleased with both of us."

* * *

Apart from the bits of plaster and mortar still stuck to it, the stone Elen placed on top of the sizable cairn was just like any other.

The pile marked the spot on the little island in the straits of Mona where she'd last seen Grandmother. Over the years those wanting to show their respect, to speak her name, had come here to set their own stone down. Now the pile was up to about the level of Elen's hip.

"From the palace in Treverorum," she said. "I cut it out of the wall myself."

"She would have laughed for a long time at that," Gula said.

Elen missed Grandmother's smile almost as much as she did Eugenius' touch and had often imagined she could hear her infectious chuckle echoing down the wide corridors of Magnus' palace.

It was also such a relief to speak the native tongue. The ancient words rolled off her tongue in a way that Latin could never do. It felt so nice that she wanted to sing, even if what they had to talk about was the fate of the land.

It seemed to Elen that the long months in Gaul spent as empress had put years on her. But four years without Father had done wonders for her mother. The lines of worry on her face had almost all gone and it even seemed that she had fewer grey hairs.

Sevira had found some clump of moss and squeezed it in her tiny hand with fascination, enthralled with the strange sensation. Nothing like that grew in the grounds of the palace. She'd seen Elen place the stone, and mimicking the action, set her precious moss at the foot of the cairn.

She was far too young to start learning about her heritage, but one day Elen would explain that the stories she told at bedtime were of their ancestors, and one day soon she would start teaching her the long list of her ancestors.

Magnus might not be too happy about it, but like it or not, he was the father of a girl whose lineage went all the way back to the time of Cadwal and Gwain, the last heroes of the Ordovices. At the thought of them, she felt the usual feelings of her inadequacy flare up. They were the calibre of men that Britannia Secunda needed more than ever. Instead, it had Elen.

Maglorius, her mother's guard, looked at Sevira with longing. He'd been her grandmother's protector, and now was mother's. Her Eugenius. Looking at Sevira, the fourth generation of the family he'd known, he must have seen his own mortality in her, as he didn't have enough years left to be her guard.

Elen looked at Eugenius. The man of her life stood with the other three of her guards by the boats. She wondered if he knew how close he was to the spot they'd got married, but stopped that thought from going any further. If she was to allow herself to think of those heady days before Magnus had come to Britannia, or the ones when they'd chased Gratian, she wouldn't be able to help herself running down to the beach and throwing herself into his arms. It had already been the most part of a year since the last time, and in every quiet moment she would still feel herself wrapped up in his embrace. But one day they could be together again. She had to believe that.

"There is unrest here," her mother said.

The words made her slam back into her role as empress. "Unrest? What do you mean?" she asked with an unwelcome sense of responsibility that stifled her like a heavy cloak.

Gula indicated that Maglorius should explain.

"The crux of it is that these soldiers have been at Segontium for so long that they think they run the whole place. Taking over local businesses, and such like, causes conflict with those in the vicus, as every man takes offence at being treated as lesser class."

"That's not really something that..." Elen started, but didn't really want to say that she was empress in Gaul and matters in this little corner of Britannia Secunda were for her mother to sort out.

Gula knew what Elen was thinking though. "I am not my mother. I was never who she wanted me to be. And now, with her gone, and you gone, I am not strong enough to do anything about it. So..."

Elen understood what her mother's look meant. "You want me to control a garrison of five hundred soldiers? What can I possibly do?"

"Your husband could do something about it," Maglorius added. "What with him being the emperor, an' all."

Elen shook her head. "My influence with my husband is probably a lot less than you imagine it to be. It certainly doesn't extend to directing military matters."

"Ha!" Gula scoffed. "What would your grandmother say to you if she could hear you now? She'd be telling you that you are much stronger than you think, that you can do anything you want. Whether your husband is the emperor or not."

Elen looked at the pile of stones. Perhaps Gula was right. And she remembered how an emperor had died in her arms.

"Especially if he is the emperor," Maglorius added, and it was so strange for him to assume that he was a part of the conversation between mother and daughter that Elen knew instinctively that the two of them were much closer than just a high-status woman with her guard. She wondered how long they'd been together. Since when father was alive? She hoped so. Her Eugenius, indeed.

Gula might not have been all Grandmother had hoped, but she could read Elen like an unwound scroll, and she reached out to slip her hand into Maglorius'. He looked terribly nervous, until Elen nodded and smiled.

"Thank you," he said, but Elen couldn't think that her mother needed her permission for them to be together.

"But that is not all of our troubles," Gula said. "A little further away from here, but no less important. Padarn's baby died."

Elen burned with the guilt and shame of condemning the baby to death. Ever since she'd received the note confirming it, she'd held some little hope that it hadn't been her hand, that he'd died of some natural cause.

"Unfortunately, there is suspicion among some powerful men in the tribe that it wasn't a natural death." The way Gula looked at her, as though her eyes were the red hot pokers of a torturer urging her to spill her truths, she knew. Yet she wasn't offering judgement or condemnation. "And, as well as that, Padarn is a very ill man."

Padarn couldn't die yet. Not without someone strong and loyal to Magnus in charge. "How long does he have?" she asked nervously.

"All reports say not long," Gula said.

Another hot flush, but this time it was one of anger at Magnus for refusing to bring back the thousands of fighting men he'd taken to Gaul the year before. Grandmother wouldn't have allowed that. She was just as disappointed with herself that she hadn't managed to convince him to keep his word as at him for breaking it. "And what do you want Magnus to do about it?" she asked

"Magnus?" Gula scoffed. "Not everything can be solved by a sword or a shouted command."

"Me?" Elen gasped. "What do you think I can do?"

Gula shrugged. "I have sent entreaties to Padarn, and as well, Coelius of the Sixth has been sending men up to try and get some agreement made, but Padarn is even more stubborn than your father was. The problem is that he doesn't know who to trust, and he seems content to let those he thinks might have killed his boy to fight among themselves, to whatever outcome that may be. And he hates Edern with a real ferocity. Betrayal means a lot to men like him. Up there, they live and die by honour."

Elen caught Maglorius' eye and nodded to let him speak. "You need to talk to Padarn," he said. "You need to convince him to hand his leadership down to Edern before he dies and everyone else starts fighting."

Elen laughed. "I was there the day he made his blood-oath. But when he arrives for the council, you think Magnus would let me open my mouth in front of such men?"

"Well," he said with a big grin that reminded her of Grandmother. "I have an idea of how we could convince him."

* * *

Magnus strode through the soldiers lined up in the street in the middle of the fort of Segontium. All stood stiffly to attention. He hoped that he was at least projecting a look of confidence, as he certainly didn't feel it.

He'd been sitting quietly in the praetorium, waiting for some inspirational thought to pop into his head for what he could do about Padarn, but nothing had come.

A row of swords were stood up at the side of the principia door. Magnus would keep his.

The tradition for an emperor to receive his guests was for him to be waiting for them sitting serenely on his throne, looking close to a deity. They were to walk up to him as though he was the Statue of Zeus at Olympia, and bow in supplication. Magnus was late for the council though and the principia in the small fort was no grandiose reception room, and so instead of shooing everyone out just so he could be there when they went back in again, he entered as the only one standing.

The eight men who were about to decide the future of Britannia were seated on big chairs on either side made especially for this occasion. Seeing him come in, Andragathius, Coelius and Aed Broc jumped to attention. Edern, paying attention to his son as though he was on a family outing rather than in a meeting to secure the future of the province, saw the others rise and scrambled to his feet. A couple of heartbeats later, the two bishops, of Londinium and Eboracum rose, a little laboured. Hopefully because of their cumbersome and restrictive attire rather than any reluctance to show him subservience.

Not Padarn, though. The hard-faced man with him had begun to rise, but seeing his ruler remain seated, he was caught in an awkward hunch-backed pose where he managed to disrespect both Padarn and Magnus.

Magnus was almost ready to shout out a curse at the stupid barbarian for making no effort to show respect, but caught his gaze. It was hard not to stare at those piercing ice-blue eyes, but even with the huge bearskin over the old barbarian's shoulders, he looked shockingly thin. It didn't look as though he could get up even if he wanted to. He waved at the old man to remain in his seat and got a respectful nod in return. Under the bearskin, Magnus could see a little red of the cloak he'd given him a few years ago.

Magnus' chair, bigger than the others, was set at the far end. Elen stood next to hers, straight-backed, her hands clenched before her. Large drapes of cloth hung behind it to block off the door to the tribune's office and the strong room where the detachment's wages were kept. He was used to much more luxurious things, but for a small fort of a few hundred men in the arse end of the empire, they'd at least done half a job.

He could have simply sat down, but all had known him only as the Dux Britanniarum. Now he wanted them to know him as Imperator Caesar Dominus Magnus Maximus Pius Felix Augustus. He had the idea that flashing the cloak he was so proud of in front of them would be the best way to do it, so while turning around, he tugged it out to the side to make it billow out. As soon as he started, though, he realised how ridiculous he looked. With a hot flush of shame, he'd managed to remind himself of Gratian. How the young emperor had preened himself in front of him when they met in Treverorum, the day he was made Dux Britanniarum, had made him feel more pity than respect. The thought that he'd just done the same with the most important men in Britannia made him want to disappear behind the drapes rather than sit in front of them.

He was expecting the look of sheer disdain that Elen cast him, but it still stung.

He looked around. Just like counters on a ludus board, he knew how to arrange the men in front of him so that everyone, most importantly himself, was happy. It would be easy to get rid of the bishop of Londinium. An offer of some position in the imperial court in Treverorum would allow him to promote the other one from Eboracum to his place. They'd both be more than happy with the arrangement. With Aed Broc's people settled and safe from the enemies that had hounded him in his former land of Hibernia, he had pretty much all he wanted already. He was about to be asked to give many men to Magnus' army, which he surely wouldn't be too happy about, but that couldn't be helped. Young men needed to feed the army.

Coelius was about to be the recipient of a significant amount of gold so that the walls of Eboracum could be shored up and Andragathius, was about to be sent to the Wall to set up a heavy cavalry detachment at Vindolanda, which would bolster the stripped-down forces up there.

The only real problem was Padarn. His Votadini tribe staying strong north of the Wall was critical to the future safety of Britannia. Meddling in the power structures of tribal matters needed a very delicate touch, though, and Magnus knew that simply offering the old man more gold wouldn't make him forget the blood-oath he'd made to kill the son who sat opposite him. Although he'd seriously considered it, simply stabbing him where he sat and announcing that Edern was now the leader would cause a lot more trouble than it would solve. He looked again at what was left of the once vital and fierce old man. He would have to come up with some solution fast, but still didn't have any idea where to start.

Elen leaned over, probably about to give some more of her senseless words that she believed were ones of advice. As though a woman could tell an emperor what to do. "There is a man behind you with a sword a finger's width from your spine."

The words were so unexpected and so shocking that it took him a moment to register them, but before he was about to shout for the guards, he felt a sharp prick in his back and it was as though all the blood had suddenly left his legs.

"Do not move," she hissed. "Not a muscle. If you open your mouth to disturb me. The man behind you is under my command."

Magnus couldn't help reaching behind him, but as soon as he felt something cold and sharp, he snapped his hand away. There was blood on his finger. "What are you doing?" he seethed.

"We've done things all your way in Gaul for a year and I was always silent. But we are in my land now."

"What are you...?" he started as she stood up, but with a finger pointed at him as though she was training a puppy, she warned him to stay where he was, and the sword pressed a tiny bit harder to his back. He was stuck in his chair as helpless as Padarn seemed to be in his.

And then, almost as shocking as finding that he was held at sword point, Elen spoke in a foreign language. To hear his wife talk like a barbarian made him squirm in his seat more than the blade did.

There was more though. Elen dropped her shawl from her shoulders and reached up to unpin her intricately styled hair. Shaking it loose, she looked how she did the morning after one of the infrequent nights she stayed in his bed. It was an absolutely outrageous sight for an empress, but he was looking at a girl who was still tied to the old ways.

"We are here today for the future," she said to the assembled men back in the imperial tongue, her voice as confident as that of an emperor's. "The future that all of us here hold dear."

Both the bishops stared at her as though the devil himself had appeared before them. The bishop of Eboracum turned to look at him, and if looks could kill. If he thought Magnus' soul was badly stained for negotiating his way out of his baptism, finding out that he was married to the abomination before them was even worse.

He probably wasn't wrong. And Magnus was close to shouting a command to put an end to the nonsense. Whoever was behind him with the sword could sense his movement and pushed the blade a tiny bit further forwards. The pain in his back made him grasp the arms of his chair, but he didn't dare move.

"The empire is in a critical state," Elen continued. "From beyond its borders, and within. Goths, Alemani and Sassanids, you have all heard reports of armies being sent to confront. But the real threat are the Huns, as the horsemen from the east grow in strength they push the Goths over our borders. Their choice is very simple; to die at the end of Roman steel or in a hail of Hun arrows. My fear is that if, or when, this threat becomes more acute, and the imperial authorities have to commit more men and resources to this, Britannia will become isolated, perhaps even cut off from the rest of the empire. So today, I stand before you to talk about our security. The Deisi," she held her hand out to Aed Broic, "have made our coast secure from Scotti raids. And he has just welcomed a son, one born here in Britannia."

Next, she indicated Coelius, and dared to address a Roman officer as an equal, "And those of the red, you serve my husband, the emperor, with honour and diligence." Then she turned to Padarn. It was a huge effort for Magnus to stay still as the stupid bitch spoke to the man he'd risked so much to install as foederati.

"Keep still," the man behind him growled.

Slowly, Magnus turned his head. "I will have you crucified for this," he said.

"So be it. The security of my land is worth a lot more to me than my life."

Magnus caught Andragathius' eye. The Batavi looked back with a hawk-like stare. He knew something was wrong. Coelius noticed how the master of cavalry was ignoring Elen and seemed to be poised to leap out of his seat and as soon as he saw the rigid way Magnus was sitting.

There wasn't anything Magnus could do though. If he called out for his men to attack whoever was behind him, the sword would be poking out through his stomach before they'd even got to their feet. Maybe a Moor could waggle his fingers in a certain way to order a man to go around the back of the principia and sneak up on the swordsman, but all he could do was wave a finger and slowly shake his head. Elen had complete control.

"Padarn," his wife continued. "I hear that your breath is laboured. I can see that your days begin to draw to a close."

"Not him," the old man said, nodding weakly towards Edern.

"I understand," she said. "But the foundation of the land of ours cannot be allowed to be threatened by hate and distrust."

"Not him!" he said again, icy blue eyes burning. "Sons do not betray their fathers."

And wives do not betray their husbands Magnus thought, but did not speak it aloud. But while Magnus was thinking of skinning her alive as the mob had done with Hypatia, part of him was intrigued to know what the plan she was risking so much for was. What had she thought of that he hadn't?

She went over to Edern and held her arm out to take his boy's hand. Little Cunedda was timid and tried to draw away, but Edern set him down and with a smile wider than she'd ever given him, she convinced him to take her hand. He was the same age as Victor, and whereas Magnus' son had his rainbows, Magnus saw that Cunedda had a toy draco in his hand. Its head looked expertly carved. Its open mouth had rows of teeth, and it even had some streamers down its back. Unbidden, distant memories of Magnus' own childhood came back, when he used to dream of being a draconarius himself, the dragon's head screaming as the air was forced through it.

Elen led the boy a few steps over to Padarn, and where Magnus would have had a sword to threaten the stubborn old bastard with, she went to him with a small child.

"I mourn the loss of your son," she said. "As a mother, it is a tragedy I cannot even imagine suffering."

Magnus had heard the rumours that it had been at her command the child had been killed. He'd dismissed them as nonsense, but now he looked at her, wondering if it was possible that she could speak so nicely to the man whose son she'd ordered murdered.

"But this is Cunedda, your grandson," she said softly as though she was telling some story to get Victor to go to sleep.

Padarn scowled, refusing to take him–and so after everything she'd done, everything she'd risked, the stupid bitch's plan had failed. And now she would have to face Magnus' wrath.

"Your father was a priest?" she asked.

Padarn looked up at her confused.

"Tegid ap Iago was his name, wasn't it? And he would have known a child is absolutely innocent of all and any sin. Is this true?"

Reluctantly, Padarn sighed. "It is true."

Magnus listened carefully. Some pathetic men did believe that a child was born into sin, but he didn't know where she was leading with such words.

"Cunedda is your blood. And he is innocent." She held Cunedda's little hand out to Padarn again. "Innocent of the sins of the father."

This time the Votadini leader took Cunedda's little hand in his big, rough one. Magnus watched as a curious thing happened, the icy look completely melted, and the hardened warrior in him gone, Magnus saw a dying man staring into the small eyes of the future of his line. Someone who would speak his name. The giant wheel of life the uncivilised believed in, turning in front of him.

In a broken voice, he said, "Cunedda is a good name. A strong name. I claim him as of my line." He held the boy close and with an effort, leaned over to kiss his little forehead.

The man next to him uttered some protest, but as weak as Padarn looked, his backhanded punch was fast enough to catch the man unawares and hard enough to make his already crooked nose bleed.

"And Edern," she pressed gently.

"And Edern shall rule until the boy comes of age. But not one day more. So be it!"

Padarn then forced himself to his feet. As the huge bear skin dropped from his shoulders Magnus could see that whatever illness he was suffering from had ravaged his once proud body and now there was nothing left but skin and bones. The red cloak looked far too big on him. "Up!" he snapped at Edern.

The Areani shook his head.

"Up! As your father I command it!"

Magnus was glad that the Areani looked to him for permission. Despite the blade at his back rendering him a mere observer of the proceedings, he could still nod his consent.

As Edern stood, Padarn pulled out a dagger from a sheath strapped under his arm.

The guards at the principia doors would get the flogging of their lives for allowing him in with it, but Elen didn't look too concerned, it was almost as though she knew exactly what was about to happen.

Magnus watched confused as Padarn turned it around to offer the hilt to Edern. "Not for you, but for Britannia. And for Elen," he said in a croaky voice.

The Votadini man to the side protested again, but was ignored this time, rather than punched.

Edern reached out to reluctantly take the blade. Magus wondered if it was some barbarian ceremony for handing over power, but as soon as Edern had his hand on it, Padarn jerked his son's arm forwards and the dagger sank into his chest, in through a rib in his sunken cage.

Edern's cry of, "No!" echoed around the principia and the other Votadini fell to his knees to cradle his dying leader.

Elen reached forwards to put her arms defensively around Cunedda, but the boy was a bit too young to understand what the crumpled form of Padarn on the floor meant. Every pretend sword fight he'd had would have ended up with his fellow opponent getting straight back up unharmed, a smile on his face.

The crumpled form of Padarn wouldn't be rising. Magnus had been shocked at the spectacle of his last blood-oath, but this one was even more impressive. Definitely an effective way of exchanging power.

The other Votadini stood up and Magnus wondered if there was about to be a fight in the council, but all he wanted to do was to lay the bearskin over Padarn's body, like an ancient form of a funerary shroud. The blood from his nose dropped onto it. Then he knelt before Edern.

Magnus had seen enough powerful men taking the knee when they had to. He'd learned to tell who was sincere and who wasn't. This man wasn't.

Aed looked on impassively, Coelius, aware of the strange ways of those from above the Wall had gritted his teeth but judged it best not to interfere in the affairs of tribesmen. From the way he was sitting in his chair, he was ready to leap up to protect Magnus, if that was needed. Although, if it was, Magnus would be dead before he got to him.

The bishops both stared, horrified, mouthing prayers for protection as though druids were right in front of them, cutting the mistletoe with silver sickles by the light of the full moon.

Edern sank to his knees, and hunched over to hold Padarn's head in his hands. The old man might have hated Edern for siding with Rome in the Conspiracy, but it was still his father bleeding out before him. The man who'd at one time cared for him as he now did for Cunedda.

The other Votadini, cradling his bleeding nose, looked crestfallen. He'd probably been expecting to take over from Padarn and with everything taken away from him, he was a very dangerous man. Probably more for Edern and his son than for Magnus, but it would be best to get rid of him, just in case. He'd have to be quick though. Both the bishops and his wife would be dragging him out of the principia to the river after the council was concluded to baptise him in the river.

It was Elen that Magnus watched though. As she looked up to the sky, his first thought was that she had the power to see Padarn's soul rise, but he was sure that heaven was not where the old man's soul would be going. She was looking up to ask for forgiveness. When she looked back at Padarn's body she mouthed the word 'sorry'. Magnus flinched, as though the sword had pierced him after all, but it was the shock of realising that Elen had made this moment happen because it really was her who'd killed Padarn's child the previous autumn. The bitch had been meddling in a province he was the emperor of, ordering a killing that could have easily have caused disaster for the whole bloody place. She was more like him than he'd ever suspected. Apart from one notable difference: Her actions were done for the benefit of other people rather than for herself.

Grudgingly though, he had to admit that she might just have solved the problem of the Votadini, which was something he might not have been able to do. And if she'd explained her plan beforehand he'd have thought her mad and probably had her confined somewhere out of harm's way. The only way she could have done it, was the way she had done.

"And this concludes matters of the Old Ways," she said.

As Aed stood up, Magnus was worried he was about to attack his wife, but both he and Edern dropped to a knee before her, to pay her honour. She spoke the strange language of her land again, touched both of them on the tops of their heads, and then finally returned to Magnus's side. She picked her discarded shawl up and held it out to him. He took it and, nervous that the swordsman might not understand that his wife had given him permission to get up, he rose and put it back around her shoulders, like a loving husband.

"Is that all?" he asked.

"Not quite. I need to have all of the soldiers in the fort of Segontium changed."

Even with all she'd just said and done with Padarn, she still managed to shock him.

"Aed is reluctant to give you men for your army. It is this land they agreed to protect, not to guard some outpost in some far-distant province. The solution is to put his men in the fort in Segontium and take the men from here, men with many years of service and experience in the Roman army, with you back to Gaul."

It wasn't just a suggestion, it was inspired.

"Is that all?" he asked.

She smiled sweetly. "One more thing."

"Of course there is."

"To seal deals and treaties with tribes here, it is customary to exchange gifts. You gave Padarn your cloak, right off your back as a show of respect."

"And what do I have that I can give to Edern?"

"Maybe you can offer your sword. What better symbol to gift a man who will protect our most important border?"

"My brother gave it to me," Magnus said. "It is special."

"Then it will be perfect," she smiled.

He would find some way to punish her for her actions later, but it seemed he wouldn't be cutting her head off her shoulders. He pulled the blade out far enough from its scabbard that he could read the inscription. TO HIM UNCONQUERED. It was the perfect gift for Magnus Maximus, a man who had never lost a battle or a fight. Apart perhaps from this one. Although Elen had won a victory for him.

Last look taken, he slid it back into its sheath and held it out for Edern.

The new leader of the Votadini said, "A true gift. And in return, I swear on my life to defend Britannia." He took the sword, a look of awe on his face. "Does it have a name?" he asked.

Another barbarian tradition. "We don't name our weapons in..." He stopped himself from saying 'civilised' places. "Call it 'Hard Cut'," he said.

"So it will be," Edern smiled.

"And now, good husband, isn't it time for you to be baptised. Symbolically, of course."

She was good. Too good. She'd even arranged it so that he couldn't really punish her, as in a few moments he'd be a true Christian, and all sins committed from that moment forever on would be strictly punished.

Rather than congratulate him for being the one who taught her well, he berated himself for not learning all he could from her.

* * *

Elen stood on the bank near the river's edge, keeping a tight hold of Victor's hand as Magnus waded into the water. He should have been unclothed, his nakedness representing the status of the re-born, but he was so stupidly proud of his purple cloak he'd insisted on wearing it. And with the weight of his armour, if he was to lose his footing in the mud, the bishops wouldn't be able to pull him back out.

The current pulled the cloak and as he wanted, it splayed out behind him, as grandiosely as he'd hoped. But while his soul might be about to be cleansed, the cloak would have to be washed so thoroughly afterwards it would probably need to be re-dyed.

All the townsfolk behind her were kept at a suitable distance away from the empress, but they jostled with each other to get a better view. Further down the bank, the soldiers of the fort were also keen to watch. For everyone in Segontium, an emperor being baptised was something they'd only get to see once in their lifetimes.

While Magnus renounced Satan and his evils, the two bishops in the river with him had a hand each on his shoulders, ready to support him as he was submerged. But as much as the Christian ritual was an intimate ceremony between man and God, Elen felt that it was missing something. It was probably a heretical thought, but she wondered if it might be better if Magnus had one foot in the river, one on land, while breathing the air and feeling the heat of a small fire against his lower legs. Earth, fire, air and water. A ritual performed with the elements as witnesses.

But what it wasn't missing was ceremony. No one could choose which of the bishops would perform the emperor's baptism, least of all the bishops themselves, and so both of them were in the river. Neither had wanted to look any less spectacular than the other on such a momentous occasion, so they'd both gone in the muddy waters in full regalia. Their clothes would be as hard as Magnus' armour to clean. They incanted the sacred words somewhat in unison.

She wondered how many of those who'd come to watch knew it was about to be a real baptism, not just a symbolic one. And if both bishops knew, or just one of them.

"Papa?" Victor mumbled in a worried voice, concerned that something bad was happening.

As the bishops placed their hands on Magnus' head, ready to duck him under the water, Magnus cast her a hateful look. The fact that he did it in the presence of the bishops, under the gaze of God, made her wonder if the river waters really were about to wash all of his wrath away. She'd counted on that to be immune from revenge for what she'd just done to him in the principia. She hoped the expression on his face would be different when he emerged.

It had been worth the risk though, as she was confident she'd got what was needed to keep Britannia protected. But baptised or not, she knew he'd never forgive her for the way she'd done it. And from now on, she'd never be let anywhere near his inner circle.

"Papa?" Victor cried as Magnus went under, but then he was out again. As he wiped the dirty water out of his eyes, Elen wondered how different he'd see the world now. To the enthusiastic applause of the onlookers, Magnus waded out of the river, but not with Godlike grace. With his lower body covered in alluvial mud and dirty water pouring off him, he looked like some kind of monster of the deep.

Victor was understandably frightened, and as Magnus held his hands out for his son. He tried to burrow himself away under Elen's arm. When Magnus grabbed him, he began to scream and by the time Magnus was stepping carefully into the river again, the poor boy was wetting himself in terror.

She'd told Magnus that Victor was too young to understand what was going on, so that he'd have to be careful not to frighten him too much. As usual, he'd paid her no attention, and now what should have been the most wondrous moment of Victor's life was about to be the most traumatic. Magnus often had that effect.

If being held above the river was bad enough for Victor, getting lowered into it was even worse, and then the bishops were asking him pressing questions about Satan and the Holy Ghost. He could even understand them, let alone answer, and he was screaming and kicking so much, he couldn't breathe properly.

There must have been a thousand people watching, but she couldn't imagine that too many of them thought that Victor's reaction could be a good omen.

Magnus pinched Victor's little nose as the bishops dragged him under. But he still didn't stop struggling, his tiny hands splashing the water, like a fish caught on a line. Nor did he stop screaming, and when they pulled him up again, he was coughing and choking.

Magnus lifted his son above his head to show him to the crowd, "I declare my son, Victor Flavius Maximus to be my co-Augustus!"

With river water in his lungs, Elen hoped that the new emperor wasn't about to catch a serious cold. But with his destiny now entwined with that of his father, she worried, with a warning chill, that might end up being the least of his concerns.

PART III

XVI

TREVERORUM. SUMMER 387

The sounds of swords clashing together rang through the courtyard. Even if they were only wooden ones, for Magnus it was a beautiful sound. It was the irregular rhythm of a dance of death. Victor was getting better with the blade and shield and was starting to get the hang of the techniques of defence and counter attack, his movements beginning to become more fluid, more natural. Not bad for a six-year-old.

His sword was small but heavier than one of a similar size made of metal would be. Daily sparring, long runs out in the country whatever the weather, Ausonius teaching him letters and numbers, and Magnus spending long evenings explaining battlefield theory, one day he would be an emperor with a reputation worthy to be spoken of in the same breath as his greatest predecessors.

And all Magnus had to do to make that happen was win two battles with the other two emperors.

He held the little piece of parchment. It seemed too small for the weight of the words written on it. It was a strange situation to be the only one who knew that the quiet days were over and the empire was at war.

Victor noticed Magnus watching him and even though he was flagging, doubled his efforts against Nannienus. His master of infantry was a good teacher and let Victor get close with his wooden sword a few times so that the boy's enthusiasm wouldn't waver too much and he'd keep trying that little bit harder. He allowed Victor to graze his leg with the wooden blade and cried out in what sounded like distress. As he pretended to limp away, Victor should have gone in for the kill, but a few more half-hearted stabs and he looked close to tears.

Yet while there was the urge of a father to protect his son from the harsh and myriad cruelties of the world, before he was a father, Magnus was emperor. Valentinian the First had spared his sons the rigour of army training and he'd made two weak little whelps that did nothing for the empire. One was hopelessly dominated by his mother, the other had died at the hands of a woman. The next few years were not going to be easy for Victor. Magnus couldn't allow them to be. As a weapon has to be forged in the fire hammered into shape and sharpened with the file and whetstone, he had to make Victor strong so he could protect the borders from outside threats. And ones from the inside. Against men like Magnus.

The note from Constantinople meant that Magnus' four years of being an administrator were over. It was time to be a soldier again. Theo had chosen war, not recognition.

As Victor took a step back to catch his breath, Magnus handed the note to Fraomar. Countless messages came in every day from all over the empire, from Edern on the Wall, to Egypt, where a statue of Magnus had been erected, and plenty from Mediolanum that were just gossip.

This one was different.

The words written on this parchment were ones he'd been waiting for ever since he'd taken the purple.

Fraomar began reading incuriously, but then got to the part after the salutations, and gasped, "Two thirds of Armenia to the Sassanids!"

It was the same reaction Magnus had just had. Fraomar passed the parchment over to Nannienus, who instantly understood that all the training was over and set his wooden sword down.

The attendants, all quite adept at reading the needs of those they served, stood stiffer to attention. It was an atmosphere Magnus was very happy with. It had been far too long since he'd been in an army camp the evening before a battle, giving out the commands that were the difference between life and death.

"What is it, papa?" Victor asked, his sword lesson instantly forgotten. He rested the tip of his training sword on the flagstones, as for him it was still quite heavy.

Magnus ignored him and waited for Nannenius' response.

"It sounds as though Theo kneels before Shapur the Third, as Valerian did for his grandfather," he said.

It was a good answer.

Shapur the First had skinned Emperor Valerian. Whether he was alive or dead at the time didn't matter, it was still the most grievous insult the empire had endured since Arminius had led Varus into the forest. Giving away so much bitterly contested territory indicated how desperate Theo was to come west. He wanted to confront Magnus, no matter the cost.

Magnus was a much more skilled fighter than an administrator, but even so, he couldn't help feeling disappointed. In choosing war instead of the two of them ruling the empire in tandem and ushering in a new golden era, whatever was to happen after the conflict, the winner would have to spend the rest of his life picking up the pieces.

Theo had shifted the game on the ludus board. There was only one move open for Magnus. To face Theo he needed the armies of Italy.

If Elen hadn't sent word south to get the mountain passes blocked as soon as he'd beaten Gratian, Magnus would have had control of Italy for the last four years. He'd be ruler over a force larger enough that Theo wouldn't have dared mobilise against him. At the beginning of his journey to the purple, she'd been his greatest asset. Now, she could be the cause of his downfall.

"This note arrives the day after Ambrosius does. I don't believe that can be a coincidence," Nannenius said as he folded it behind his armour.

Magnus agreed, "But he hasn't come from Valentinian with any offer that will be for our benefit."

"And if he is here to discuss your cousin's next move," Fraomar added. "It means that Valentinian has at least two weeks head start on his preparations over us."

Magnus wondered at just what a disadvantage he was at.

"What's wrong, Father?" Victor whined.

One day he would be the sole emperor, making his own plans for war, but now was not the time for children. "Go to your mother," he said, a little bit more severely than he'd intended. To the others, he said, "I will meet the bishop and see what nonsense he wishes to pollute my ears with this time, and then we will have a council. Send for the others!"

They saluted him and left.

"Papa?" Victor persisted. "What's happening?"

Magnus looked down at him and wondered how many times in his life his son would have to hear the same words. "We are at war."

"But-"

"Messenger!" Magnus shouted,

A terrified-looking eunuch who'd been waiting by the door came in. "Augustus?"

"Inform the bishop I will meet him in the consistory. Immediately."

A deep bow, a few scraping steps backwards, and the slimy little man ran off.

Magnus shouted for his cloak and armour and another attendant scurried off to fetch it.

He hadn't worn his lorica squamata for a long time, but for the battle of words he was about to have with the Bishop of Mediolanum, he wanted to wear it. It was purely for show, but would be a good visual reminder for the bishop that if he'd come to talk about war, Magnus was one of the most successful generals to have ever graced the empire.

The last time he'd met Ambrosius, he'd been soundly defeated. Magnus hoped the bishop would find him more worthy opponent this time.

The first attendant came to him with his immaculately polished scaled armour, another followed behind with his cloak.

Before he was out of the palace grounds the eunuch, red-faced and sweating, ran up to him. "Forgive me, Augustus. The bishop enquires whether you might be mistaken about the meeting place."

"I am not mistaken," Magnus said and, with a look of terror on his chubby face, the grovelling eunuch skulked off back to the bishop.

* * *

There were so many people around that Elen was close to screaming at them all to leave and allow her some moments of peace. It was always the way. Attendants, guards, nurses and nannies, messengers, slaves; everywhere she went it was always crowded. She'd come to think that being an empress was similar to a queen bee in the middle of a hive, surrounded to the point of being smothered by the workers. Another similarity was that the only function she was required to perform was to produce the emperor's offspring.

She cradled the sleeping Maxima, her third child, already almost a year old. Sevira laughed with Aigla as they played a game that involved patting their hands together in some sort of pattern.

Victor came in, face flushed, forehead sweaty from his daily sword lesson. In one way, he was still her baby, one who'd made such an effort to soil as much of his swaddling as he could, but overlaid on that was an image of him standing proud in his father's cloak, diadem on his head, and the two conflicting images of the same boy made her head swirl. All she wanted was for him to be just a young boy, his days spent doing nothing more than boyish pursuits; a boy whose days weren't tormented by the weighty future that was expected of him.

Magnus had raised him to co-Augustus though, so a normal childhood was not something he could hope for.

Victor looked at Publicus, who was peering timidly around his mother's legs. The two boys had been playmates since before they could walk, but born of a freed slave, Magnus had made it very clear the pair should never be seen in public together.

She waved Victor over and before he got to her, his tears came. "What is it?" she asked, ready to tell him he could play with Publicus again as soon as the bishop had left the city.

"I don't want to be a soldier," he said. "I don't like it."

It was one of the most heartbreaking things she'd ever heard. The mother in her wanted to tell him that everything would be all right, that when he grew up he could be anything he wanted to be. The empress in her though almost flew into a rage as incandescent as her husband's. These days, a boy born to the purple had to be the strongest fighter in the world, and the thought of her and Victor ending up like Valentinian and Justina, surrounded by enemies who wished them dead, almost made her weep.

"Why do we have to fight?" he cried.

"Who is fighting?" she asked. "No one is fighting."

"Father is."

"What?" Elen gasped.

"He got a message. He says it's war!"

The shock of the words was almost enough to make her drop Maxima. Eugenius was concerned enough at her reaction to take a step forward.

Since they'd last been in Britannia, Elen had been relegated to the role of distant wife with barely any access to Magnus' court. She stood up, waved Aigla to come and take Maxima, then in the voice grandmother had taught her, shouted, "Out! Everyone *out*! Now!"

From it being just another day of watching children play, panic swept through the small crowd as people began moving out.

"You too," she said to Victor.

"But..." he protested and then puffed his chest out in an effort to look like his father. "I am co-Augustus!"

"To everyone else, you are," she nodded. "But to me, you are my little boy who needs to do what he is told."

There would come a time when he'd have the authority to order her around, but that wasn't today.

When it was just her and her four guards, she said, "Something important has happened. I need to find out what that is."

Two of her guards nodded and left. Two stayed. Eugenius was one of them. He would never leave. She looked at him, trying not to let her sorrow or fear show. "We need to find a way of getting back to Britannia and taking Victor with us," she said.

"Some will see that as kidnapping the emperor," Eugenius said.

"If Magnus goes south, it will not be safe here."

"It will not be safe anywhere," he said.

* * *

The first time Magnus had met Ambrosius, the bishop had almost dazzled him with his attire. The robes of high ecclesiastical office, richly embroidered with gold thread, had far outdone those of a mere emperor in his purple toga. This time, Magnus was a little less impressed. He was four years an emperor now, not just two weeks, and he knew Ambrosius had been set against him since the very first, so wouldn't be wasting any breath trying to win him over.

He took his seat in the room next to the cathedral, wondering why it was always cold in old buildings.

Ambrosius, his beard longer and with a few more grey hairs in it, walked slowly, deliberately. Fewer attendants followed him in than the last time. The same as Magnus, as only Nanninius stood at his side: another little demonstration of contempt.

Magnus rose and invited the bishop up to the steps of the small dais and gave him a perfunctory kiss on the cheek in greeting. The bishop's demeanour was instantly belligerent though. "Why do you offer a kiss of peace to one who you do not acknowledge?" he asked as he stepped back.

"What do you mean?" Magnus replied, trying his best to sound genuinely confused.

"If you had acknowledged me, you would not have seen me here in the consistory, but rather in the basilica."

"You are angry?" Magnus asked. Years ago, he'd have been terrified about insulting such a powerful man. Now, seeing he was making the bishop fume, he had to be careful not to let his smile spread.

"It is not anger I feel, but shame at appearing in a place unsuited to me."

Magnus continued his feigned innocence. "Yet on your first mission to see me, you were received right here."

"True, but the blame rests on him who summoned, not on me who entered."

"Then why did you not make your disagreement known the last time we met?"

"Because then I was suing for peace on behalf of one who was inferior to you, but now I appear for your equal."

Magnus scoffed with genuine surprise, the echo amplifying his mirth. "By whose favour does Valentinian consider himself my equal?"

"By that of Almighty God!" the bishop said defiantly. "Who has maintained Valentinian in the empire he bestowed on him."

"And how do you think I have ruled from Treverorum so successfully these last four years? Do you think that I wear this purple cloak by the power of Satan?"

A few of the bishop's men grumbled their discomfort at the mention of the enemy of God.

"The ways of the Lord are forever a mystery to us mere mortals," the bishop sighed.

Magnus remembered how Ambrosius had effortlessly directed the discussion last time, so slapped the bishop's old words back at him. "What do you want?" He expected that the bishop's next words would be related to Theo's obvious plan to come west. Some plan that he would insinuate was a benefit to Magnus and Valentinian both.

"I come here for Gratian," he said, which threw Magnus for a moment, "so that he may finally be restored to his brother, as Marcellinus was to you."

"That's it?" Magnus scoffed. "If that is all you have travelled so far to ask of me, I'm afraid you have had a long journey for nothing."

"Do you allege that you are worried, lest the grief of the troops should be renewed by the return of those remains? Ambrosius mocked. "Will they then defend after death, one whom they deserted in life? Why do you fear him now he is dead?"

"You *have* heard of Theo's moves, have you not?" Magnus asked. "Giving the most part of Armenia away to the Sassanids can only mean war? And all you ask of me is for the bones of a forgotten emperor?"

Magnus wasn't expecting the flash of confusion on the bishop's face. He hadn't imagined that he'd got the news before the bishop. He motioned Nannenius to pass him the note. As Ambrosius read it, he coughed nervously and his face began to turn red. "You trust the author of this letter?" he asked.

"Why wouldn't I?"

"Because..." and for the very first time, it seemed that the great Ambrosius was lost for words.

"Because," Magnus said, "a clash of Christian emperors is upon us, yet you have chosen to serve a heretic."

The bishop obviously still supported Valentinian, as he clearly wanted to race back to Mediolanum as quickly as he could.

"If Gratian was really all you came here to discuss with me, you are free to hasten back to the heretic child," Magnus said.

"Christians should not fight Christians," Ambrosius growled.

"I suggest that you tell that to my cousin," Magnus shrugged. "I have been content here in Treverorum for years. It is Theo who makes the moves to come west for confrontation."

"What will you do?" the bishop asked with a much softer tone.

Magnus leaned slowly forwards, the scales of his armour making the sound of a soldier. "Such a thing, I would tell to a man who was to fight with me. Tell me, bishop, here in the house of the Lord, will you fight with me? Or against me?"

"I err..."

"Exactly! I suspect you will want to get back to your heretic child as soon as you can. In fact, you should leave this very instant."

"We have other things to discuss."

Magnus stood up. On the dais, he towered over Ambrosius. "We are at war."

It would take him the best part of two weeks to get back to Mediolanum. Magnus could have Andragathius in the mountains and an army on the march before then.

He could win.

XVII

Andragathius tugged the hood of his cloak tighter around his head. It was much easier to look no further than the back legs of the oxen pulling his wagon up the mountain track, than over the massive drop to the side.

He'd grown up in a land where burial mounds of the ancients were the highest points in the landscape, and so even in Britannia the craggy hills and the mists that blanketed the valleys had sometimes left him gawping in awe. The giant mountains that stood between the lands of Magnus' Gaul and Valentinian's Italy were something else though: a home of the gods.

Immense snow-capped peaks of sheer rock jutted up higher than the clouds, higher than anything he'd ever imagined before. Waterfalls cascaded down sheer rock faces and the rivers ran in foaming white torrents, great streams of elemental rage that he was scared to drink from in case the waters were to pitch him into a blinding rage. Every now and again the wagon he was driving would turn a corner and he'd come to a place where he had a view up the valley, and every time, the mountains carried on as far as he could see. It made him so dizzy that with the sheer cliffs on one side and the sheer drops on the other, he was worried he'd lose his balance and slump out of his seat. And if he did, he'd be falling for quite a while.

The mountains were almost as bad as the sea.

He pulled his hood down even further and wondered if he'd be happier in the back of the wagon with the others, unable to see anything.

They'd been climbing for days, and were still going up. A few days before, they'd passed the last little farm perched on a steep slope where hardy goats were herded, but they were so high now the only signs of life were nothing but stunted bushes and some strange flowers poking through the snow.

Andragathius looked over the side, down to the road they'd just come up. A defending army in a good position could fight an invading one like stabbing fish in a barrel. No wonder Magnus had chosen to take his army on the much longer route around them.

For a man who'd spent most of his life on the back of a horse, the drudgingly slow pace of the oxen felt painfully slow, each laboured step seemingly one of protest. All he wanted was his horse so he could ride quickly out of the cold and breathless air, back down to the plains where the farmers were. They had to maintain their guise of traders though, right up until the patrol came to pull back the hide to check what was inside. With Magnus seemingly settled in Treverorum for the past few years they'd perhaps got a little lax with their security measures. They weren't expecting that the goods being transported would stab them in the throat.

Some men preached that all men were equal. In the eyes of God, maybe that was true, apart from slaves and women, but for Andragathius it was a very different feeling to kill Roman soldiers compared to the invading Goths that had usually found themselves at the end of his sword or spear. Especially so close to Italy.

The bodies made little rock falls as they tumbled down the almost sheer drop. The sounds of their bones smashing against the rocks echoed around them.

The wagon creaked on even higher. The rain came again, cold enough to be mixed with snow. Andragathius' heart pumped hard from the killings, enough to keep him warm, but surprising a couple of unsuspecting guards was nothing compared to what was about to come and he couldn't help testing the sword hidden under his thick cloak.

How Magnus had won the battle against Gratian, without spilling a single drop of blood, was the stuff of legend, but no matter how much faith Andragathius had in Magnus' military capabilities, he couldn't believe that the same thing would happen on the other side of the mountains.

A few more tight turns, the oxen struggling to pull the cart around, slipping on the slush of the winter snow that still hadn't melted, and finally they were at the pass.

"Ready now," he called to the men behind him. For the last several years, only hardy traders and shepherds had crawled up the switch-back road and Andragathius was happy that nothing but the gate itself was manned, and that it was open. The wet whelp that was the empress' brother had been right. Andragathius had a deep distrust of the little runt, but a good part of his grim mood was because deep down he feared a betrayal. He hadn't trusted Kenon since he'd fished him out of the river with Padarn. Perhaps as a scout he might be on his way to earning a bit of redemption.

He shuffled on the flat shield he'd put face down on the bench and felt for the hand grip. He lashed the sullen oxen to take the last few steps through the dirty snow, pulling a little on the sword to make sure it would slide out of the scabbard without impediment when the moment came. He was going to have to act fast.

"Get ready," he hissed to those behind him. "The gate is open."

When they weren't fighting, soldiers always looked deathly bored. It was the same everywhere he'd been all over the empire. Good commanders knew that the only real threat they had to keep guards sharp was death. One man executed in front of the others for dozing off kept the rest wide awake for months. But even that wasn't enough sometimes. The pair who walked over to inspect the wagon looked as though it was only their bodies here, that the spirits were away dreaming somewhere of fields with soil and things in it that a man could grow and live off. Some place a bit easier to live than huddling for shelter between windswept rocks.

One held his hand up, as he'd probably done to hundreds of wagon drivers before. Neither paid any attention to the fact that the wagon harness wasn't connected to the oxen in the usual fashion, that there was just a single thick rope connecting them, one that Andragathius had been staring at all day, imagining how best to slash through it with the one stroke he had.

"Halt," one shouted, annoyed, but not frightened.

The oxen were so slow. The gate was only a couple of heartbeats away on a horse, but pulled by the lazy beasts, if the soldiers beside called out a warning to their companions, the gate would be shut long before he got there. He was at least thankful for the windswept rain. The shower was bad enough that the other guards were taking shelter.

"Oi!" the second guard yelled and then they realised something was wrong.

"Now!" Andragathius called out over his shoulder, but by the time Baccus had lifted up the sheet at the side of the wagon, the guards had their swords drawn, and his men jumped into a pitched fight. And ahead, suddenly heads were popping up over the wall in front.

Andragathius lashed the oxen and screamed curses at them, but nothing encouraged them to move any faster. He knew that his life depended on a couple of draft animals dragging him a few more feet. "Come on!" he yelled, but the guards were already running to get the gates shut. He wasn't going to make it.

Sword drawn, cloak dropped behind him, he leapt forwards, took a couple of steps along the back of one of the oxen, then was charging at the gate guards. Alone. He engaged them both, drove them back, ran back to the oxen to drag them forwards, fought a man one-handed while still pulling the reluctant animals behind him and then he was in the gate. A hard strike at the guard, who staggered away, then he turned to slash down at the neck of the nearest ox. Spine severed, it slumped to the ground. The other, panicked, tried to keep moving, but one of the wheels of the wagon was wedged against the side of the gate. Then one of his men, blade bloodied, was scrambling over the back of it. They were through.

A massive pain in his shoulder knocked him to a knee, but the arrow skidded off his armour at an angle, so it hadn't cut him. No man could beat him with a sword, but his chances out in the open against an archer were much slimmer, especially as his shield was still lying useless on the wagon.

There were plenty of large rocks to hide behind, so like the greatest coward, he leapt behind one and quickly looked around to try and spot the archer. There, he realised a terrifying thing about fighting in the mountains; as well as left and right, he had to defend himself from above as well.

His men had their shields though and Baccus led the charge at those firing arrows, catching them harmlessly in the layered wood.

Andragathius set his sword down, unwound his sling and put a lead bullet in it. There wasn't much space to swing, but the first guard wasn't too far away and the bullet screamed through the air with its high-pitched whistle to smack into his back. It didn't kill him, but it hurt him enough to make him drop his bow. His companion turned and pulled his bowstring back and fired. Andragathius saw the arrow coming and ducked under it, so it clattered off the rock behind him. He rose again, already swinging the next bullet. He watched the guard notch another arrow, but he wasn't fast enough. Andragathius' next bullet hit him in the arm and he doubled over in pain. Andragathius could then get his sword again, a proper weapon. He looked around, scanning the area for threats, but it seemed that the fighting was done. "We need some alive!" he shouted. Baccus was still shouting though, and was pointing to something behind him.

The sudden pain was unimaginable, as though someone had cut his skull open and was bashing his brains about like a village woman in the river with the laundry. He tried to work out what had happened and thought that the mountains had turned against him and were trying to crush the life out of him. But that was only because he was lying face down on the cold ground.

Shouts of panic came from all around. He tried to move. He didn't believe in any of the old gods, but was sure that Zeus was striking him in the back with a lightning bolt.

As a soldier, he knew that lying down, wounded, was death. He managed to turn his head and saw the arrow shaft sticking out of his back. That was a horrible enough realisation, but what was worse was that he couldn't move his legs.

Baccus threw the archer down and with his face pressed down on the ground he stared at Andragathius with terrified eyes, which screwed up in pain as Baccus turned his foot to grind him into the dirt.

"Kill him!" Andragathius managed to gasp, but Baccus didn't move. "*Kill him!*"

"He's the last one," Baccus sighed.

Andragathius groaned into the dirty, blood-stained snow. It felt like he'd just lost two fights, one with an arrow, and another with fate as he couldn't kill the man who'd taken his life.

Andragathius nodded his reluctant consent.

"Your lucky day," Baccus snarled at the soldier. "You're going to run all the way out of these cursed mountains to tell your commander that Magnus Maximus is coming through the high passes with all of his army behind him, heading straight for Mediolanum. Do you understand?"

"Yes, sir," he cried, now respectful to the men he'd just tried to kill.

Baccus moved to let him up, but Andragathius managed to say, "Take his fingers." If the lad was to live, at least he'd never get to fight any of Andragathius' men again.

The man's screams made strange echoes off the rocks around them and seeming to come from everywhere at once, they filled Andragathius' head. Then it was his own screams he heard as someone started to work the arrow out of his spine.

"Am I err..?" Baccus started nervously. "In charge now?"

Despite the agony, Andragathius growled. "The day. You are in charge. Is the day. I die."

"But... I don't..."

"Do I sound fucking dead to you?"

"No."

"Right then. Shut up and find a way to get me to Mediolanum. Without me ripping your head off."

XVIII

Magnus had been sitting on the back of his horse, ready to ride, since the first glow of dawn had lightened the eastern sky. The ancients might have thought that the sunrise was their sun god awakening, but in Magnus' soldier's mind, it looked like a large city was on fire on the horizon.

The sun highlighted the line of jagged mountains to the east so they looked like the teeth of a draco.

It was a stunning morning. Almost as though it was the dawn of a day of destiny.

Behind him, the dots of light were the hundreds of small fires the soldiers were boiling their breakfast oats on. In the near darkness, the camp was already beginning to come to life.

In all of his long years in the army, he'd never grown bored of witnessing the spectacle of a full army on the move. Tucked into his armour were a couple of messages that had come in the night before. If what was written in them was true, this might be the last time he'd need to put an army on the march.

One more battle to come and then there would be no more.

First to file out of the gates, and between the ditch and the gap in the sharpened stakes were the scouts. Any traps or ambushes, or if Valentinian dared to risk a confrontation on the far side of the mountains, it would be these three hundred riders who would find him first. All nodded their respect or gave a full salute as they rode past. Next out were the four hundred riders of the vanguard. The most experienced and trusted fighters. These would be the men first into the fight, the ones who would hold the line while the rest of the army caught up with the engagement. Side by side, it took such a long time for them all to leave that the sun was well over the mountains before the sounds of their horses finally started to trail off into the distance.

A little pause, in which one of his camp attendants brought him a steaming bowl of porridge and nuts sweetened with honey, and it was the turn of the surveyors and the engineers to file out. Swords and shields on the hips and backs of each man, their heavy packs also included tools like spades, picks, axes and saws. It would be these who would mark out the camp, dig the ditches and construct the perimeter wall of the next camp, some twelve miles south.

His horse stomped a foot impatiently. Magnus leaned over to pat it on the neck soothingly. He understood its desire. He also wanted to run, to feel the wind in his hair as he charged at full pelt towards Italy. Both notes said the same thing; that Valentinian and his bitch mother had fled east, and that Italy was Magnus' for the taking, like an autumn apple ready to fall. It was excruciatingly tempting to snap an order to turn and march up through the high mountains straight to Mediolanum rather than taking his army all the way to the coast and then turning north to go around them. It was still too much of a risk though. He couldn't be absolutely sure that the messengers weren't actually Valentinian's agents trying to lure him into the mountains where he'd be exposed to ambushes in places impossible to manoeuver into a battle formation.

He wouldn't put such a ploy past Ambrosius.

But if it was true...

Marcellinus pulled up next to him and, as the standard bearers shuffled into position at his side, his brother leaned back in a large yawn. "We share the same parents," he said, still sounding sleepy. "But I still have no idea how you could rise so early every day. Some men say that sleep is *good* for you!"

Magnus smiled. "And I never understood how you could sleep half of your days away."

He hadn't told anyone what was written in the notes, but he turned to his brother and said, "Perhaps this is a day to be awake for."

That got Marcellinus' attention. He looked around to see who was in earshot. "What do you know?"

"When I am sure of it, I will tell you."

Magnus could see that his little brother wanted to ask more, but the general in him respected his superior officer and so he kept his mouth shut. Once the war was over they'd have plenty of time to be brothers again—although if Marcellinus was to be the Eastern Emperor in Theo's stead, as Magnus intended, they'd be kept far apart by their different concerns. "I enjoyed our last ride to Mediolanum all those years ago," Magnus said. "Perhaps soon we can do it again."

Marcellinus' expression changed from confusion to realisation, but he didn't press for any more information. "With one slight difference," Magnus added.

"You will be emperor in Italy this time," his brother smiled.

Fraomar and Merobaudes came to take their positions behind Magnus, as did Felix the bishop of Treverorum. He'd come on the march on the pretence of administering to the needs of the Christian soldiers, but Magnus had suspicions that it was Ambrosius he took orders from. He had men watching him, making sure that no note he wrote could get out and find its way before Ambrosius' eyes without Magnus knowing what was in it. That no one had found anything just made him suspicious that Felix was more cunning than Magnus had assumed.

A trumpet sounded. Magnus' horse was so well trained it knew it was time to head out, so started forward without any other input. The jingle of tack, the sounds of hundreds of hooves on the ground and then he was out of the gates. A nod at the men on duty and the hundred and twenty Moor riders in his escort were on the road again. Behind him, the main body of the light cavalry would soon follow, and behind them, the infantry auxiliaries would begin their long trudge on foot. Then the cumbersome baggage train with the camp slaves, spare horses and finally the rear guard. It would take so long for the whole army to leave that before they were all out of the camp, the vanguard would already be halfway to the new one.

With the notes suggesting that Mediolanum and Italy were his for the taking, the slow pace of the army felt monotonous, and his mind wandered to think about which great generals in the past, the best military commanders the empire had ever known, had worked out how to move tens of thousands of soldiers in the most efficient way. The glory days of the legions were long gone, but now he had the entire fighting force of the Western empire at his command, so once the coming war was won, he could concentrate on issuing levies to recruit men and get them properly trained. No Goths would ever threaten Gaul again.

Yet again, he couldn't help feeling frustration towards his cousin, as he was still unsure how Theo would react to him taking Italy. If he was to accept that the cousins were equal, and together not only would they be the progenitors of the Theodicean line, they could be the architects of Rome's glorious revival. For hundreds of years, Magnus' name would be spoken of with reverence in the same breath as Diocletian and Constantine. Maybe even Caesar. He could hand over half an empire that had enjoyed a long and stable peace to Victor, while the east was run by Theodosius' sons Honorius and Arcadius. The empire's golden years really could be restored.

It was no foregone conclusion though. Ausonius, and a few other trusted advisors, insisted that Theodosius held a deep resentment for the way Magnus had taken power from Gratian. The way he'd handed Armenia over to the empire's most despised enemies was proof that he was doing everything he could to free himself up to come west and face Magnus. If Magnus really did have control of Italy's armies, and Theo chose confrontation, the battle to come would be one that echoed down the centuries. Whichever way it turned out.

He caught sight of movement through the trees at the far side of a field. Long shadows cast by the low sun of men speeding as fast as their horses would carry them. His first instinct was that it was an attack coming straight for him–but the men were riding in parallel to the column of soldiers, not towards it, so it must just be a scout on the flank. But then there was shouting and his guards closed in around him, taking shields off their backs, drawing swords and readying spears.

Magnus pushed himself up in the saddle to get a better view of what was going on so he could shout appropriate orders. A track led down the side of the field and a handful of riders approached. More Scouts. Magnus' stomach turned at the thought of what news they were about to relay. He was good with faces though and before anybody else recognized him, he saw it was Baccus, and so shouted for his men to let Andragathius' second-in-command approach.

Baccus had a dust-covered face that was streaked with tears, a sign he'd been running hard and fast. His horse, pushed far beyond the point it should be rested, staggered and tossed its head as Baccus aimed it through the gap Magnus' guards made for him. He obviously had some very important news, but before that, Magnus had a more important question. As Baccus pulled up, he asked, "Why do you ride to me without Andragathius?"

"He lives," Baccus said breathlessly.

"But?"

"He is wounded."

"Where?"

"At the high pass when we took the gate."

"Where on his *body*?"

Baccus blushed with embarrassment as the most important men in Magnus' army laughed at him. "In the back. He can't walk."

"And where is he now?"

"We left him in Mediolanum. With a doctor."

Andragathius was in Mediolanum. That could only mean that Valentinian wasn't. The ruse had worked. Valentinian had sent his army into the mountains and now Magnus was closer to the child emperor than Bauto was.

Murmurs of surprise and joy spread through the men. Magnus had won, and again without a single drop of blood being spilled. Apart from Andragathius'.

"Valentinian has fled?" he asked, needing to make sure.

"He has, Augustus."

Marcellinus shouted, "Your reputation alone has caused another emperor to flee! If Caesar himself were here to witness this, he would do you honour."

He'd expected Valentinian to put up some kind of resistance, so knowing he'd fled as a coward felt like a bit of an anti-climax. But it was a victory nonetheless. "We have won!" Magnus called out and shouts of appreciation spread through the men. It sounded like an echo as it made its way along the line of soldiers which was long enough they were lost in the distance.

"The passes are clear?" Magnus asked Baccus.

"Guarded. We came from the west, so no one stopped us."

He needed to get to Mediolanum as quickly as possible, but the momentum of an army on the march was not something he could simply steer off into a completely different direction. It was akin to a river of ice in the high mountains; almost impossible to change it while it was in motion.

It had been a long and gruelling march from Treverorum, so tonight he'd let his men rest and would source more cattle from nearby farms for a real feast while they waited a day or so for the advance scouts to check the way up through the mountains. If everything went without trouble, he'd be in Mediolanum within a week. He smiled at the thought of receiving Ambrosius in the smallest and rudest church he could find.

He turned to look at Felix and wasn't unsurprised to see that his face was blanched. He'd have him watched even more intently over the coming days.

"Ride to camp with us," Magnus said to Baccus. "Rest, eat, then on fresh horses ride back to Mediolanum as fast as you can. I don't want Andragathius to be left unguarded there."

XIX

Kenon was in Rome. It was a lifetime's dream, but being in the Eternal City was nothing like he'd expected. He came in the entourage of the sole emperor of the West, but it was no moment of glory, no sense of triumph was in the air. Quite the opposite. Kenan rode with his detachment of scouts through the deserted streets. All the gates to the houses were closed, probably firmly bolted on the inside, and all the insulae in the less affluent part of the city had the shutters pulled closed.

It seemed everyone was terrified of the new emperor who was riding into the city.

In the years he'd been a scout, he'd learned to see imminent threats in things other men would deem mundane. Signs in disturbed undergrowth, the way the calls of certain birds changed when men were close to their nests. In the city, how a shutter opened a slither, just wide enough for an arrow, how a man turned his head to mumble a warning to his hidden companions. In Rome, the only threat he sensed was to himself. He'd always believed that an emperor cared more for normal people. The population had paid their taxes in the understanding that in return those in power would keep them safe from the threat of invaders, so their children could grow up safe and prosper. As soon as Valentinian had found out that the force he'd sent to the north had marched against nothing but a ruse, and that there was only the mountains between him and Magnus, he'd simply left everything behind and run for his life. Like a coward.

It made him nervous as it demonstrated that lesser men who had nothing to offer were easily dispensable. It served as confirmation, if he needed it, that as soon as Emperor Theodosius or the Bishop of Mediolanum didn't need him, neither would hesitate to discard him.

With a stab of apprehension, he knew it wouldn't matter too much soon, as he was so close to getting absolutely everything he desired. At last. Ursula had finished her three-year-long pilgrimage around the holy sights of the empire and had come to Rome so that they could be married. After three years of writing long letters, he was now in the same city as the girl who would be his wife, the mother of his children. In his whole life, he'd never wanted anything more.

The fact that he would get his baptism at the same moment, was almost too much to believe.

A flash of movement from the corner of his eye, a crashing sound, some curses and a couple of soldiers were smashing their way through the doors of an insulae. A few moments later they dragged out the boys who'd dropped the roof tile down on them. Maurus had blood on his face—and ignoring the screams of a hysterical woman who followed him out, looked as though he was about to execute the lads right there.

In the terrified faces of the boys, helpless in the grip of such strong men, Kenon was struck with the uncomfortable memory of once being in a similar situation. He was so tantalisingly close to being forgiven for it, to having the nightmare exorcised from his head that he shouted, "Leave them!"

Maurus wiped blood from his forehead and cast a challenging look. He didn't dare to openly question Kenon though, so he didn't have to repeat the command.

"They are afraid of us. We are invaders here," he said. Maurus was a believer in Theodosius' vision for the future of the empire, not Magnus', and so knew the truth of the words.

It was still with some reluctance that Maurus allowed the boys to scurry back to their mother. But then a strange thing happened; the woman not only called out her thanks to him, but once she'd ushered her sons safely inside, she dared to come to him, and took his hand in hers to kiss the back of it. It was so opposite of the nightmare he'd feared was about to be repeated, that he was dumbstruck.

But the feel of the woman's lips on him brought back memories of all the girls who touched him in a similar way, ones he'd paid for. Such a thing was only for Ursula now and so he snatched his hand away in disgust.

So close. It was an effort not to kick his horse into a gallop and right through the street shouting her name.

The further they got away from the main road, the poorer the neighbourhoods became like a warren. And the whole place stank. But at least Magnus seemed a welcome emperor, a Nicean returning to the city that an emperor should be in, so there were no irate mobs needing to be subdued. Most people brave enough to be out knew to press themselves up against the wall or cower in doorways when they saw imperial guards riding through the narrow streets. There was no threat to Magnus. Kenon waved for one of his men to ride to the thoroughfare to give the all clear.

Kenon was the threat.

At the forum, he completely forgot to look for any fermentation of dissent among the populace as he gawped at the incredible buildings he'd only ever heard stories about. He'd grown up believing that Deva was the centre of civilization, had almost been overwhelmed by the imperial city of Treverorum, and the same for his brief visit to Constantinople. The buildings of Rome were something else. Something far beyond what he'd ever imagined.

And that Magnus was now the emperor of it all, seemed horribly unjust - and all without a fight, as though everyone had given way to his irresistible righteousness.

The emperor's procession was a sight to behold. Perhaps it would have been glorious if the man at the head of it deserved to be there. Others might have been smiling at the impressive sight of the hundreds of riders with perfect uniforms, not a speck of dirt on a single one, nor a blemish on a single piece of tack, but not Kenon. He smiled as well, but not from the spectacle, but because one day he would have the opportunity to take all of this from the usurper.

By the end of the day, when whatever formalities of investiture that needed to be performed had been done and at last, Kenon was free.

He shouted impatiently at the bathhouse attendants to hurry up, screamed at the boy wrapping the toga around him, and didn't feel the slightest bit guilty–in a few moments he'd be forgiven everything.

Pope Siricius[1] had welcomed the emperor, and was now administrating to Kenon. He stood before him with the same feeling of knee-weakening awe he'd felt when he was in the presence of Theodosius and the Bishop of Mediolanum. But the feeling of being in the presence of a man of such power paled in comparison to what it was like to be next to Ursula.

"Those boys attacked a soldier. Bad enough that there was blood," the Pope said solemnly and Kenon had to tear his attention away from Ursula. "The outcome of such a situation could have had a much different outcome, had it not been for your timely intervention."

"I er..." Kenon started, but held his tongue before bragging about it. He should be a humble man from now on.

Ursula squeezed his hand. To Kenon, that delicate little touch was worth more than anything the Pope could do for him.

"That woman is known to me," he said. "She assures me that due to your actions, her boys were spared harm. Ambrosius himself recommended you to me, but without you passing through a period of catechumen, I had my concerns. But will now welcome you into the fold without any reservation."

"And I will have a good and godly husband," Ursula said. She had such a beaming smile. The light in her eyes reflected the cathedral's candles looked so incredible, that he almost didn't mind that she'd spoken out of turn.

---

[1] https://en.wikipedia.org/wiki/Pope_Siricius

So many changes were about to come.

Ursula's white and yellow dress accented a few curves of her body. Three years he'd lived in a self-inflicted celibacy in anticipation of the night that was about to come. He couldn't even remember the last time he'd been with a woman. He shivered. Less from a sense of divine connection, more from the fact that it was soon time to strip down to only a loincloth. Getting too excited in front of the Pope about what he and his new wife would do later that evening would be the absolute worst thing in the world.

Toga and tunic off, held reverentially by Ursula, one of the Pope's assistants had rubbed some oils on him. They smelt exotic, but somewhat similar to those he'd experienced in a few of the better brothels he'd frequented in the past.

"Know, my son," the Pope intoned, "that this regeneration must be approached with reverence and repentance. Now is the time for you to be born anew and enter into life. Repent, therefore, in your heart of all your wicked deeds, known and unknown. Repeat after me, I renounce you Satan, and all your servants, and all your works! Say it!"

"I renounce you Satan, and all your servants, and all your works!" Kenon wailed as the Pope grabbed him with surprisingly strong hands.

More oil, more shouting, then another man, dressed almost as wonderfully as the Pope, clasped him by the shoulders.

"Do you believe in God the Father Almighty?" he asked, so close that hairs of his wiry beard tickled against Kenon's face.

"I believe!"

More water, or oil, he couldn't quite tell.

"Do you believe in Christ Jesus, the son of God, who was born of the holy spirit of the Virgin Mary, and was crucified under Pontius Pilate, and was dead and buried, and rose again the third day, alive from the dead, ascended into heaven, and sat at the right hand of the Father, and will come to judge the quick and the dead?"

"I believe!"

And then it was over. His heart was beating hard, but that probably had more to do with the men touching him than any divine connection. Ursula still smiled at him, as though she was in ecstasy, but Kenon had thought that would be a bit more to the process; a complete change. He should have been a completely different person. Reborn. But he felt just the same. With a flash of panic, he almost asked if something had gone wrong, if he'd been rejected, or maybe the ceremony was just the appearance of the true baptism because Theodosius or Ambrosius didn't think him worthy of a real one. Had powerful men betrayed him again? He looked at Ursula again and judged her smile to be genuine. She was still gripping his hand. At least she believed it. That was enough.

He wanted to wed her so much that he decided not to ask if anything was amiss.

XX

Andragathius uttered another curse.

Despite reclining on enough cushions to make an empress jealous, they didn't do much to dampen the constant jostling of the carriage on the seemingly endless journey. After a month, which felt more like years, travelling across the width of Italy, they were finally close to Magnus, although he wasn't particularly enthused about meeting the emperor again. He was sure he was about to be presented with some reward for his sacrifice up in the mountains, but knowing Magnus and what the army meant to him, it would probably be a promotion–and that was absolutely the last thing he wanted.

The carriage jolted again, hard enough to make him wince in pain. He wondered how he could say no to a man powerful enough to make two emperors scatter and flee before him. All he wanted to do was escape the agony in his back and have a farm in the flat lands he'd dreamed of every one of the days he'd been in Mediolanum.

He didn't remember too much of his months as a guest of Ambrosius. Pain, it seemed, has a way of making a man forget things. He could recall lying in ungodly agony, in a cold palace room, of being in unspeakable pain when the Bishop of Mediolanum came to visit with his whispered promises of a God he claimed to speak for–the price for which was only to betray Magnus. He had a vague recollection of Magnus coming to sit at his bed a few times as well, now somehow the emperor of Italy, again without a fight. He'd offered equally empty promises of glory, riches and power, as though a man who couldn't stand would wish for anything more than a good pair of legs. One offered him spiritual wonders, the other worldly ones. He wasn't particularly interested in either.

The greatest pain was realising he'd never ride again.

The only pleasant memory over the winter of his convalescence was the servant girl who'd brought him strange-tasting brews. They took some of the pain away, but they gave him dreams that seemed so real he woke up wondering why he was in a palace and not on his cosy farm. Before the next cup, he'd lie in a fugued stupor, unsure what was a dream and what wasn't, and when she wouldn't bring any more, telling him fearfully that the doctor had said he'd drunk too much, he realised he didn't even have power over a serving girl.

And he couldn't even be a farmer.

"At last!" Baccus called out as they pulled up to the city gates of Aqualaie.

Andragathius looked out of the carriage as they trundled through the town. It was a nice place, but one that Magnus had commandeered as a staging post for his giant war with his cousin and so everything about it was geared for the ten thousand or more men staged in the camp nearby. The smell of hundreds of cooking fires, latrines and leftovers, was a familiar, if not entirely welcome, aroma.

The basilica was nothing like the one in Treverorum, but Magnus still sat on a big chair on a raised dais as though he was divine. Being an emperor suited him, but Andragathius' entrance was equally as grand, as he was carried on a chair borne by four slaves. Those who didn't know he was just a former master of cavalry and what had happened to his back, might have thought he was Theodosius, come from Constantinople to discuss a power-sharing treaty.

Despite Baccus trying to persuade him to stay reclining, Andragathius would not stay seated for people to think he was a complete cripple. He'd learned to use the sticks quite well–except, he'd never practised with them on flagstones as smooth as a mirror. As soon as he had all of his weight on them, one slipped and he only just managed not to fall flat on his face in front of everybody. Through the searing pain, he tried to pull himself straight, but when he looked down at his right foot, he saw it was twisted half way around, pointing at his left one. No matter how he tried to get it turned back, or to twist his hip to swing it, he couldn't get it straight.

Seeing him struggle and perhaps wanting to spare him the ignominy of becoming a spectacle for the able-bodied men in his court, Magnus came down to embrace him, an honour an emperor did not bestow on most men. "Everything I have in Italy, I have because of you," Magnus said loud enough for everyone to hear, "for what you did in the mountains."

Andragathius wasn't really listening, though. He could see that there was only one chair on the dais, and that was not a good sign. If Elen was still in Treverorum, Magnus would be making plans to face his cousin without the restraint of an advisor whose words of caution could keep him in check. If there was a way to prevent a confrontation between the two halves of the empire, it would be Elen who would find a way. He'd never found out exactly what she'd done in Segontium, but with the sword point shaped hole Magnus had in his cloak afterwards, he had his suspicions that she was more than a match for her husband, and if Magnus had left her alone with her lover together in Treverorum, it probably meant he'd given up on her. Not a good sign at all.

"Not only are you one of my closest friends, you are one of my most valued commanders," Magnus said, continuing to espouse his platitudes while gripping Andragathius' shoulders. "I wish to honour the sacrifice you have made for me by giving you an even greater command than you ever wished for yourself."

Any other man would have been deeply honoured to hear such words spoken to them by an emperor. Andragathius' thought was that he didn't really want to be involved in what was coming. "I... err... as master of cavalry, I think my days are done," he said.

Magnus nodded. "But you can still command, can you not?"

"Not from the back of a horse," Andragathius replied.

"Granted, but you are my most trusted man. Master of cavalry, no longer, with sadness, I agree, but admiral of the Adriatic Fleet is a bit of a promotion, don't you think?"

As he realised Magnus wanted him to be on a ship, not just for a sea crossing, but to stay on one for days and weeks at a time, what little strength he had left in his legs left him and he slumped back into his slave chair.

"What do you say?" Magnus asked.

Andragathius looked up and saw a flash of desperation on Magnus' face. He couldn't deny the emperor now, not as he was amassing his strength for the battle to come. "A ship is not a horse," he tried.

"But they do have their similarities," Magnus smiled.

In the short silence, Andragathius wondered how long he'd last if he said no. "An honour I can hardly believe," he said, and saw how Magnus almost wilted with relief.

The man who'd won every battle he'd ever entered wasn't at all confident he was going to win the most important one of all.

"Admiral Andragathius, commander of the Imperial Adriatic Fleet," Magnus announced to the small assembly, pushing out his cloak so it twirled out behind him. The stone walls did a good job of amplifying the applause, but just the thought of being on a ship was enough to make him curse.

He felt that instead of being rewarded, he was being punished for surviving the arrow.

XXI

AQUAILEIA. SUMMER 388

The air had changed. It felt like a storm was about to break.

It was close now. The final confrontation was drawing nearer with a momentum and inevitability all of its own. Magnus could do as much about it, as preventing the dawn rising on a day he didn't want to see. They were at the point of choosing battle sites now, ready for a fight that would either leave him the undisputed master of the whole empire, known forever as Magnus the Great... or his head on a spike. Theo's choice of confrontation meant there could be no other outcome.

The safety that the walls of Aquileia had offered all winter, was far behind his army now. A few days earlier, he'd watched a little more than half of his forces march north to the site they'd found at Poetovio, where they'd block the northern route into the mountains.

Stripped of half of his force, he felt oddly vulnerable.

From the camp his six thousand men had occupied for nearly a week, he looked across the river at the town of Emona silhouetted against the setting sun.

Next to him, Fraomar spat a curse at its inhabitants. "We will have to leave men behind us to protect our rear."

"Unless the garrison of Emona decides to follow us," Magnus added.

"Bah," Fraomar scoffed, unconcerned. "A few men on the road a few miles away and we'll have plenty of warning if they plan to bother us."

Magnus nodded his approval.

The thousand soldiers inside against Magnus' remaining six thousand weren't any kind of threat in numbers, but it meant that he was opposed. That a town had shut its gates and chosen Theodosius over him, or maybe even Valentinian, didn't sit well at all. "But not all bad news." He tapped the note he'd received from Andragathius. In his new role in command of the navy, the Batavi had staved off Theodosius' ships and had them pinned to the south.

"He didn't find Valentinian and Justina, though."

Having the young emperor in his power would have been a priceless bargaining tool, but it wasn't to be. They had probably crossed back into Italy; a problem he'd have to deal with later.

"It matters not," Fraomar smiled. "You flushed them out like turds once before. You can do the same again," he said in the straight-talking way the Goths were known for, "but we should drink wine for your new admiral because thanks to him, we won't be fighting on two fronts."

"Is that all that is making you nervous?" his master of infantry asked.

He wasn't sure if Fraomar was gently mocking him or was genuinely concerned, but couldn't help a smile.

"Scouts?"

Magnus nodded. As many men as he could spare were out looking for a place to the east to arrange his forces. Others were ranging out even further, to offer gold to detachments of Theodosius' army so they would come and fight for Magnus instead. He didn't say it to Fraomar, seeing as he was one himself, but although Goths could be easily bought, they could never really be trusted.

"Double crossers?" Fraomar asked, pressing Magnus' thoughts away. "Aye. Not what you want in the middle of an army, but keep a guard on them. Have them surrender their weapons in camp, and put them in the front lines when the fighting starts. Or, if you really can't trust them, keep them unarmed and away from any action; no good for you in battle, but at least then they won't be fighting against us."

Magnus clasped Fraomar's shoulder. "I am lucky to have you."

"Aye, you are."

"And you are not nervous?"

He shrugged. "I am quite interested to see this last fight of yours. This last battle the empire will ever see. I've been a soldier for more than half of my life, so I can't believe it, but it should be good to watch. If you do the same to your cousin as you did with Gratian and Valentinian, I will enjoy watching the birth of such a legend."

Horns blew. Incoming riders. Magnus listened for the shouts from the guards to relay who it was that was approaching. It was Marcellinus, so he shouted, "Let him in!" The order was passed down through the layers of command until those at the bottom pulled the fences of sharpened posts back from the fort entrance. The smile on Marcellinus' face as he trotted towards him set Magnus' heart at ease.

Fraomar handed Andragathius' note back. "More good news," he said.

It was only his brother Magnus trusted enough to send out to choose the site for the battle, the place where he'd meet his fate, and with his brother's happy demeanour, Magnus knew he'd found the location.

Marcellinus' horse was filthy and foaming at the bit, as he'd obviously pushed it to its last reserves to get to Magnus before sunset. "A perfect place to array our forces," he said breathlessly, then quickly added, "Augustus," and sat up a bit straighter. "Wide and open enough for you to easily manoeuvre and cover whatever attack Theodosius can attempt. Behind a shallow part of the river, thick trees to the rear. Near Siscia."

It sounded like just what Magnus was looking for. "How far?"

"Four days at a push."

"And how far away is our cousin?"

"Easily more than a week, perhaps closer to two... at a guess."

Magnus didn't like guesses, but trusted that Marcellinus was competent enough in the ways of war to know what he was doing.

Official duty done, Marcellinus slipped out of his saddle, winced at how much his legs and hips ached from his long ride, and despite the purple cloak over Magnus' shoulders, embraced him as a brother. "Emona holds for Theodosius?" he asked, surprised.

"Or for Valentinian," Magnus shrugged, which made his brother laugh.

"Never mind. It was good for the men to rest here for these days, and when we come back this way, you'll be the one and only emperor, so the heads of their commanders will be flying over the walls before they've even got the gates open!"

His brother always had the knack of being able to cheer him up. Some light words were good for a heavy heart, but the thought of assuming such power, such responsibility, was almost too much to contemplate. It also meant that those in Emona had no faith he'd win.

"We will go north tomorrow," Magnus said. "You'll oversee the defences at Poetovio."

"You have ten days at least," Marcellinus said dismissively. "Your most trusted scouts told me this. Talking of which, I met your favourite person, your wife's brother. He serves you well these days. He was far to the east."

At the idea of the little weasel being in his army, Magnus almost sneered.

"So relax, breathe, brother. Drink wine and enjoy your ride east towards glory. Just keep the men rested!"

To Fraomar, Magnus said, "Give out the order. At dawn tomorrow, we march east."

"Sir!" Fraomar snapped and hit his balled fist to his chest.

Despite Marcellinus' uplifting words, the mood was tense over the next few days, as Magnus' half of the army marched through the hills of Illyricum. First thing every morning was always the worst part of the day, as it was when the number of deserters was read out. As they got closer to Theo, it was always more than the day before. A couple had been caught and without Magnus' permission, had been nailed to crosses just outside the fort gates. The torture was supposed to act as a deterrent to anyone else contemplating trying to slip away, but Magnus wanted his six thousand men to be in a determined, jovial mood, looking forward to the fight, the victory of which was already a foregone conclusion. Starting their daily march with the agonised screams of their comrades in their ears was not the best way to achieve that.

It was a hard march, eighteen miles a day on average, but just as Marcellinus had said, it took four days to get to the place he'd found near Siscia. Birds sang, the wide glade was full of flowers in the short grass. Everything was green and vibrant. It seemed a tranquil place for women to come for an afternoon of lounging in the summer sun, safe enough to let children run around, barely supervised. Magnus had come to turn it into a place of death and destruction.

Despite walking since the crack of dawn, the engineers were already almost finished digging the defensive ditches in a large rectangle and Magnus breathed in the smell of the freshly disturbed clay. It was a special scent and it took him back to the days of his childhood, when he'd only dreamed of the flowing tails of the draco, not the purple cloak.

So close to the enemy, all of them hacked away at the earth in full armour, but by Marcellinus' count they had the better part of a week to get everything ready, perhaps longer, and as Valens had found out at great cost to the empire, exhausted men didn't fight well. To learn that lesson had cost two-thirds of Rome's standing army in a single day at Adrianople, so he gave the order that they could work bare-backed. As soon as he'd spoken, though, something moved against the line of trees behind them. With a hammering heart, he was about to shout a warning, but it was just a spooked deer. As he willed his heart to slow down, he realised he was a lot more nervous than he could allow the men to see.

With a good part of his guard in tow, he rode out to look at the topography around the camp near where the vanguard had taken up sentry positions. He took a few steps into the trees. Tangled young growth, so no chance of anyone riding through it. Then he checked the depth of the river and the height of the banks. Ideally, the water would be a bit deeper and the banks higher, but Marcellinus had said that this was the best place, and as he listened to the sounds of trees being felled to make the defences with, he knew he was where he'd meet his cousin.

Merobaudes, his master of infantry, the man he'd raised to the consulship, the only man to be so honoured three times, was on his horse near the command tent, waiting patiently for an order. Magnus was quite pleased that he had none to give, although he still couldn't stop the feeling of deep unease.

For the rest of the day, soldiers filed into the half-finished fort. When the lumbering wagons of the baggage train and the rear guard came in and the tents went up, he felt a little more secure, but still not confident.

No battle was ever ordinary, but in all of the fights he'd commanded over his long military life, he'd never been in one where one Roman army was pitched against another. He wondered if that was what was worrying him. He looked around at his busy soldiers. Apart from the officers, there was hardly a Roman citizen between them. Most were Gauls and Goths, complemented by some Franks and the detachment of men from Segontium he'd brought from Britannia. The days when Rome was protected by a dozen iron-strong legions were in the distant past. Armies these days were made up of foreign fighters who could be cajoled to hold a sword and guard a wall with promises of gold. If he was to beat his cousin, that was the first thing he intended to rectify.

He tapped his horse with a foot and it turned so he could look over the river, towards the east, the direction Theo would be coming from... and saw movement.

"Riders!" someone shouted, which prompted those with the horns to blow an alarm and to a man Magnus' army noisily dropped tools, grabbed weapons and sprang to attention, awaiting orders. It was only Kenon though, followed by his handful of scouts. Magnus watched how easily his horse waded through the river, the water was not even halfway up its legs at the deepest part, and it easily jumped up the far back.

The guards at the perimeter let him in and Magnus' personal guard parted to let the runt ride up to him.

"Augustus, Theodosius approaches," he said. "A week away at least. But he is slow and there are many desertions."

Theodosius was moving slower than what Marcellinus had said, but Kenon's intelligence was many days younger. Maybe it had rained in the mountains in the east and slowed his cousin down. There could be many reasons, but at least now he'd have plenty of time to fill his side of the river bank with a forest of sharpened stakes and get plenty of large rocks thrown into the water to make it harder for Theodosius' horsemen to cross. All the advantages seemed to be falling to him.

"Also, I have a whole detachment of riders ready to come over and fight for you. They wait not far from here. I promised I would bring them gold."

Magnus would give all of the gold in the empire if enough men changed their allegiance from Theodosius to give him victory. "How many riders?"

"About a hundred and fifty."

Magnus nodded. Not an insignificant number. Kenon had done good work. Maybe he'd been a bit too harsh on the boy. "I will give you the gold. Half now, the rest after the fight."

"Of course, Augustus,' Kenon said, as though he was a normal officer and not just his wife's brother fobbed off with a horse and a handful of men to command. Victor playing in his sand pit had more authority and was more useful, yet he was a little impressed at how far the wretch had come from the day he'd nearly had him crucified. Maybe being part of his entourage was good for a man.

He waved to Merobaudes, who went to fetch the coin. It was a bulging bag he handed over. If it was any other man, Magnus might have been a little suspicious at the greedy way Kenon eyed it, as though it was the finest whore he'd ever seen and he could barely control himself. Not Kenon, though. He was far too soft and timid to have any thoughts about not serving Magnus properly. The only reason he'd become a scout was so he could get as far away from people and the complicated politics at court. He would not be involved in intrigues. The only ones he killed were little girls.

As though Kenon couldn't stand to be near Magnus for a heartbeat longer, after his salute he rode through the camp so fast, it was close to being reckless.

Fraomar shook his head, unimpressed, and Magnus considered the look the runt had given the gold. It had been smug... self-satisfied, as though Kenon had won some secret victory only he knew about. Or maybe not. He dismissed it. It was just Kenon. No one cared about Kenon.

Magnus continued his ride slowly around the busy camp again, a confidence in his heart starting to bud like a tree after a long winter. He looked around at the men who would fight for him in the next week or so. He marvelled at how quickly the smiths had got their forges up and running and were working on all the pieces of horse tack and armour that needed repairing after the few day's march from Emona. He wished he had the special sword his brother had given him in his hand. To Him Unconquered. He hoped that Edern was looking after it properly in Britannia, keeping it out of the never-ending rain, at least.

He stayed a while to listen to the relaxing sounds of hammers on anvils, then nudged his horse to take him to the gate facing the river and stopped before the rigid-looking gate commander. "I am expecting riders to come in before sunset," he said. "They are coming over to our side, so don't engage. Welcome them."

"Yes, sir," the soldier snapped.

"Good man," Magnus smiled.

He ordered a couple of centurions to tell their men to relax. As the battle was a week away at the earliest, it would be much better for them to lie under the sun with bare chests than to sweat in full armour. He needed them all at full strength for when the fight finally happened.

Pitched in the centre of the camp, where the principia would be in a fort, his huge tent was almost finished. Fraomar was waiting for him. Over the desk, he was putting the finishing touches to a big map that Magnus would use to better plan the defences. There was plenty of time for that though. He draped his cloak over the back of a chair, and it felt wonderful to take his outer shirt of scaled armour off. He could breathe easier.

"So this is it?" Fraomar said, sweeping his hand over the map. "This will be where the last battle the empire will ever see will take place? The war to end all wars?"

"You speak as though you don't believe it."

"Men fight," he said. "Always have, always will."

The old foederati commander had said he was bored with guard duty in Treverorum and wanted to be part of the battle that would make Magnus sole emperor. Magnus hadn't hesitated to leave Nannienus in charge of the Rhine defences and welcomed Fraomar in Aquileia as master of infantry. He was capable and qualified in the role, but if Magnus was honest with himself, he knew Fraomar had agreed to take on the role and come south only because the rewards for fighting for such a man would be immeasurable. Magnus wondered what he was secretly hoping would be his payment, but decided that it probably wouldn't matter; after he'd won, he'd be in a position to grant almost anything to anyone. At the thought, a shuddering thrill coursed through him. He really was only a few days away from being as powerful as Constantine had been–as Caesar himself.

Would he raise Fraomar to Augustus, to control Italy? If Marcellinus was to have the East, Fraomar would be a good, pragmatic ruler. Yet the thought of handing almost equal power to another man made him uneasy.

"We're not fighting then?" Fraomar asked with a look of puzzlement.

"My scouts say Theodosius is many days away. A week at least."

Pewter cup of wine paused at his lips, Fraomar set his cup on the table at the side of the map. "Which scouts?"

"Marcellinus told me."

"And who told Marcellinus?"

"Kenon."

"Bah," he scoffed. "Why you put so much trust in that little runt, I will never know!"

Magnus wasn't quite sure how to react to words that from almost anyone else he'd deem as insubordination.

The worried look still on his face, Fraomar went to stand at the tent entrance, and looked out as though he was trying to taste the air. "Something doesn't seem right to me," he said.

A heavy weight settling on his chest, Magnus went to stand next to him and watched as Fraomar climbed onto his horse. Once he'd got his balance to stand on the saddle, he looked out over to the other side of the river.

"Not right at all," Fraomar mused. He pointed to the near distance. "Look."

From where he was, Magnus could see the flock of startled birds fly from their perches in the trees on the other side of the river.

"Get me a horn!" Fraomar shouted at his nearest attendant. "A *horn*!"

A lad started to scurry off, but Magnus stopped him. "It's just some deserters from Theodosius' army. Kenon just told me. I am expecting them."

"Fuck that little bastard," Fraomar spat. "Get up on your saddle so you can see what I see."

It was an order given by a superior to someone he commanded, but Magnus was too panicked to bring Fraomar up on it. As he tried to keep his balance on his horse, horns blew in response to the fast-approaching riders. They came and full tilt, bursting out from behind the trees on the other side of the river. And they kept coming. Hundreds of them. If Kenon hadn't told him they were deserters paid with his gold coming to pledge their swords to him, he would have assumed it was about to be a real attack.

They splashed through the river without slowing.

"Tell me that's not a full attack!" Fraomar spat.

They were no ordinary riders, either. Dark-skinned, riding their horses with their legs, and wearing strangely circular hats, Fraomar spat another curse. They were Huns. Kenon had neglected to mention that. As the men who'd been allowed to lounge in the river to cool down were shot in the backs with arrows fired from horseback, Magnus joined in with the curses.

He slid down into his saddle, and snatched the horn from the servant's hand, but others were already blowing, and the shouts of panic had started to ring out through the camp, mixing with those of pain from outside. He tossed the horn to the ground and at the top of his voice yelled, "Attack!" But looking around, no one was ready. It seemed half the men didn't even have their armour on. He didn't either. Just his padded shirt, and the first Huns had already made it across the river.

"The little bastard," Magnus seethed. The realisation that he'd been betrayed by Kenon, the little shit he'd raised far beyond what his station should be just to keep his wife happy, hit him like a mortal blow. It didn't seem possible. The runt who'd pissed himself when he'd been fished out of the river with the Votadini, had done some kind of deal with the Huns! It seemed unreal.

As he strapped his helmet under his chin and drew his sword, his

Moor bodyguards closed ranks around him, shouting orders among themselves, their commanders trying to second guess what Magnus' next action was going to be. "With me!" he shouted.

"Augustus!" one of them shouted. "Your armour!"

There was no time to run back to his tent and fumble around with his lorica squamata, so he ignored the call and charged towards the camp perimeter in just his padded shirt. At the gates, he shouted, "Keep them in the river! Do not let them get a foothold on our side!"

But the Huns had already ranged around to the ground in front of the camp, assembling there to protect the others who were still crossing. Unlike an army forming rank, they were all constantly moving, a seething mass of angry horses and Magnus' had no idea where to look, as though he couldn't focus his eyes. The chaos of it was an ugly sight, but even though there seemed to be no coordination, the bastards were deadly accurate with the arrows, even though they were shot from the back of a galloping horse.

With his sword raised high, Magnus hoped he looked the part to spur courage into his panicked men, but without his special cloak spilling down his back he felt near naked.

His guards, Gildo's best men from Africa, some hundred and twenty strong, fanned out on their horses around him.

"Formation! Formation!" Magnus bellowed. "Stop them getting a foothold on our side!"

"How many of them are there?" he shouted. He obviously couldn't trust his scouts, so for all he knew, Theo's army could be following right behind.

To fight against horses, especially the lightning-quick ones of the Huns, he needed his own riders, so screamed for his cavalry to get out of another gate and ride around to engage them from the side. Before he'd even finished shouting, he saw that about fifty of his riders had already readied their mounts and were charging, swords drawn. It was gladdening to know that he had such capable soldiers fighting for him, although barely half the horses had armour on them.

Magnus was close enough to see the scars on the Hun's ugly faces, marks the savages gave to their newborn babies so they knew pain before their mother's milk... and the strange way they seemed to be raised above their saddles so they were standing on something.

His Moor guards, aware that Magnus was the main target of the arrows, crowded around him, shields raised. They protected him, but blocked his view, and in the confusion and press of horses, he was pushed from the fray. He had to order those in front of him to drop their shields so he could see.

The Huns had a strange way of fighting. He'd heard about it many times, but seeing it in front of him was something else. They charged in sweeping arcs of riders, close enough to loose a few well-aimed arrows, but they moved so fast that they were elusive targets for those trying to fight back. When they saw Magnus' cavalry coming at them, they didn't think to engage, just turned around like cowards and galloped off like flies avoiding a swat, but then they peeled off and others were charging... and arrows flew... and men fell. Even if Magnus' riders weren't taking arrows, they were fatally confused. All their training was for full engagement, not dealing with seemingly uncoordinated lightning sorties and feigned retreats. Some faced the wrong way and rode into their colleagues. Two men even knocked each other from their saddles.

Next to Magnus, a horse took an arrow through its armour into its flank. It raised its legs to kick at the air, its wild hooves dangerously close to Magnus' head.

Screams came from the fight as more Hun arrows found horse's hides, and in a desperate panic, they turned away from a threat that couldn't be defended against, pressed into their own ranks, making it harder for the others to manoeuvre.

Trying to muster in the camp, in amongst the tents and supply wagons, wouldn't work, and they'd already lost the ground between the camp and the river. And Theo's army could be just behind. 'Charge and attack' were well-used words in Magnus' vocabulary, but now he voiced another, one he'd never had to shout at any man he'd commanded before. "Retreat!"

He ordered it a few more times and heard the command repeated through the ranks, so shouted an order at his cavalry to stay between his foot soldiers and the Huns to protect them. He knew they'd be leaving almost everything behind, but couldn't risk Theo catching him.

Slowly, with more men dying all the time, Magnus' men made their hurried way to the safety of the trees, all as spooked as the deer he'd seen earlier.

He pulled up at the trees and shouted at those running to him to hurry, that they were safe and that they'd regroup soon. But even to his own ears, his words seemed hollow, as the whole camp and all of its supplies, along with the wounded, had been left for the Huns.

He noticed that his horse was agitated and limping and looked down to see an arrow sticking out of its back leg. It was shallow, in at an oblique angle, and it was sobering to know how close he'd come to taking one. Being de-horsed in that confused melee wouldn't have ended well. It was very warming how many men came to offer their own mounts for him to take, as though it was a great honour to give their horse away to their emperor.

Magnus looked back at his retreating army. The Huns seemed content to hold the river crossing rather than to keep attacking, but many were in the camp, ransacking it, starting fires. All that the fleeing soldiers hadn't brought with them was lost.

"I want reports," he shouted, but to no one in particular, trusting that whoever was in earshot would pass the command along. "I need to know what is coming behind them."

If Theo's heavy cavalry were about to come charging across the river it would be a complete rout.

He watched the men come in, some without helmets, others without shields or armour. Normally such dereliction of duty would have resulted in strict punishment, but today no man would feel the lash of the whip for losing his equipment. The blame for everything rested fully on Magnus' shoulders. Then he remembered that he was without his lorica squamata. When he realised he'd retreated without his purple cloak, his heart almost stopped dead in his chest. At the thought of what the savages would do to it when they found it, he was almost ready to charge back at them alone.

Merobaudes undid his armour and handed it over. "It's a good fit," he said.

"*You* need it," Magnus shrugged.

"I serve the empire," he said, holding a steely gaze. "Take it!"

At Magnus' slow reaction, Fraomar nudged his horse against Magnus', got the armour over his shoulders and leaned over to help do up the toggles at his side. Fighting in another man's armour was always a bad idea, as for it to work properly it had to fit like a second skin, but all Magnus needed was to protect himself from arrows, and for that, Merobaudes' would do fine. Without his cloak, he still felt lost, though.

As he adjusted the armour, trying to tug it away from the pinch points where the shape of Merobaudes body differed from Magnus', he wondered at how all the shifting alliances seemed bewilderingly confusing. An enemy like Merobaudes, who Magnus had spent years dreaming of killing slowly, was now risking his life with no outer armour in front of the Huns, while his own wife's brother had gone from a nervous wreck to almost single-handed costing Magnus everything. Not knowing who he could trust, which of his men were ready to protect him, and which were waiting to sink a blade between his ribs, was a dizzying sensation.

"All is not lost," Fraomar said with a confidence that seemed well out of place, although his tone was strained.

"They caught us by surprise, that's all," Merobaudes shrugged.

"Thanks to a cowardly betrayal. We should let the men know that Kenon deceived us, so they don't think it was just…" And then he stopped.

"Incompetence?" Magnus suggested. He saw a few of his men, stragglers, obviously wounded, trying to get to the tree line, so sent some of his guards out to protect them.

His options seemed limited. Every fibre in his body screamed at him to attack, to purge the empire of the scum that were the Huns, but to do that he'd have to try and fight his way back into his own camp. And he knew exactly how well his engineers had dug the ditches and arranged defences of sharpened sticks.

"We regroup or march north?" Magnus asked.

"None of the intelligence we have about Theodosius can be trusted," Fraomar said, echoing Magnus' fears. "Not numbers. Not even where he is."

Merobaudes nodded his agreement. "We could reform ranks, but we could end up charging straight at Theodosius' main force instead of just these Huns, and that will be our six thousand against his twelve."

"And we've lost the river crossing," Fraomar added.

"North to Marcellinus at Poetovio, then," Magnus said, "but don't call it a retreat."

His two generals kicked their horses ready to run, but reigned in as soon as they saw that Magnus hadn't moved.

"We'll wait for as many men as we can," Magnus said, pointing at the infantry still making their way to them. "Every man we save now will be one more to fight Theo with."

He was twitching to turn and run, but watched as a sizable detachment of his cavalry charged at a group of Huns who were trying to pick off fleeing foot soldiers. Their horses were faster than his… and in that charge Magnus also learned that the Huns could shoot arrows behind them while they were riding away. Then his riders had been lured too close to the Hun's main group, and before they could wheel around were caught in a hail of arrows.

"Augustus!" Fraomar said impatiently.

Magnus was about to give in, but saw a man with his cloak and his hands. Not only had he managed to save it in the midst of the raid, he'd respected the cloth so much that he even folded it. With it around his shoulders, he could turn the tide of the battle. "You shall be rewarded!" Magnus called out in joy. "Richly!"

The man didn't get to him though. Cloak still held out in his hands reverentially, he slipped to his knees. When he fell forwards, Magnus saw the arrow sticking out of his back. It had gone deep.

"Send riders to Marcellinus," he shouted. "Get as many cavalry down here as he can spare. With supplies!"

XXII

Kenon listened to the sounds of battle in the distance. He should have been glad that he was paying back his bitterest enemy, a revenge he'd waited years to exact, but all he felt was a weighty worry that his soul would be eternally condemned for unleashing the godless Huns in Christian lands.

Even with no understanding of the ways of the church, using Satan's spawn to fight for God seemed very wrong. It was Theodosius' command though. For the greater good, the worst things could be done, the Bishop of Mediolanum had told him that.

He looked at the men around the small fire they'd made at the edge of the woods, and his stomach churned. Even from a distance, the sight of the Huns disgusted him, so actually being in the presence of some made him feel as though he'd fallen into a latrine pit. Their swarthy skin and beady eyes gave them a rattish look, but what disturbed him most was how close they were to their horses, as though part of their soul was animal… and therefore not entirely human. They spent so long on horseback that they even walked with an odd waddle, as their legs had taken the shape of the saddle.

And how they reeked. A Roman with even the lowest modicum of dignity went to the bathhouse once a day to have the dirt sweated out and scraped off his skin. The bow-legged bastards from the grasslands stank as though they were unaware of the concept of hot water and a strigil. Vile creatures.

He tried to recall the scent of Ursula's perfume, but didn't want to sully her memory even by just thinking of her while in the company of such brutes.

It was no companionable sharing of the fire. The Huns were here in case Kennan had double-crossed them. If they were to ride into a trap, the archers a few paces away would kill him.

The five other scouts that Kenon commanded seemed equally as uncomfortable, especially Maurus who guarded the gold they'd tricked from Magnus. Kenon looked at the bulging bag. A few short years ago he would have taken all those coins and in the taverns and brothels of the nearest settlement would have drunk and screwed himself silly, but what he dreamed of now was worth much more than any coin could buy. He had a wife he loved, and who loved him. Soon they'd have a whole province to govern together. Imagining that they would make their own little Britannia in Amorica still had an unreal quality to it.

Soldiers, about to become veterans after their next fight, had been granted their plots of land there, and from the two hundred Goth women Theodosius would send, they'd have their pick for wives. Never mind that he was baptised now, cleansed, it would be a paradise on earth. And it was almost within his grasp—as long as Theodosius won.

He listened again to the shouts and screams from across the river, the Huns he'd set against Magnus' completely unprepared army, were sowing chaos and causing casualties. With every scream Theodosius' victory got closer.

One of the Huns spoke some Latin. "So half your world thinks that this Magnus is emperor?" he asked, sounding confused. "But another half thinks that this Theodosius is emperor?"

"Yes," Kenon said. It seemed a fair approximation of the situation.

"We know who our emperor is," he grinned. "We only have one. You fight for this Magnus Maximus?"

"He *thinks* I do," Kenon answered guardedly.

"Yes, thinks. But you really fight for the other one?"

"Theodosius, yes."

"This is not clean. This is dirty," the Hun said.

To be called unclean by such a man was a deep insult. After his baptism Kenon was cleaner than the Huns could even conceive. But perhaps he did have a point. Politics was truly a filthy art. "Magnus is nothing but a usurper," he offered, but trying to explain such a concept to a man with no real understanding of the intricacies of civilization was probably a waste of breath.

"What is this? I don't know this word."

"He just took power for himself, not because it was granted to him."

"Because he is stronger? He can fight better than others?" the man scoffed.

Kenon nodded.

"Do you know what we call a man like this in our land?"

"What?" Kenon asked, uninterested, but he forced himself to at least appear polite.

"Emperor!" he laughed. When he'd translated it to the others, they cackled between themselves. Kenon's skin crawled at the chorus of guttural hacking, and at how the scars they all had on their faces made them even uglier when they grinned.

It really did not sit well that Theodosius was using Huns for his fight. Surely an agent of God shouldn't need to tarnish his battlefields with the worst, most degenerate, of the barbarians. Any glory that came from it would surely be tainted.

He looked at his men again. Four of them were staunch supporters of Theodosius, their pouches full of the Eastern Emperor's gold, and now with a fat bag of Magnus'. They were all looking forward to the land and wives in Gaul that Theodosius had promised: apart from Fidelis. His face showed scorn. Contempt. Not for just the Huns, but also for Kenon, and the raid against Magnus he'd just arranged. An insult to God and all that is good, he'd called it. He wasn't wrong about that, but he'd also complained that he couldn't present himself to Saint Peter, when the time came, with dishonour in his heart for breaking his sacred vow. The only way Fidelis could get back to Magnus without being suspected of being involved in the betrayal was to go back with Kenon's head.

Fidelis had to die.

Kenon was so tantalisingly close to having everything he wanted. He was not going to let anyone take it away from him.

He felt the handle of the knife at his hip and tried to undo the knot of conflict in his mind. Killing in cold blood was the weightiest sin, one that would damn a man's soul for all of eternity. But Fidelis was loyal to the usurper. As well as saving his own skin, killing him would mean one less soldier standing against the true God-chosen emperor, whose mission was to make Christianity stronger in the face of all who threatened the one true faith.

For the greater good, the worst things could be done.

He went over to a tree and hiked his tunic up, pretending to take a piss. It wasn't his cock he took out though, and before he thought too much about it and talked himself out of it, he crept up behind Fidelis and carefully reached towards him, knife in hand. But he couldn't do it.

Despite the Bishop of Rome performing the ceremony, despite marrying Ursula and spending a week with her in bed, he'd never managed to rid himself of the suspicion that it hadn't been a real baptism. That the bishop, the emperor, and the Pope hadn't deemed him worthy of true absolution; that it had been an empty ceremony, a gilded coin, only gold on the outside.

And, he couldn't risk living with the guilt of taking a life again. Not after the years of torment from the poor little girl. "Give me the gold," he said to Maurus.

Fidelis twisted away from Kenon, and looked around at the others at the fire, wondering what was wrong.

"What? Why?" he asked, gripping the bag tighter.

"Because we have already been gifted enough by Theodosius. And this bag is from Magnus, so it is filthy."

"Looks bright and shiny enough to me," Maurus said, but at Kenon's threatening look he reluctantly handed it over.

Kenon marvelled at the power he had. Maurus had just given back enough gold to make his life very comfortable for many years, He still hadn't got used to having men to command.

"We all agreed to kill you," Kenon said to Fidelis. "Go and give this back to Magnus. With it, he will be convinced of your loyalty to him and no harm will come to you."

As Fidelis' confusion turned to fear, he got up, grabbed the gold and was riding away before he'd even got properly in his saddle.

As he disappeared, Kenon wondered if he was really a Christian now.

XXIII

It had been a difficult decision for Magnus to decide when to give up on the wounded who hadn't made it from the camp to the safety of the trees. Huns weren't known for the mercy they showed to those they'd captured. It was also equally hard to decide when to stop marching that evening. Panic pushed him on like the blade Elen had had set at his back the last time they'd been in Britannia. His instinct was to put as much distance between them and the Huns as possible, but building defences for their camp in the dark was far from ideal.

As the sun was beginning to set, he called for the men to assemble on a grassy hill and get trees down so they could get a rough perimeter defence up. Watching the men work, Magnus had the sinking feeling that he'd have to set men to guard as much against those trying to leave the camp as the Huns trying to get into it. He couldn't blame them. Their commander, their emperor, had failed them and they had a very hard march ahead before they were safe. It would be very tempting to slip away to Theo and be assimilated into the side they believed would win, one with plenty of food, and proper defences to spend the night inside of. To stop them, Magnus knew he had to inspire them, but the only words he had to offer that evening were if they didn't walk far and fast enough, they'd be dead.

Felix, the bishop of Trier, was doing his part, laying his hands on the shoulders of any man he could find, intoning over and over, "Although the righteous fall seven times, they rise again!"

Morale was more important than gold now, and so the bishop was priceless. Magnus wondered if he'd been wrong for the past few years about distrusting him, assuming he was an agent of Ambrosius. He'd trusted Kenon. Having no idea who was loyal and who wasn't, was like finding out that the mosaic which had had a clear picture and pattern, was just a pile of tesserae.

As darkness fell, his fears rose. Some said just two hundred Huns had crossed the river, others swore it was closer to a thousand. None had seen any other elements of Theo's army, though, only the Huns, but whatever number they were, they'd managed to rout all of Magnus' six thousand... which at roll call was now down to under five and a half.

He ordered no fires, but anyone pursuing them would have known exactly where they were by the screams of the men having arrows pulled out, or pushed through, their bodies.

The first few days of the march to Marcellinus were the worst of Magnus' life. Five and a half thousand men with a severe lack of equipment and food, only what could be foraged and pillaged from farms along the route, men sleeping in the open, on the ground in the rain, and twenty miles of marching on empty stomachs, day after day. Then hours of building defences sturdy enough to keep any enemies out, and far enough away from camp that no arrows could be shot in to land on sleeping men.

The scouts on the flanks were kept busy, but their swords weren't bloodied by Huns, only those trying to desert. Many died this way. How many more managed to slip out and make their way back south to join Theodosius ranks, he didn't know. He didn't waste time with the morning roll call.

On the first day, he'd given his horse to a pair of wounded men and as he trudged along, his mind wandering from one morbid thought to another like a wild animal pacing in a small cage, he imagined that his army was a single body, and it was limping and bleeding from hundreds of small cuts.

Magnus understood now why some generals chose to die on the battlefield rather than retreat or surrender in shame.

A few miserable days in and some of the Huns overtook them. Instead of fighting, the cowards set fire to farms and the columns of smoke rising into the sky were desperately needed grain and livestock going up in flames. They didn't attack though. Neither Magnus nor his generals had any idea why that should be, as Magnus' men were certainly vulnerable enough. Unless Theo had ordered them not to. Perhaps his cousin knew that a Christian emperor using the worst of the Eastern savages to win his war was not a good look.

His men were already seriously hungry, and after a few days of drinking river water, the inevitable flux ran rife through them, and added to that, those who couldn't keep their wounds clean, fell to fever and if they weren't already dead in the morning, had to be left behind.

Now they were just over five thousand sick men marching north for their lives.

Shouts came from in front. Magnus was instantly alert and his guards immediately pressed around him. They'd indulged him in his long sulk and let him walk, but now they insisted he get onto a horse, both to better command and to be able to flee faster from any threat they couldn't defend against.

The wounded man groaned as he slid off Magnus' horse. Magnus tried his best to ignore the blood all over the saddle.

"Riders incoming," was the message sent back along the line.

Magnus could see those in front take defensive positions, but couldn't see who was coming at them. If Theo's vanguard had managed to outflank him, they were now cut off from Marcellinus' forces.

A path to him was cleared for one of his scouts. "Fifty riders. About two miles out. Running fast," he said.

"Huns?" Magnus asked nervously.

"No, Augustus."

"Heavy cavalry?"

"Yes, Augustus."

Magnus almost fell out of his saddle with the relief of knowing Marcellinus' men had arrived and he almost wept in relief at the sound of the cheer that swept through the men as they knew they were saved. Magnus looked beyond Fraomar and Merobaudes to Felix and gave an appreciative nod.

The next day some of his scouts managed to ambush a band of Huns and when their ugly severed heads were tossed to the ground, the frenzy of hatred as the soldiers jostled to spit on them, then crush them underfoot, showed that they still had some fight left. It wasn't all over.

The next day they made it to a camp Marcellinus had used on his way north and to be inside the ready-made ditch lined with sharpened stakes felt wonderful. The smell of roasting meat from the cows they'd herded in and slaughtered made his stomach twist in knots in hunger. He was not the first to eat though. A young girl on a windy mountainside in a far away land had taught him how to win the hearts of men, and he walked among them, stopping at their fires as they roasted their chunks of fresh meat, recalling as many names as he could.

He actually wished Elen was with him to give him some wise words... although she'd probably just berate him for being so blindly ambitious, and from Elen, his thoughts turned to her brother. If he was ever to catch the little bastard, he'd hammer the nails through his hands and pull the cross up himself. He'd also order a damnatio memoriae to make it as though the runt had never even lived: wiped from history, forgotten forever. A fate most men feared worse than death. Even that wouldn't be enough.

"We'll be with my brother the day after tomorrow," Magnus repeated as he made his way around the camp, gratefully accepting a few morsels of scolding hot meat here and there until he was full.

The walls of Poetovio rising up the hill on the far side of the river was a sight sweet enough to bring a tear to Magnus' eye. They'd survived the near disaster, had time to regroup, and now he could get fire back into his men's hearts before he faced Theo. The shock of being routed by a handful of dirty bastards had surely galvanised them, and they wouldn't allow themselves to be humiliated a second time.

He could still win.

When they got to Marcellinus' camp their dishevelled appearance, days old stubble, missing weapons and walking wounded was no great morale booster for the six thousand under Marcellinus. He ordered double rations for them for two days and sent them in groups to the baths in the city to relax, and more importantly, recuperate. They didn't have too long, though, as scouts kept circling in with reports that Theodosius was quickly approaching, and then he was sighted.

Magnus mused over the memories of all the fights he and his cousin had been in together, hunting the traitor Firmas down through the deserts of Africa, back to how they sparred together with heavy wooden swords under Theodosius the Elder's appraising gaze. Now one of them would have to die. It seemed such a waste. They could have built so much together, made the empire stronger again. Opposed, there was so much they would destroy.

His cousin pitched his army a mile or two down the valley, but although Magnus waited hopefully, no emissary was sent with an offer of parley.

The days drew slowly on, the tension and frustration growing. Marcellinus, as positive as ever, suggested it meant he was open to negotiation, or even that it was because Theo was too afraid to engage. Magnus knew the wait was only because Theo had also learned from Valens' mistake at Adrianople. He would only fight with well-rested men. There would be no negotiation.

At the dawn of the fourth day, the soldiers, already in armour and with weapons ready, were called out into formation to match Theo's movement. Magnus was almost sick with trepidation.

The bishops and priests, led by Felix, offered the men kneeling solemnly before them absolution before they headed out to the battlefield. Magnus wasn't too sure he agreed with the ritual. Men who were eager to offload their sins were those worried they were about to die.

Some twelve thousand of Magnus' men lined up to face Theo's equally large army, but once the rattle of armour had died down, an uneasy quiet settled, as neither front line advanced. It turned into an uneasy stand-off. Soldiers just as reluctant to engage as their emperors were.

As the sun rose higher in the sky and the day's heat grew, Magnus began to sweat and if he was hot just sitting on the back of his horse, then those standing in full armour would be sweltering. Slaves were ordered to pass out water canteens through the lines and laden like over-packed mules, they never stopped running from the stream to the soldiers.

The smell of what nervous men had to do where they stood began to catch Magnus' nose and soon the flies began to cause a nuisance.

The tedium was broken only in the afternoon when one of Magnus' infantry strode to the open space between the formations and was met with the challenger from the opposite ranks. The cheers for both, as they fought to the death, was as though the entire army was fighting. But while it was good that the men weren't mindlessly bored, when Magnus' fighter fell, he judged it a very poor omen. The fact that Theo's didn't make it back to his line without collapsing from his wounds didn't do too much to restore morale.

At sunset, horns were blown and the army trudged solemnly back to camp.

The next day, apart from the one to one combat, the scene was repeated.

At night Magnus and Marcellinus stood on the walls of Poetovio together, looking out at the fires of Theo's camp. Neither could sleep. All discussions about what had happened during the day and what they could do on the following one were done, there was nothing left that needed to be spoken about. All they could do was to wait for the sun to rise.

"After this, I think I will have a villa, back in Hispania," Marcellinus mused. "I will make my own wine and will raise horses until I am too old to ride them."

"You will have a lot to do as my second-in-command before then," Magnus laughed. "With the Eastern Empire added to my domain, it will be far too much for one man to run."

"I don't fancy dealing with the Sassanids, though," he sighed. "Nor the Huns. Maybe I could just be governor of Hispania?"

Something twisted uncomfortably in the pit of Magnus' stomach. He'd just offered Marcellinus the Eastern empire, to rule from the vast palaces of Constantinople, and he'd brushed it aside as though it was a glass of cheap wine. His brother dismissing such an honour was a painful rejection.

He looked at the lights of Theodosius' camp again, cooking fires twinkling through the darkness between them, wondering what else he didn't understand. "At least you will be consul next year," he said quietly.

"There will be plenty of time to talk about it after the battle," Marcellinus said.

Another great honour dismissed.

A few moments of strained silence passed between them before his brother asked, "So we'll have to do it then? No way out of fighting?"

"We sent messengers. He didn't give a reply to a single one."

"Settled by blood, then not diplomacy?"

"Do you think I am a fool to have brought us here to this?" Magnus asked.

"Glory is never given, brother. Glory always has to be earned." They were good, strong words, but seemed a little forced. Something a eunuch would say in the palace to appease a superior. Not words he needed from his brother at that moment.

"Tell me about our father," Marcellinus asked. "It has been long since we spoke of him."

Magnus began one of their favourite stories, but couldn't help the awful sinking feeling that he was recalling meaningful memories to someone on their deathbed looking back at better days in their final moments.

It felt like the dawn took forever to break, as though the sun was reluctant to shine on the day that was to come.

As it slowly rose, Magnus walked through the massing ranks, thousands of perfectly polished helmets catching the morning light. The Seguntienses he'd brought with him from Britannia, saluted him as he passed their ordered rows. They were men who'd been in the fort the day he'd first laid eyes on Elen. That felt like such an impossibly long time ago.

He thought of his wife. Elen of the Roads, or Elen of the Hosts, as she was known in that strange island. Soon she'd be married to Magnus the Great. If God was willing.

In neat lines, the civilised antithesis of the Huns, the first detachments of cavalry rode off to the open ground to the east of the town.

Magnus checked the armour on his horse, pulling at the straps to make sure that the scales over its face were positioned correctly so its vision wasn't obscured. Then, once he was in the saddle, he adjusted himself until he was comfortable, as it might be another long day. One of his attendants held up a canteen of water and he downed it. With his head tilted back, he saw that there was not a cloud in the morning sky. It would be a baking hot summer day and he didn't know when the next opportunity to drink would be. He waved for another canteen and downed that as well, but his stomach clenched and he came perilously close to throwing it back up. The only thing standing between winning the coming fight and disaster was his superior skills in battle and his bravery. If the men were to see their Augustus being sick in front of them, it would be an absolute disaster for morale.

The neat rectangles of his infantry auxiliaries advanced. Thousands of feet stomping forwards in a rhythm, all in coordination with one foot then the next, it was like a hammering heart of some giant mythical creature.

Days had been spent discussing plans, the interplaying array of cavalry and infantry, and every soldier had had the plan related to them and had been practising drills, so everyone knew what was coming and what was expected of them. The very last thing the auxiliaries needed was some strong words from their emperor. Something about reclaiming their valour and dignity with the blood of every last Hun, Magnus thought as he trotted around to the front. The rising sun warmed his face as he rode across the flattened grass to face Theo.

This time there was no idiot running across the open ground, arms flapping like a fledgling trying to take flight, to stop the battle before it was allowed to begin. The thought of Kenon made him angry and he realised he was making his horse nervous by pulling on the reins as they were a rope tightening around the little bastard's neck.

As he rode around the flank he saw that Theo's army in formation looked worryingly like staring into a reflection. Whatever was about to happen, it was going to be an evenly-matched fight. He was keenly aware that it could easily go either way. Rather than superior tactics, fate could be the decider. Or God. And he wondered which cousin the Lord would favour. Theo with his Godless Huns, or Magnus who'd got to where he was by bribing bishops to lie for him.

If there was no clear victory, then the fate of the empire hung in the balance. What he'd promised never to risk, he had brought to be.

He trotted along with Marcellinus, but wished it was his cousin with him at his side rather than his brother.

Just as he pulled up in front of a cohort of infantry, all eyes on their leader, he felt the long-familiar churn in his stomach that nerves often caused. He'd come close to spewing up sometimes, but had always managed to keep it under control–until the most critically important moment of his life. Trying to stop it coming up, some of it went down into his lungs, so when all the water he'd just downed came gushing out in such a fountain, it did so with a choking cough, and for a few moments it was a desperate fight to catch his breath. By the time he'd managed to control himself and had wiped his chin clean, he saw he'd splashed over several men in the first row.

In the muffled whispers and groans as they repeated what had just happened to those behind them, he felt a cold draft waft over him as the fire in men's hearts went out.

"We will end this day together in glory!" Marcellinus shouted, but it was too late. He watched as the men marched forwards, sure that instead of filling their hearts full of courage, he'd left them full of doubt.

Just as was his own.

Cursing himself for handing Theo such a huge advantage, he rode back to his place at the rear, nestled safely in amongst his mounted Moor guards and watched as the wooden blocks he'd moved on the table a few days before had become a little more than ten thousand men riding and walking, closing the space between them, about to unleash death and destruction.

A whistle, the sound of spears banging into shields changed into a roar as hundreds of men shouted as loud as they could in guttural voices for courage. They rode at little more than walking pace at first, but some groups ran faster, getting a bit too far ahead before their centurions managed to hold them back so it was a unified line that struck Theo's men.

Magnus heard the change of sound as the shouts of the charge were replaced with those of exertion and pain. The sounds of hundreds of shields smashing together was like a clap of thunder. And then everything was out of Magnus' hands, the outcome down to the bravery and fighting skills of each individual soldier. He was watching either the last conflict from which was ushered in a golden age of peace, or a savage bloodbath in which so many soldiers were to die that it would precipitate the fall of the empire.

Fate would soon fall one way or another. The die was cast. Odds or evens.

Over the stomach-churning melee, Magnus tried to spot Theo, but the sun was in his eyes and the cloud of dust kicked up by the scuffling of thousands of men was so thick it quickly obscured everything but Magnus' rear line.

There were no Huns involved and Magnus wondered if perhaps his cousin was as disgusted as Magnus at the thought of such barbarians fighting in his name and in the name of God.

The sound of thunder was another detachment of cavalry heading into the fray and although his fists kept clenching as though he was wielding a sword in the heart of the fight, there was nothing for Magnus to do but sit on his horse and watch. And hope.

It didn't take long before men began to limp and crawl back to camp, one with a face covered in blood from a bad head wound, another missing a hand, waving his bloodied stump until a medic ran to him and roughly bound the wound. Many others would be staying on the ground where they fell.

The dust made Magnus cough, the sounds of anger and agony made his horse nervous, as it shuffled about under him, stomping a foot.

The battle drew on, hundreds of helmets flashing in the morning light, both sides evenly matched.

In his mind he was back on a ridge in Britannia overlooking the lands that were about to become his, the day the Votadini had raided and made it so that his men had declared him Augustus. Another memory and he was in the heart of Gaul, victorious over an emperor without a single sword being drawn, riding into an abandoned Mediolanum to take Italy. Getting to this point had been so easy. It had all flowed like a leaf on the stream of destiny.

Theo had stopped that advance, though.

His cousin had been raised by the same man who had brought Magnus up, and suddenly it struck him as utterly tragic at how much

Theodosius the Elder would have wept to know that his son and nephew were ripping the empire apart in their attempt to kill each other. Each of them throwing men, who were desperately needed to defend the borders, at each other for nothing but their own glory. Maybe Theodosius had brought up a pair of monsters.

Whether it had been Africa, Britannia, or on the Rhine, it had always been the greatest thrill to outwit, out-manoeuvre and outfight a worthy opponent and to have him beg for mercy on his knees, or his head put on parade. The Battle of Poetovio was not like that. It was less of a glorious fight and more of a disgrace.

He threw up again.

As he tried to peer through the dense cloud of dust to see what was happening, he felt such a weighty grief that he almost ordered a retreat there and then.

"Sir!" one of his guards said, pointing to the side, and with a sinking heart, Magnus saw the Huns. Although they weren't in anything close to a formation, they milled around in a group. Perhaps it was because they were on the field with Theodosius' army, not running around, charging in several different directions at once like something out of a nightmare. They stayed well to the side, out on the flank, but even so far away they were enough to make his guard nervous. They moved around so that there were more men between them. Magnus didn't think there was too much point as the Huns could probably run around them to attack from the other side faster than the Moors could arrange themselves.

They stayed where they were waiting for some signal, or some change in the fighting, and Magnus realised he'd underestimated the depth of his cousin's ambitions all these years. Theo had never intended to leave him in Treverorum. He'd probably been grateful to Magnus for flushing Valentinian into his clutches, eliminating the boy as a rival to his power, and had wanted this fight to happen to get rid of Magnus, so Theo could have it all. In a way, that seemed reasonable, but using the Huns to win his war? Magnus didn't want to believe that his cousin could stoop so low.

Something splashed in the river. Magnus couldn't see whose men had been driven in, but with their weighty armour on, arms dead tired from stabbing a sword and holding a shield, they wouldn't last long.

A riderless horse, its armour dragging under its hooves, charged past them.

Because he couldn't see anything, he had to rely on the sporadic reports that came to him. Where the line was threatening to buckle, he ordered cavalry to sweep in

The fight was still dead even though, with no movement signifying a breakthrough anywhere. It could go either way... until Marcellinus said, "Enough of this waiting. I will win the day for you, brother! And for it, you will grant me my villa in Hispania!"

When Marcellinus drew his sword it caught the morning sun in a particular way and Magnus understood the flash as a warning, but before he could say anything to stop him, his brother was charging away, leading a cavalry detachment into the heart of the fray, disappearing into the dust. So sure it was the last time he'd see his brother, Magnus almost keeled over in the saddle.

And now there were fewer men between him and the Huns.

To Magnus, they looked like nothing more than a pack of hungry, yet nervous, dogs.

A loud roar rose from somewhere to the side, from the direction Marcellinus had ridden. The thought of what it could mean made him heave up the last bit of water, but all he could do was to wait for the next report.

To the side, he saw movement and cursed at the Huns. Their leaders were pointing at something animatedly. From the fight at Sisica, he knew they were too fast to bring any infantry against them and too accurate with their arrows to ignore, but he didn't know enough about them to predict where or how they would attack. He was about to ask Merobaudes how best to arrange his Moor guards against them when a blanche-faced rider pulled up at his side. He shouted above the din, but Magnus couldn't understand the words. Dead, he said... Then his guards were pressed in so tightly they blocked his view of the charging Huns, and he heard more words shouted at him. Retreat. Lost. And his guards forced him away from the fight, away from his brother. He tried to turn back, but the guard commander reached over and grabbed his horse's bridle and so he was dragged away.

A couple of arrows zipped past him. One flicked harmlessly off the horse's armour.

But as he rode, he didn't care much about his own life. It was just the messenger's words that pounded in his head. He tried to hold onto the reins but his hands were weak.

Marcellinus was dead.

Gildo's cavalry kept urging him to run, a couple of men even leaning over to slap his horse on the rump with the flat of their blades to get it to go faster.

The horse in front took an arrow in the front leg and it went down so quickly that for a moment its unfortunate rider was sitting in the air. Magnus' horse jumped over it, but staggering on the flagstones, it only just managed to keep its balance. The shock of almost being pitched from the saddle, being left on foot amongst the Huns, woke Magnus up. He looked around. The dirty bastards were on both sides, charging through the wheat fields, either side of the road Magnus was on, slowed a little by the irrigation channels they had to jump over. The only positive was that they weren't in front. Yet.

But no matter how much Magnus' men pushed their mounts, they weren't going to outrun the Huns.

"What's the plan?" Merobaudes shouted, and it struck Magnus as very strange that although they were running as fast as they could, he had no idea where they were heading. All he knew was that there was no way back now. Theo had already won. It was over. He'd lost. Whatever remnants of his army were left behind would have to either surrender to Theo or fight for their lives. All Magnus had left were his guards... who were getting picked off one by one.

And Marcellinus was dead.

Merobaudes drew near him, fierce eyes staring out between the nose plate of his slightly skewed helmet. "What plan?" he shouted again.

Magnus tried to think. His life depended on it. He could still muster more men from Gaul, could send messengers to Hispania for men to ride to him, but that would take time. Weeks. And he didn't have weeks. He wasn't too sure if he only had a few moments left.

He still had Andragathius and a naval fleet, so Aquileia was the obvious place to muster. A fortified place where he could make a stand before reinforcements arrived. It wasn't a great plan, but it at least meant it wasn't all over. Not yet. "Aquileia," he shouted, and heard the message get passed through his guards. A week's ride for a hundred men, with no provisions and Huns hounding them all the way; it wasn't a great plan, but it was all he had. And so he ran.

A single Hun could pop up beside them, loose a well-aimed arrow into one of his men, and disappear again before anyone could do anything about it. More and more of those with Magnus fell and it was with a blinding terror that they rode, not knowing where the next arrow would come from. Every now and then a group of his guards would peel off and charge at the Huns. It served to keep Magnus out of arrow range for a few moments, but each time it cost a few riders.

But on a rise, they saw that a band of swarthy-skinned riders had managed to get ahead. They were surrounded. Merobaudes reigned in at Magnus' side, his horse tossing its head, its eyes wide with terror. "We have to fight them. It's the only way!" he shouted. "And you will make a run for it."

"They'll kill them all," Magnus said.

"And maybe we will live because of it. The two of us alone can find horses to change, so we'll be much faster that way!" He spoke with such authority that the soldier in Magnus obeyed.

"Hold them back!" Merobaudes shouted. "We ride to Aquileia."

Side by side, he and Merobaudes charged off together, Magnus holding his shield up in his right hand, his former enemy holding his in his left, and hunkered down, they charged, flinching at every branch near the road in case it was an arrow. And then they were free.

He urged his horse on, but it was flagging. A sharp pain worked its way to his attention. An arrow had pierced his shield dead centre, the tip cutting into the back of his wrist. He'd come so close...

A small settlement lay ahead, and the large building next to the road would be a mansio. All they had to do was get fresh horses, and to make sure that nobody following behind could do the same, and they would have an advantage. He urged his horse on, unconcerned if it died in the next mile.

They charged into the courtyard and Magnus had his sword out before his feet touched the ground. "Horses!" he bellowed as he ran into the stables. A startled boy grabbed the dagger at his side but in a well-honed soldier's instinct, was dead at the end of Magnus' blade before he could strike.

Three horses were saddled ready so that an imperial messenger didn't have to waste a moment in the change. As soon as Magnus was in the saddle he kicked his new mount into a charge across the courtyard... but then the innkeeper was blocking his path, a long cudgel in his raised hand, to strike. In an unthinking reaction, Magnus pulled the reins to jerk the horse into him. The man was slammed to the ground and trampled underfoot... and then Magnus was back on the road again, and cried out a challenge to whoever might be chasing him as no horse, a Hun one or not, could outrun a fresh one.

At the next mansio, some twelve miles further, Magnus made an effort not to kill the next stable hand and just yelled him into submission by waving his purple cloak around, as filthy as it was. Although it troubled him deeply to do it, he stabbed the necks of all the other horses, just in case a couple of Huns had managed to make it around his guards. He was running for his life, so had to take every advantage he could get.

"You could have just cut all the saddle straps," Merobaudes shouted as they galloped away.

With Merobaudes still at his side, they swapped horses and rode them half to death to the next mansio until it was too dark, and only long after the sun had set and they could hardly see where they were riding did they find a stand of woods to conceal them.

Still panting, sweat rolling down his face, Merobaudes offered Magnus some bread he'd taken from the last inn. Magnus was ravenous, but before he could take a bite, he doubled over to dry heave. He was shaking like a leaf. To try and calm himself, he took his blade out to clean... and saw the blood of the stable boy all over it. Stabbing children for a horse and some bread like an escaped slave was what got a man crucified... and what got his soul damned for eternity. He decided that the moment he stopped running, he'd find a priest... although he had no pouch of gold to pay for his absolutions.

Darkness fell and no one passed them on the road.

For three days they did nothing but ride, change horses and sleep near the side of the road, each taking turns to stand watch as though they were the raw recruits they'd been some thirty years before.

Instead of dazzling his inferiors with his special cloak, Magnus lay on it on the ground, using it to keep the worst of the cold off him. Not that he could sleep anyway, as whenever his mind slowed down enough to think, all he could see was an image of Marcellinus, his brother's bloody body being trampled into the dirt by Theo's cavalry. When he did eventually drift off, he was back at his baptism in the river outside the fortress of Segontium, except he was bathed from head to foot in the blood of the stable hand he'd killed without thinking

They wasted a lot of time going around Emona, but he couldn't risk getting caught by any of the men who'd rejected him. Two ragged men running for their lives would attract the attention of any scouts out on the road around the city. Especially one with a purple cloak draped over his back. He wouldn't take it off though. If he was to die, he would be wearing it. And the Hun probably couldn't follow them so far, as any garrison who saw them would have sworn an oath to cut men like them down on sight.

Finally, the familiar high, whitewashed walls of Aquileia, his home for the winter, were on the horizon, the azure blue sea beyond where Andragathius would be. While he waited for his admiral to respond to his summons, he'd be safe inside the fortified city, where people knew him well.

The soldiers on duty recognised his purple cloak and he was ushered inside by men with worry on their faces.

He dragged himself out of the saddle and limped up the steps of the reassuringly large and sturdy gatehouse tower. Leaning against the wall for support, he looked back towards the mountains they'd come from. A few miles away he saw dust rising and wondered if it was Gildo's men, the last battered remnants of his once glorious army hurrying to protect him... or the Huns coming to tear his head off.

He called out for a scribe and messenger, but there was no one to carry out the order.

Merobaudes then walked calmly to him. For years he'd been the man Magnus had hated the most, and for almost the same number of years he'd been his most competent advisor and general. "Get the gates closed and the walls manned!" Magnus ordered. "We need the city sealed."

Merobaudes looked far too calm and made no move to do anything.

"Hurry," Magnus snapped. "We don't have much time!" he pointed at the approaching riders. "They could be Theo's men!"

"It's over," Merobaudes said. "We won't be fighting anymore."

Magnus pointed urgently to the horizon as though his general had gone stupid. "They will be here soon!"

"They come only for you," Merobaudes said, and Magnus knew that the roles they'd had since the day Merobaudes had brought Gratian's purple cloak to him had just been reversed. The butterfly that was power had flittered off Magnus' shoulders so that the most powerful man in the empire was now the man next to him.

There were other men around. For a moment Magnus thought they were grabbing his shoulders to congratulate him for something, even though they should have been doing the opposite. But then he realised that they were pinning his arms to his sides, holding him secure. He tried to twist free, but they held him tightly, as though he was a prisoner. "Get your hands off me!" he shouted. "I command you! I will have your heads!"

Merobaudes was unmoving, though.

"I let you live!" Magnus snarled. "Despite what you did to my uncle! Serve me now!"

Merobaudes looked him straight in the eye and said, "I serve the empire." He nodded to someone behind Magnus and he felt the cold iron of a pair of manacles being clamped around his wrists.

"Keep the gates open!" Merobaudes called down. And they stood in silence as Theodosius' men arrived, and the city guards let them in. At least they weren't Huns.

His body was so tired from the battle and the long ride back to Aquileia, that with his hands cuffed behind his back, it was almost impossible to stay in the saddle, especially as the rain was heavy enough to make the leather slippery. The ugly sneers of his captors kept him upright as he couldn't bear the thought of keeling over in front of them like an overworked slave.

He pulled at the metal around his wrists with some daft hope that in the last few moments since he'd last tried they'd somehow come loose enough for him to undo. The fact that it was the killer of his uncle who had put the chains around his wrists really riled him. He decided that the first thing he'd ask of his cousin before asking for him to keep Britannia and Hispania was that he would be allowed to kill Merobaudes. Or perhaps just being Governor of Britannia would be enough. Every single soldier on that island knew his name. He decided that it would be best to gauge Theo's disposition before asking him for anything.

They came to a mile marker stone set at the side of the road, where the man in charge ordered the other couple of riders to leave them. Being alone with the general gave Magnus a very bad feeling, and when he was pulled out of the saddle and forced to his knees on the wet road, Magnus began to think that he might not get to hash out a deal with his cousin after all. The mile marker said that Aquileia was three miles away. Far too far for him to run to, even if his hands weren't bound behind him. Even if it wasn't a city full of men who'd had just betrayed him.

"Do you know who I am?" the big man towering over him asked.

Magnus shook his head.

"I want you to know my name. Arbogast. Is it one you have heard before?"

"It is," Magnus said. The man's reputation was at least as fearsome as Andragathius'.

Arbogast bent over to undo the clasps of Magnus' cloak. "Your cousin thinks to rule the whole of the Empire by himself. Like Constantine," he said as took the cloak away. "I know, and you must know even better than I do, no one man can do that. It will be a disaster."

"So you want the West?" Magnus scoffed.

"Why not?" he shrugged.

Magnus pulled at his bonds again. They were just as unyielding as they'd been since Aquileia. "You are a Goth," he said. "Unless you hadn't noticed, there are one or two rules that prevent you from wearing that cloak of mine."

"A Goth may rule in Rome sooner than you think," he said. "But I will find a senator to raise to the purple."

As the rain ran down the back of his exposed neck, Magnus squinted up as Arbogast folded the cloak. The rain still fell, but the sun had come out. "And why are you telling me this?" he asked as it was not considered a great strategy to tell your plans to your enemy.

"Because you won't be telling anyone..." he said as he folded the cloak away.

At least he didn't throw it around his own shoulders.

"I submit my life to you," Magnus said. "But I beg you, please, as a good Christian, make sure that my son is spared. He is too young to know the horrors of politics."

Arbogast shrugged. "You raised him to Augustus. It was *you* who lifted him high above the parapets for all of your enemies to see. So it will be because of that he will die. Because of *you*!"

He could have his army taken from him, his palace and even his purple cloak, but leaving him as a man unable to protect his own child, *that* was the greatest insult.

Arbogast drew his sword and held it before Magnus. The blade caught the sun. The way it was angled, the rain drops running towards the tip, glimmered as they caught the sun, turning them into tiny little rainbows, from red, through yellow and blue, to the colour of his cloak. It was the single most beautiful thing he'd ever seen in his life, and he wished he had someone to share it with. He saw Victor in the palace gardens staring in innocent wonder at the same rainbow in the dew drop only he could see.

"You die once here, now," Arbogast said, "but you will die again. Theodosius has ordered a damnatio memoriae against you."

At such a thought, it felt like the blade had already fallen.

Every enemy he'd ever faced, fought and beaten. He'd trade victory in every fight he'd ever had to tear the heart out of the man in front of him, but bound as he was, he didn't even manage to get a foot under him.

"Wait!" he gasped, but the blade swung. From the corner of his eye, he saw the flash of rainbow colours again... but then just red. A blood-soaked rainbow.

XXIV

A horse. All Andragathius wanted was a horse. Perhaps a few straps to hold him in the saddle, and he could ride and ride and be free. A nice farm in the flat lands of his birth, a son or two to raise. Peace. Thoughts about planting seeds that he would watch germinate rather than ones about to kill as many of his enemy's men with losing the least number of his own, waking up in the morning from a wife's whisper in his ear, rather than someone barking an order.

Instead, he was a crippled commander on a ship that made him sick to look at. He could hardly stand on solid ground with his sticks to keep him upright, but on a deck that constantly moved under him, he had no chance. Just as much from his spinning head than from the wallowing of the ship.

It had taken most of his life to come to the conclusion, but a man could have enough of fighting.

It was a calm day, but his stomach wasn't helped by the smell of the sweat of five hundred men wafting up from below decks; men who sat at oars, ready to row into battle at a moment's notice.

Andragathius enjoyed his station as naval commander about as much as he enjoyed being a cripple. All he wanted was a horse. Horses were lithe, gorgeous, powerful creatures, and being on the back of a well-trained one, a warrior had almost divine amounts of speed, range and power. There had never been a moment when he was in the saddle that he'd ever thought of doing anything else. All there was to naval fighting was blocking off the attempted movement of your opponents. An endless game of ludus with big, slow-to-manoeuvrer ships instead of counters. A nudge of the knee and a horse would turn and gallop in another direction, the ship turned so slowly that sometimes it drove Andragathius close to tears of frustration.

There had been an initial confrontation, a few boats ramming each other, one of Theodosius' sunk, which had been a sight so awful Andragathius would never forget it. The screams of the men being drowned out one by one as it went down, had haunted his dreams for weeks

A few times they'd been close enough to throw spears and shoot arrows – but with the superiority of Magnus' fleet established, the war had turned into nothing more than a drawn-out stand-off. Andragathius was at anchor guarding several of Theodosius' ships that were trapped in a harbour. All he had to do was make sure they didn't slip around him and get north.

Theodosius' men held the town, but steep mountains surrounded it and Andragathius had enough men on the slopes so there would be no column of men abandoning their ships to march north to fight against Magnus.

So he did nothing but take endless supplies of food and fresh water and pray for continued calm weather, something which made his life a little easier. And that's what he would have carried on doing– until he'd heard the roars of jubilation carrying over the water the day before. They'd unsettled him deeply and now the enemy ships were raising sales and rowing south. It was a bad sign.

Baccus asked why they weren't getting ready to follow them, but Andragathius was sure that the only reason they were leaving was because the war had ended. He was also sure that there would be a message for him on the small supply boat that was making its way towards them.

With a dull thump, the two ships bumped into each other and the moment caused another wave of nausea. Ropes thrown, they were tethered together, and as the amphorae were bundled over, the rowers were all happy to receive the fresh water and food. Andragathius suspected that there was a more pressing cargo. As he expected, the messenger scrambled over from the smaller craft and from the look of terror in his eyes, Andragathius knew exactly what was in the note.

He wondered what instructions he could give to Baccus and the men that would help save their lives. Follow Theodosius' ships back to Constantinople and surrender there? To sail around the south coast of Italy and go to Rome? Men were most needed in the north, as with so many soldiers drawn into Magnus' battle, the borders would be in desperate need for reinforcements. It was early September though, so they would have to hurry to get over the mountains if they didn't want to be caught by the weather. Or they could sail to Massilia and march through Gaul to the west of them. But then he realised it didn't really matter. Nothing was his concern any more.

"I need a shit," he said and had Baccus help him hobble over to the stern rail. He despised the sight of his wasted legs, so didn't hike his tunic up. He handed the unopened note to Baccus and his last thought was that he wished he could have a drink of the infusion the servant girl used to make for him in Mediolanum that made him dream so vividly. He wanted to be on his farm in the flatlands, the happy shouts of the sons he'd never had mixing with the clucking of the chickens.

As he leaned backwards and began to fall, he said to Baccus, "You're in charge!"

XXV

Kenon tried not to look at the semi-naked slaves in the cage.

"They don't speak Latin, only some barbarian tongue!" Maurus said, with disappointment as he roughly inspected one of the women – one that would perhaps soon be his wife.

"What do you want them to say?" Iutus laughed as he tried to pull open the dress of the next girl in the line. "It's only what they *do* that bothers me, not what they say! You can teach them that easily!"

"And you'll be happy with your sons speaking like barbarians, will you?" Maurus asked. He grabbed the jaw of the girl he was looking at in his big hand and angled her face up and to the side, the same way a horse trader would inspect the teeth of a prospective purchase.

The one in front of Kenon was beautiful – or at least she would be when the bruises on her face had healed and her tussled hair was made less wild. "What is your name?" he asked, trying to show that he wasn't a monster. She pulled up the collar and shrugged her shoulders in a gesture of futility. Kenon understood it to mean that seeing as she was a slave, he could call her whatever he wanted.

"Your name?" he asked, a little softer.

"Dareca," she replied, but pulled an ugly face.

"See, they will learn. You will teach them," he said to his men, trying to be the best Christian he could. He knew he was being a little optimistic about the situation, though. For their service to the empire, his men, and about a hundred and fifty veterans, newly retired after the glorious battle of Poetovio, had been granted land in the far west of Gaul. The women, captured or traded from somewhere east of the Rhine, had been gifted to go with it. With coin and diplomas in hand, all were very enthusiastic about the calm days ahead of doing nothing more than ploughing their new fields and wives in equal measure.

Kenon was certainly no expert on how women saw the world, but he was pretty sure they appraised what was happening a little differently. Instead of looking forward to the prospect of being married to men they'd be glad to bring up a family with, they'd just been sold as slaves to those they considered enemies.

The chains binding them together by the collars around their necks suggested that perhaps they had the more accurate understanding of the situation. Some had been in their collars for so long, or had struggled so hard against them, that they had ugly red chafe marks around their necks. It would be the Christian thing to do to unlock them and give them some balm for their wounds, but it would be a long walk across Gaul. They were barbarian slaves, though. He was a scout, so could track them down easily enough, but he would rather get to his new life as soon as he could without wasting time rounding them up, so decided it would be best to keep them chained until they got there.

"Can you understand 'suck my cock'?" Maurus mocked at one. In case she didn't understand, he demonstrated the action.

Some of the men probably wouldn't unlock them once they'd got there.

The girl Maurus was taunting might not have understood his words, but could probably understand what he meant as she spat in his face. She should have expected to slap, but Maurus hit her so hard a couple of girls she was chained to were jerked to their knees, the one in front of Kenon included. The chorus of screams and barbarian insults sounded like something out of the tales of old his mother used to tell him. Harpies, and barbarians who had women fighting for them.

Kenon was about to put a stop to the commotion, but through the chaos, he saw a stiff-backed messenger running straight for him.

Flush-cheeked, eyes watering and breathing hard, he'd obviously ridden as fast as he could, and for quite a way. As soon as he handed the folded parchment over, Kenon knew it was bad news. He broke the seal and ignoring the screams from the women beside him, unfolded it. 'With regret to inform you... Tragedy... Incursion over the border... Dead... Ursula.'

"Tell me this is a lie!" Kenon screamed, but with a dagger buried to the hilt in his throat, the messenger couldn't speak. As he slumped to the ground, choking to death on his own blood. Kenon was as surprised as everyone else who'd just seen him do it, that he'd just killed someone.

He saw everything that he'd dreamed of for the past few years bleed out just like the messenger, the empty void he'd been pretending hadn't still been inside him since his baptism in Rome, enveloped him in dark arms and swept him away from the false light he'd been basking in.

Everyone stared at him in shock, his men with their swords out scanning around for threats, but Kenon told them to stand down.

He'd always harboured the suspicion that his baptism hadn't been real, either that God had never accepted him, or the pope hadn't performed a real ceremony, and with Ursula taken from him in such a way, he reverted back to his old self. No pretences. And the best way to do that was with death–which was marked suitably as the messenger's foot stopped twitching.

The slaves had stopped screaming, but there was still a high-pitched shriek of pain coming from somewhere. As Kenon reached down to pull his dagger from the messenger's throat, he realised it was in his head. He knew a way to stop that, but couldn't do it with anyone watching.

He gave the crumpled note to Iustus. "Burn it," he said.

Barbarian invaders. Raided across a weakened border. As much as he blamed God for destroying all of his hopes and dreams, the reason the border was so porous was because Magnus had stripped the garrisons along the Rhine for the army he'd taken south. It was as though the bastard had cursed Kenon from the grave.

Her cheek turning red, the slave Maurus had slapped stood up and started screaming at him, insults in a language he didn't understand. It made him wonder if Ursula had heard the same words just before the raiders had killed her. They sounded disgusting and had no place in the civilised world. Iustus was right about not wanting their sons to speak like barbarians. Or maybe she was laying curses on him. He'd had enough curses in his life.

"Hold her," he said and Iustus pinned her arms behind her back while Maurus grabbed her hair to hold her head still. As she continued to scream her curses, Kenon jammed the handle of his dagger between her teeth and fished around for her tongue. When he had it, he turned the knife around, put it into her mouth, and sliced.

She still screamed, but now her disgusting words were unintelligible even to those who spoke her language.

"Next!" Kenon shouted.

There were nearly two hundred of them. He'd have to work quickly if he wanted to start marching before midday.

XXVI

Elen had known him since he was a mewling newborn, watched him take his first steps, had heard his first words–and now she would watch him die.

One more sacrifice, one more death, one more horror to endure and she'd be freer than she'd ever allowed herself to dream. Magnus was dead, and when Theodosius' men who'd come to kill Victor had done their bloody work, she could go back to Britannia and have the life with Eugenius she'd prayed for for years. Except she didn't think she could go through with it. She was already packed, the carriage was ready, a good portion of Magnus' treasury was safely buried so it could be recovered in more stable times, but huddled in her room, wondering if the next footsteps would be a soldier with malicious intent, her mind flitted from one pointless plan to another. She could bundle him in the carriage and try to make a run for it–but they'd never outrun the soldiers, and so she came back to thinking that poisoning him or smothering him herself was the best idea. It would be a more merciful end than cowering away from a hulking soldier.

She finally decided that doing it herself would be better, but her indecision had cost her all the time it would have taken to do it, as screams and raised voices announced the arrival of Theodosius' men.

"What is it?" the innocent little voice asked from beside her.

It was all she could do to keep the scream from escaping her chest. "Hush," she said as calmly as she could. "Nothing to worry about. It will all be over soon."

For years she'd been accustomed to people tiptoeing around her, affording her deference as wife to one emperor and mother to the other, so when the door burst open with a shove of a shoulder, the loud noise made her jump, and a memory of her irate father come to teach her another lesson in appropriate behaviour for a young girl flashed in her mind. The terror was not for herself this time, though.

The soldier was filthy. It looked like he'd done nothing but ride and sleep in ditches for days. The stubble on his chin made him look as rough as a barbarian. It had been years since she'd met anyone who hadn't come straight from a bathhouse on their way to see her.

The brute nodded to whoever was in the corridor, stepped in, and with his foot shut the door behind him. Eyes roaming around the room, he took a cautious look behind the couch before deciding that the only threat in the room was him.

"So this is the former Emperor Victor?" he asked, the leather straps of his armour creaking as he rolled his shoulders as though he was limbering up for some exercise. "My name is Arbogast. I assume that you know why I am here?"

"Don't hurt him," Elen couldn't help saying, even though she knew such pleas would fall on deaf ears.

"It won't hurt at all," he replied with a predatory smile.

The poor boy tried to nuzzle himself into the folds of her clothes, but she had no protection to offer. "He is just a child. Innocent!" she sobbed.

"Not *just* a child though, is he?" he said with a horrible grin. He slowly slid his dagger out and turned it in the light to check the sharpness of the blade. "And you can thank your husband for that. I told him I would do this."

"You were the one who killed him?" she asked.

"I was," he nodded, and his smile spread. She saw that he felt pride. but while that seemed shocking for Elen, perhaps for a soldier who'd taken the life of an emperor it wasn't such an unusual thing. "And now I'll do the same with his son," he added, still proudly, even though it was the killing of a small boy he was talking about.

"Noooo..." came a plaintive little wail from under her arm. The poor boy knew something bad was about to happen, but she was glad that he was young enough so that he couldn't understand the true horror of it.

"Come on. You know it has to be like this. Hand him over."

"Have mercy," she begged. "Mercy on your *own* soul!"

"Just be glad that Theodosius is merciful enough to let *you* live. Or else I'd be here for the both of you."

"You are killing me today, as well. Be sure of it," Elen spat.

His relaxed chuckle seemed so out of place in such an unbearable situation. "You can't possibly think he can leave this room alive, do you? You cannot be so naive! If it's not me now, it will be some other bastard tomorrow."

Sadly, it was a truth he spoke. Neither Theodosius nor Valentinian could afford to leave a child emperor alive. There was no place in the world for a failed usurper's son, never mind one proclaimed as co-emperor. Magnus had doomed Victor just as much as he had doomed himself.

"No blood," Elen whispered, and at agreeing to allow such a horror to happen had to clench her fists to stop the scream that was ready to burst from her chest.

"Women!" Arbogast scoffed and rolled his eyes as he unbuckled his sword belt. "The quicker the better," he shrugged, and actually had the audacity to hand his heavy sword to her. It was both an insult and a gesture to demonstrate that she had absolutely no control. Or worse, that she was a willing accomplice.

A big hand on a tiny shoulder and Arbogast looped the belt around the boy's throat before he knew what was happening. His sweaty little hands grabbed at Elen's tunic, but as Arbogast pulled on the ends of the leather strap, the tendons in his neck straining with the effort, the boy let go of her to pathetically claw at Arbogast's arms, as though someone so small could hope to fight against such a monster; one that even Magnus couldn't defend himself against. She dropped the sword, slumped to her knees and tried to put her hands around the small body in some vain and useless attempt to give some comfort in the final moments.

He died in silence. Arbogast pulled on the belt so hard he couldn't even gasp. Mercifully it was only a few moments before, with blue lips, swollen tongue and rolled back eyes, his lifeless body slumped to the floor and it was over. Yet Elen knew it would be a moment that would haunt her waking days for the rest of her life.

Arbogast buckled his sword back up as casually as he'd just come out of a brothel. As he walked slowly away, she hoped to God that he would suffer terribly for his actions. An eternity of unremitting burning agony wouldn't be enough. She knew it would be best to just keep quiet, to let him skulk off to whatever brutality he was commanded to commit next, but the words rose in her chest and spewed out in a cascade she couldn't control. "I curse you, Arbogast the Frank. I curse you that you will be the most hated man in this entire broken Empire. That when it comes crashing down and is overrun by blood-thirsty barbarians, all raging for the slaughter of all that is good, all that is *Christian*, those alive to witness the fall will spit on your name as the cause of the doom they see and the darkness to come."

She had no idea where the words came from and it felt more like she was listening to them rather than speaking them, as though it was her *Grandmother* who was speaking. She braced herself for a kick or a slap, but when she managed to focus her eyes through the tears, Arbogast was staring at her, open-mouthed and ashen-faced, shocked as though he'd just seen his own son killed in front of him. She thought he was about to say something, to offer some crass retort, but thought better of it and just turned away, and her keening cry drowned out the sounds of his receding footsteps.

She couldn't bear to stay next to the body, so as soon as she managed to get her legs under her, she staggered down the empty corridor, steadying herself against the walls as though she was blind drunk. At every step, her legs threatened to give way and it was hard to breathe as though it was her throat Arbogast's belt was around. Outside, she felt the summer sun on her face and breathed in the fresh air, yet there was no comfort in them, and might never be again.

Her carriage was ready, her four guards at attention waiting for her, Eugenius with his jaw clenched tightly shut.

"Is it done?" Aigla asked.

"It is," Elen noted and it took the very last of her strength to look her devastated friend in the eye. "I am so sorry," she cried.

If any of Theodosius' soldiers heard Aigla's heart-rendering cry, hopefully they'd think it was a woman broken at the death of an emperor, not that of a mother mourning the loss of her son. In her uncontrolled grief, she grabbed Elen, and they fell, holding each other, to the cobblestones together.

"We need to go! Now!" Eugenius said and in a way he would never have dared if Magnus was alive, picked Elen up and set her on the seat in the carriage.

The noise of the wheels on the stones drowned out her cries and when she'd managed to control herself enough to look out of the window, she saw that they were already out of the city. No one had stopped them at the gate, and so after eight long years, they were finally free of Magnus.

"Mama!" she heard in a muffled voice from under the seat.

She opened the door and called for Eugenius to come in. He lifted the seat up and pulled Victor out of his hiding place. And as they rode back towards Britannia they all held each other so tightly that her arms soon began to ache. She didn't let either of them go.

EPILOGUE

Aigla came in with a basket full of fresh eggs she'd taken from the coop Eugenius had made. Elen was sure that she'd never cease to wonder at the sheer enjoyment of making breakfast for those she loved.

Outside, workers had already started their day building the new church from the remains of the old mithraeum near the fort of Segontium.

Only one thing made the morning less than perfect; Victor was still in the foul mood he'd been in for the past few days. "I am Victor!" he wailed.

But with the sweet smile Aigla gave her, she couldn't mask the pain that was just under the surface. And suddenly, Elen remembered what her happiness had cost.

"We have to call you Peblig now," she said softly. "I've told you, it is very important."

"What is Peblig?"

"It's how we say Publicus here in Britannia," she said.

Eugenius held his hands out, but their son didn't want a hug. "I want *Papa*!" he shouted.

"Well," Eugenius said with a smile Elen would never be tired of seeing. "About your father..."

THE END

OVERLORD

Book 4 in the Foundation of the Dragon series.

Due out in summer 2024.

Go to http://www.robbpritchard.co.uk/ for more details!

AUTHOR'S NOTE

Amazon reviews!!!

If you enjoyed Enemies of the Empire and would like to play a little part in its success, as well as that of the coming sequels, perhaps you could do me a little, but lovely, favour. Nothing benefits an indie author who has to compete with the tens of millions of other books on Amazon more than a rating. Or even better, a review. It doesn't have to be a treatise, just a few words would be fine.

Also, if you sign up for my infrequent newsletter via my website you can get a free short book, Blood of the Druids. Set seventeen years before Brethren, it is based on the true story of the Battle of Mona.

www.robbpritchard.co.uk

ACKNOWLEDGEMENTS

To my wonderful girlfriend, Jana Goetzova, for all of the support and for not getting too mad at me when I need to scribble ideas down at 3am. It's such an honour to be your second favourite writer...

Elaine Borges-Ibanez for going above and beyond with the proofedting. Thank you so much! No one else did so much to make this book come to life.

Rebecca Robinson of First Write Editors for the brilliant editing.

Ella Pritchard for her tireless typo hunting.

Marina Kosenkova for help with the niggly little bits.

Callum Nelson and all at the incredible Park in the Past near Wrexham https://parkinthepast.org.uk/ An amazing idea, an amazing place. Well worth a visit. I will be spending plenty of time here over the next summers with these experts and enthusiasts.

Kristina Spiel for finding some spare moments to help with that bane of writers, the dreaded blurb.

For the most in-depth account of the life of Magnus Maximus, I recommend Maxwell Craven's Magnus Maximus: The Neglected Roman Emperor and his British Legacy. From the dozens of sources I pulled information from, I found his work to be by far the most authoritative. He also helped with some specific information that found its way into Usurpers, for which I am very grateful.

For historical advice and the brilliant FB page on the fort of Caerhun, (Canovium) in North Wales, David from https://facebook.com/Caerhun

For once again going way beyond the call of duty for the artwork, I owe massive thanks to Sasa Juric for the work he did on the gorgeous cover.

Anthony Mathison for his help with religious practises of the distant past.

Robert Vermaat for his excellent advice on Late Roman history.

Printed in Great Britain
by Amazon